A Novel by:

DASHAWN TAYLOR

NEXT LEVEL PUBLISHING
P.O. Box 8644
Newark, NJ 07108

•———————————————————————————————————•

Kissed By The Devil

ISBN: 0-9800154-0-5
ISBN 13:   978-0-9800154-0-9

Manufactured in the United States of America

•———————————————————————————————————•

Cover Concept & Publishing Consultation - Nakea S. Murray – The Literary Consultant Group
Photographer - Doss Tidwell
Cover Model - Aziza Anderson
Editor- Gracie Leavitt
For more info and copies log onto www.kissedbythedevil.com or call 973.634.8421

This Book is dedicated to
my Family, Friends and Fans!

Thank You For

Your Patience

Your Support

And Your Prayers

Without *You* There Is No *Me*!

-Dashawn Taylor

"Men and Women lie everyday!
They lie to each other,
lie to themselves
And even lie to God.
So what makes you think they won't lie to you?
Trust No One!"

- Heidi Kachina aka "High"

Prologue

Wednesday, November 1, 2006
Newark, New Jersey

2:14 a.m.

"Ye, though I walk through the valley of the shadow of death, I will fear no evil. For You are with me; Your rod and Your staff, they comfort me"

Heidi said a short prayer under her breath as she smelled death in the air. The blood and tears were flowing heavy from her swollen eyes but she could still see her attacker standing over her. It was her fiancé Jayson. His eyes were burgundy red and the expression on his face was almost demonic. In the seven years that she'd known him, Jayson had never raised a hand to Heidi. But tonight, without warning, Jayson punched her twice with the force of a mule kick. It had felt like every pound of his three hundred plus pound body had rushed to his cantaloupe-sized fists. The hits instantly knocked her to the ground where she was now lying on her back. It took a few moments for Heidi to stop seeing double. She regained her eyesight just in time to watch Jayson's size thirteen boot swing from her left side and kick her square in the ribs. The pain instantly rushed from Heidi's stomach to every inch of her frail body. She screamed in pain.

"Please God! Stop, Jayson. What are you doing?" Heidi's voice was weak.

As if he were hard of hearing, Jayson totally ignored Heidi's call for mercy. He reached down and grabbed her by the shoulders and pulled her face closer to his. Heidi could smell the foul aroma of spoiled alcohol on his lips. She was looking directly into Jayson's eyes when his dilated pupils sent a chilling shockwave through her body. It was almost as if he were possessed with some foreign emotion that she had never seen. He opened his mouth and the scent of his drunken breath spilled out in a rush.

"I always knew you was a foul bitch, High. But how the fuck could you do this to me?" Jayson's deep voice vibrated through Heidi's body. "Huh?" Jayson grunted. "How the fuck could you do this to me? I gave you everything." Jayson was talking really slowly. His tone was even yet angry. He didn't raise his voice once. Most of his words got snagged on his lips in a slur. Jayson's eyes began to swell with tears. "That nigga, he told me everything High!" Jayson cynically whispered. "Everything!" Heidi nervously stared at Jayson. She was petrified.

"He?" Heidi whispered. "Who is He? And what are you talking about?"

Jayson totally ignored Heidi's questions as he continued to blast her with accusations. "And the worse part about it is…I was 'bout to marry yo foul ass." Jayson shook his head. He looked down as if ashamed. "Fuck you, High. I mean that. Fuck you!"

Jayson's lips began to quiver. He was crying now. Heidi was terrified at the sight of her fiancé losing control. She sensed that something terrible was just minutes away. She tried to react but she was so weak. Jayson's grip on her shoulders was alligator tight. She didn't want to pull away from him believing that Jayson would get even angrier. She made another attempt to bargain with her fiancé. She gently placed her hands on his powerful arms and tried to calm him down.

"Jayson, listen to me. I'm hurt bad baby. I need to go to the hospital." It pained Heidi to talk. The punches to her face had caused her jaw to swell instantly. Sensing that she was running out of time, Heidi tried to ignore the pain and continued pleading.

"Everything is going to be fine, Jayson." Heidi said as the tears began to flow uncontrollably now. The pain from her face and stomach were becoming all too real. "I need some help." Heidi continued. "I don't want to die Jayson, not like this. Please."

Jayson slowly looked up to Heidi. The intensity in his eyes seemed to calm as he was becoming remorseful at the sight of his battered fiancée. Feeling like she was making some progress, Heidi decided to end the conflict there and then.

"Please Jayson. What ever I did to you, I'm so sorry. Let's work this out." Heidi whispered. "Please don't be mad at me baby."

With her last words Jayson became enraged. He smacked Heidi with a crushing force and threw her back to the floor. Jayson stood to his feet and started screaming at her.

"Don't try to handle me, High! I'm not ya fucking baby anymore! You hear me?" Jayson kicked her again. This time the toe of his heavy boot connected square on her chest plate. Heidi tried to scream but she couldn't. The pain was fierce. Jayson continued to yell at her.

"You been handlin' me for the past seven years. Never again! You hear me bitch? Never again!" Heidi squirmed on the floor. She tried to yell for help but the brutal kick seemed to take all the remaining air out of her lungs. She tried her best to breathe but nothing was coming in. Heidi instinctively turned on her side and tried to open up a passageway. It didn't help. Her body started reacting to the lack of oxygen. Heidi felt so much pain as her stomach contracted violently in search of a pocket of air. After a few moments Heidi was breathing again. A pinch of air managed to flow into her lungs. Despite feeling like she was breathing through a straw, the air felt like heaven to Heidi.

Jayson stood over his fiancée and stared at her. A devilish smirk grew on his face. He almost laughed at the fact that she reminded him of a fish out of water. The pain in her face brought pleasure to his heart. Jayson could be a cold individual at times. But tonight he was showing a more dangerous side. The mixture of alcohol and rage began to take over his consciousness. With each deep breath, more and more images of torture and destruction entered into his mind. All of a sudden he turned toward the kitchen. As if being called by some imaginary voice, he quickly stepped over Heidi's limp body and darted out of the living room. He was moving like a man on a mission.

Back in the living room Heidi was taking very short breaths to stay alive. She tried to yell again but her body wouldn't let her. The internal injuries were more severe than she could have imagined. Sensing that these would be the last moments of her life, Heidi closed her eyes. She could hear Jayson tossing pots and dishes around in the kitchen. With each crash her heart pounded harder and harder. She said another quick prayer to herself and forced the ugly images of her fiancé out of her mind.

Jayson's footsteps brought her back to reality. She cracked her eyes opened just in time to see him walk in front of her. Her vision was blurry but she could still see him pouring what she thought was water all over the living room. Her nose made a more troubling revelation. It was lighter fluid. Jayson was mumbling under his breath. Heidi made one last attempt to move her arms and legs but they were heavy as bricks. The harder her heart pounded, the more her lungs struggled to search for air. The adrenaline was too much for Heidi to bear. Her eyes rolled back in her head. The last image Heidi saw before she blacked out was her fiancé Jayson pulling out a cigarette lighter and setting the curtains ablaze.

Chapter 1

ONE YEAR LATER
Thursday, November 1, 2007
Cherry Hill, New Jersey

10:46 pm

"You ever think about how you're gonna die? Seriously? I don't mean when you gonna die or where you gonna be when you die. I mean, have you ever really sat down and imagined how it's going to feel when you pass away? It's a scary thought right? Imagine your heart stopping suddenly or a blood vessel exploding in ya head and everything just going dark. No sounds... no sights... no smell... no touch... no nothing. Just dead! That shit is so scary to me."

Heidi's soft voice was overflowing with conviction and concern. Her sleek and well-manicured hands were slightly shaking as she grabbed the wine glass from the restaurant table and put it to her lips. She slowly took a small sip of the mixed drink and continued talking.

"It's like, one minute you're here and experiencing every good and bad thing about life. And the next thing you know, BAM! You're dead! No more worrying about the good or the bad things anymore. Just dead! I don't know about you but that shit is so scary to me." Heidi's mood slightly changed as she found herself listening deeply to her own words. "And then you can't worry about nothing that was going on in your life because you can't do shit about that now anyway. I guess that's why life is so crazy. It's almost like life has to be crazy you know? Full of ups and downs and crazy turns, all to distract you from dwelling on that sad day when you eventually gotta let it all go and move on." Heidi sadly shook her head and stared across the table. She raised the wine glass above her head. "I propose a toast." Heidi continued. "To Life.........The Ultimate Distraction!"

Heidi twirled her wine glass in an effort to grab the attention of the young man sitting across from her. Twenty-nine-year-old Aaron Smith was sitting directly across from Heidi. His laid back vibe and smooth mannerisms seemed to match perfectly with his stylish button-down GLB shirt and DKNY jeans. Heidi shot the sexy young man a peculiar expression as he hesitated to grab his wine glass. Aaron was playfully staring at Heidi when a wide smile emerged on his barber-chiseled-face. A smirk grew on Heidi's face as she started waving her wine glass like a dinner bell. Aaron shook his head and decided to humor her. He reluctantly raised his wine glass in the air.

Unlike Heidi, Aaron decided not to drink excessively tonight. From the time his phone rang just a few hours earlier, Aaron sensed he was in for a long night with Heidi. He glared at a clock on the wall of the Cheesecake Factory Restaurant. A subtle feeling of regret came over him as he learned that it was quickly approaching eleven o'clock.

"This is why you called me out here tonight, High?" Aaron asked. Heidi could tell he was only slightly amused by her moment of clarity. "Don't tell me Imma miss the replay of the Knicks game for this?" Heidi grabbed his hand and forced the two wine glasses to tap together. The gentle sound caused a childish smirk to emerge on her face. She took another sip of the drink and turned to Aaron.

"No, sweetie. First off please don't call me *High*."

Aaron quickly nodded. "No doubt, Heidi. I'm sorry I forgot," Aaron humbly said. "So tell me, is this why you called me out here tonight?"

"No, Aaron. I called you out here to talk to you," Heidi said. "Sorry I'm zoning out like this right now. When my mind gets to racing, I can't stop it. This is the first anniversary."

Aaron shot her a concerned look. "First anniversary?" Aaron quickly asked.

Heidi put her wine glass down. "Wow, I guess I didn't tell you much about my problem did I?" She slowly turned away from Aaron. "Well, today is the first anniversary of my fiancé's death." Heidi paused. The sound of her previous words sent a cold chill through her body. She felt her face getting warm and tried to fight her emotions. She lowered her voice and continued to speak. "I can't believe it's been a year. I swear. It feels like it was a month ago."

Aaron was shocked. He didn't say a word. He could tell that Heidi was going through a lot more than he had imagined. He could hear the pain in her voice as she continued to explain her mood to him.

"I never talk about him in public anymore," Heidi said. "So I apologize if I never mentioned this to you. But my fiancé died a year ago. It was sort of like a freak accident. But that's another story for another day. I don't want to burden you with all the details. But I'm trying to get over it. I just can't. Somethin' about that night always bothers me."

Aaron started slowly nodding his head. "You can talk to me. I don't feel burdened at all," he said. "That's what we are here to do. You gotta talk these things through. I wouldn't be a doing my job if I didn't listen to your issues. You know what I mean?"

Heidi looked over to Aaron and pressed her lips together. She knew exactly what Aaron was referring to.

Heidi and Aaron were both participants in a volunteer support group most commonly referred to as Call & Response. The purpose of the organization was simply to assist individuals who experienced life altering and traumatic experiences by offering one-on-one counseling sessions between the members. Each member of the organization was given a list of phone numbers to contact other members of the group. If available, both members would meet and discuss their issues and try to offer each other solutions. Aaron was fairly new to the group. He joined Call & Response roughly three months earlier after a near-death motorcycle accident.

Earlier that Spring, Aaron was test driving his brand new Ducati 749 when he spun out of control and smashed his bike into a newsstand in Plainfield, New Jersey. The impact of the collision threw Aaron head-first from the bike into the concrete wall. Six broken bones and fifty-three hours later,

Dashawn Taylor

Aaron woke up in Muhlenberg Medical Center battered and bruised. Everyone on staff at the hospital praised him for surviving one of the worse bike accidents in the County's history. The senior nurse even left his helmet in the hospital room as a reminder to Aaron of how close to his own demise he had come. Although he was able to walk away from it, the trauma of the accident accounted for dozens of sleepless nights and a total change of his lifestyle. It took him close to three months to readjust to life without motorcycles. He cringed at the very sound of a screaming Testastretta engine. Some days Aaron would even turn away at the mere sight of a bike. His fear of fast moving vehicles eventually shifted to cars and Aaron found himself feeling extremely frightened to get behind the wheel again. When the opportunity to join Call & Response was made available, he leapt at the chance. After a few sessions, his partner Heidi tried her best to make him feel comfortable about getting behind the wheel again. Just three weeks later, Heidi accomplished her mission of bringing Aaron a few steps closer to facing his fears. Her long talks and natural insight seemed to help Aaron tremendously.

Tonight, it was Aaron's opportunity to return the favor. He looked over to Heidi who was still pressing her lips together. He decided to make an attempt to help her work out her issues.

"Well, what about your fiancé's death doesn't feel right to you Heidi?" Aaron asked. "Maybe I can offer an unbiased take on it."

"An unbiased take?" Heidi skeptically asked. She shot Aaron a playful mad-face. He smiled at the expression.

"Yes an unbiased take," Aaron jokingly fired back. "You know feeling like somebody died just days ago is actually a very common feeling. Even when the death happened years ago."

"Is that right?" Heidi asked. Something in Aaron's tone made her reposition herself. She listened as he continued to speak.

"I was watching something this summer about a couple in the Midwest," Aaron continued. "They were saying how their son died in a plane crash in South America. They said it happened like ten years ago, but every time they thought about him it felt like he died just months ago. To make a long story short they did a whole presentation about ghosts and supernatural experiences and they found that their son's energy was still around the house and around them. As if their son was trying to speak to them or protect them or something."

Without warning Heidi started laughing uncontrollably. Aaron was taken aback. Heidi quickly put her hands up in an attempt to beg Aaron to spare her any additional details about the story. Her silly giggling forced Aaron to laugh with her.

"What did I say? I thought I was being serious," Aaron jokingly said.

"I'm sorry." Heidi pleaded. She was still laughing. "I thought I was the one who was drinkin' too much tonight."

Aaron started chuckling harder. "Well maybe I am drinkin' too much tonight," He joked. "But I do believe in that energy stuff. I don't know, Heidi, maybe he's still here trying to talk to you. That's why you still feel uneasy about it."

Heidi was still giggling as she nodded her head towards Aaron. His words seemed to connect with her.

"Maybe he *is* still here," Heidi said as she started to straighten up. "But you definitely don't know my ex-fiancé. If he was trying to tell me something trust me, he would not be *trying*. He would find a way to do it."

The mood at the table started to change as a strange silence fell between Heidi and Aaron. Heidi blankly stared into her drink as she started to think about Jayson. Aaron immediately picked up on the uncomfortable vibe and tried to appeal to her.

"You miss him don't you?" Aaron ruefully asked.

"I do," Heidi muttered. Her choice of words forced a small grin to emerge on her face as she thought about her dreams of marrying Jayson. Aaron couldn't place the expression but he could tell that Heidi was drifting off to another place and time. He quietly observed her as she focused harder on her wine glass. A pleasant memory of her ex-fiancé Jayson started to enter Heidi's mind. She thought back to the first day she met him in 1999.

****

Dashawn Taylor

Thursday, July 8, 1999
6:18pm

Haruno's Sushi Bar & Grill in Newark, New Jersey was a very popular place in the late 90's. Corporate executives from the New York and New Jersey professional circles used this location for industry–ice breakers and impressing visiting partners. Mega-business deals, legal battles, and even political strategies were created, destroyed, re-developed, and perfected within the elegant walls of Haruno's. On this particular summer night, however, the restaurant would be the site of a different type of connection between Heidi and her soon-to-be fiancé Jayson.

A boisterous round of laughter shot from the juice bar near the entrance of the restaurant. Jayson Carter, a floor supervisor at IDT, was laughing with a few of his co-workers when his cellular phone started to ring. Jayson quickly grabbed it from his waist and glanced at the number. His first thought was to run to a quiet place in the back of the restaurant and answer the phone but something told him to ignore the call. Jayson obeyed. He selected IGNORE on his cellphone and turned back to his co-workers. A few moments later, the front door swung open and gave way to a warm sensation that seemed to seek him out. He decided to investigate the feeling. Jayson turned around just in time to see a party-of-four enter the restaurant headed by a stunning young Black woman with a confident demeanor. Her 5 feet 8 inch athletic frame seemed to tower over every other female in the group. The silky bronzed woman sashayed into the building as she moved with a genuine assurance and sharpness about her. Her name was Heidi Kachina.

Heidi was flanked by three very attractive women, all wearing business suits. Immediately Jayson was blown away by her confident swagger. She reminded him of a Time Square billboard when he first saw her. If it weren't for the leather briefcase she was carrying, Jayson would have mistaken her for a runway model. Although she didn't say much, he could see that her street mannerisms didn't match her bamboo-colored Tahari pant suit and three inch pumps. Jayson stopped paying attention to his co-workers and focused on the party-of-four. He scanned Heidi thoroughly and was impressed by her sexy figure protruding gracefully through her business attire. A devilish grin emerged on his face as he slowly surveyed every visible curve. It didn't take long for him to make his way up to her almond shaped eyes. They were amazing. Jayson was instantly mesmerized.

He stared at Heidi until she made eye contact with him. When Heidi turned to look his way, Jayson was sure that she would deliver him a smile or some other charming indication of interest. Jayson was in a very confident mood this particular day as he was also draped in his business attire. His tailor-made suit sat flawlessly atop his Zelli Classics. Six feet tall and 270 pounds, Jayson was constantly being mistaken for a professional football player. He didn't mind. It only made him work harder during the fives days per week that he spent in the gym perfecting his action figure-style body. And tonight Jayson was definitely looking his best. He could tell Heidi was very professional and older than he was. Just the way he liked it. Jayson shot her an interested gesture and cracked a wide smile.

When Heidi looked over to him their eyes met. Her dark brown eyes seemed to stare directly through him as her prior expression never changed. Their eyes met for a split second and Heidi quickly turned away. A swift chill flooded Jayson's body. When their eyes met, Jayson got a strange feeling as if he were looking into the future. The feeling didn't last long. When Heidi quickly turned away he was flooded with confusion and embarrassment. He watched as Heidi and her party searched for seats and continued to walk toward the back of the restaurant. Jayson smiled to himself and looked into his drink. The momentary rejection made him chuckle a bit. After a few moments he decided to try again and looked over his shoulder to find where Miss Time Square had decided to sit. After a few glances Jayson found her. She was sitting with her back to the door and all he could see was the back of her head. Heidi showed no interest in him. Game over.

Jayson turned around and tried to pick up his co-worker's story, but for the next hour he couldn't shake the image of Heidi's face. He tried his best not to look in her direction but he couldn't resist. Jayson took one last look over to her table but decided not to pursue it. He motioned for the bartender and asked for his check. Most of his co-workers were already gone when the bartender came back with a small napkin and gave it to Jayson.

"Don't worry about the check sir," the bartender said. "The young lady at the table in the back said to add your tab to hers. She told me to give you this too."

The bartender's words confused Jayson. He turned to the mystery woman who was still sitting with her back to the door and glanced at the napkin.

Don't Open This Napkin
until You Get Outside.

Jayson gave the bartender an uncanny look. The bartender shrugged his shoulders and walked away. Jayson wanted to confront Miss Time Square but the secrecy excited him. He obeyed the instructions and headed to his car. Once he got inside the car he quickly opened the napkin. He started to read the note and sat back in his car seat.

Hey Handsome,
The next time you decide to undress a Young lady with
your eyes,
please have the decency to ask her
For her name first.
☺
Come Back to the Restaurant on Friday
-10PM-
Ask For Heidi....and Don't Be Late!
Kisses

An enormous smile grew on Jayson's face. His stomach started folding as a heavy feeling of excitement and nervousness came over him. Jayson was feeling like a child on Christmas Eve. He slowly turned to the entrance of the Restaurant and tried to imagine what Friday at 10pm would feel like. He closed his eyes and imagined Heidi's incredible body again. Little did he realize that this would be the beginning of the ride of his life. Heidi and Jayson spent the entire Friday evening and virtually every evening thereafter together. The explosive chemistry between the two carried them for the next seven years until that fateful night in 2006.

****

(present time)

Aaron was still quietly observing Heidi as she reminisced about those seven explosive years with Jayson. She was still staring into her drink when her phone started buzzing from her purse. As if awakening from a trance, Heidi quickly sprung into action and shuffled through her Ghurka handbag. She retrieved the phone and took a quick glance at the phone number. She curled her lips up and ignored the call. Heidi tossed the phone back in her purse and looked to Aaron.

"I'm so sorry," Heidi apologized. "I'm sitting here zoning out thinkin' about my ex. Don't kill me Aaron. I'm so rude."

"It's cool Heidi," Aaron responded. "I didn't want to bother you so I just let you sit there and work it out for yourself. What did you come up with?"

"Excuse me?" Heidi uttered.

"You just told me that something didn't feel right about that night your fiancé died," Aaron said. "So I was wondering if you figured out what was bothering you."

Heidi started slowly shaking her head. "You know to be honest I wasn't thinking about that night," Heidi quickly answered. "I try to focus more on the good times we had together. But while we are on the subject, I guess I can tell you how I feel." Aaron readjusted himself. Heidi's tone gave off the impression that he was about to hear something revealing from Heidi. He paid full attention as she began to speak. "I can tell you that I know for a fact that he was cheating on me," Heidi forcefully said. Aaron couldn't help but notice that her tone was growing darker by the second. "I know Jayson was cheating on me., Heidi continued, "but I didn't find out for sure until a few weeks before he died."

- 13 -

Aaron apologetically groaned to himself. "Damn, Heidi. I'm sorry to hear that," he said.

"It's okay. I've grown to accept it. He was a very attractive man and God knows he was definitely far from an angel. We were too young to be going so hard anyway."

"I don't mean to interrupt you, Heidi. But can I ask you a question?"

"Sure."

"How do you know he was cheating? I know it's an invasive question but again, maybe I can offer another theory," Aaron warily suggested.

Heidi shot Aaron a peculiar expression. "Let's just say it's a woman thing, Aaron. Trust me, as a female you know when your man is cheating. It was little things that he started to do those last couple of months he was alive that started to trigger my intuition. First off, he started lying to me for no reason. I would ask him small questions like *could we hang out on certain nights*, and he would straight lie to me and say he had to be somewhere that he didn't go. Or sometimes he would just shut down all together. He would get quiet for like three days straight. And then one day somebody would call his cellphone and he would start bouncing around like a happy-ass puppy. And of course I didn't know who it was. He would never talk to me about his friends. But when we stopped having sex for weeks at a time, I knew somethin' was wrong then. When I tell you that Jayson was a sex-fiend! That nigga used to handle me something crazy."

Aaron started blushing and tried to erase Heidi's last sentence from his mind. She continued to talk explicitly about her ex-fiancé.

"We had sex all the time back then," Heidi said. "So when we stopped, it was like a shock to my system. I would ask him *what's wrong with you* and he would wave me off." Heidi started to get angry. Her tone grew even colder. "So I figured if we go from having sex all the time to once in a while then somebody else was definitely getting my time. Right?"

Aaron didn't agree. His skeptical expression told the whole story. "To be honest, that doesn't mean he was cheating on you Heidi," Aaron said. "Maybe he was dealing with other problems that didn't have anything to do with sex."

"That is *just* somethin' that a man would say," Heidi barked. Aaron was taken aback by her resentment. "All dudes love sex. That's y'all nature-to fuck anything that's movin'! And once in a while if y'all like somebody then y'all would fuck *them* all the time." Aaron put his hand on his chin. He was surprised to hear Heidi talk like this. He decided to keep quiet as he listened to her vent about men. "Me and Jayson would make love all the time. It didn't matter. All the time!" Heidi boasted. "I could be away on a business trip and he would find a way to drive to where I was and we would burn down the hotel. Simple as that! We didn't even discuss sex that much. We would just do it. It wasn't until that last six months or so that things started to get really strange between us. That's how I know that something was wrong. I really can't explain it no simpler than that."

"So do you have proof that he was cheating on you?" Aaron sharply asked.

"Hell yea," Heidi answered. "Not only do I have proof that he was cheating on me, I even spoke to the bitch before!" Aaron was shocked. He sat back in his chair and shot Heidi a concerned look. "Yup," Heidi continued, "862-487-8537. I remember those numbers like it was my birthday."

"What's that?" Aaron asked.

"That's the bitch's phone number," she blurted cynically. "I found that number and called it. And lo and behold it was some chick."

Aaron was afraid to ask. But before he could put a lock on his tongue, the words were already escaping from his mouth. "So who was it?" Aaron emphatically asked.

Heidi regretfully shook her head. "I don't know," she answered. Her voice was getting lower as she thought about the question. "I never met her but I called her phone a few times trying to get more details. She kept hanging up on me and saying she didn't know what I was talking about. But she knew who I was." Heidi began to whisper as she nodded her head. "But a few months ago I found out where she lives at. My peoples found out that the number was registered to a female in Newark. But yeah, that is her phone number: 862-487-8537. She had a nerve to send it to him and everything."

Dashawn Taylor

"Oh man, don't tell me you went to her house." Aaron asked.

"No, not yet," Heidi answered. "I haven't worked up the nerve. I'm scared of what I might find out-"

Before Heidi could complete her thought, her cellphone started buzzing again. Heidi quickly dove into her purse to retrieve the phone. She snatched it from her purse and focused on the name. What she saw made her aggressively release a lung-full of hot air.

Incoming Call
MOM (HOUSE PHONE)

The vibration of the phone seemed to annoy Heidi even more now that it was in her palm. She quickly answered the phone. "Mom, why are you blowin' up my phone like this?" Heidi snapped. "What's wrong?"

A gentle yet biddy voice answered from the other line.

"Now sweetie, don't get yourself all worked up," The petite voice said.

"Huh? Mom what are you talking about? What's wrong." Heidi's voice became more anxious with every word.

"Are you calm?" Heidi's mother asked.

"Come on Mom, I'm very busy right now. It's almost eleven o'clock at night. What happened?"

"It's about Rick." her mother said. Heidi slowly covered her mouth trying to brace herself for the worse. Her mother continued to talk to her from the other line. "Rick didn't come home tonight, Heidi. He called me earlier and he sounded drunk. I'm worried that he's out with somebody."

Heidi instantly caught an attitude. "What? Mom, why are you calling me about that fool? Lock his ass out."

"Please don't be mad at me honey." Heidi's mother sounded apologetic and troubled. "I just don't want to be here alone when he comes through that door. I'm sorry to do this to you, baby." Heidi sat silently on the phone. She started pinching the front of her forehead in an attempt to calm herself.

"Heidi, are you there?" her mother whispered.

Kissed by the Devil

Heidi let out a gasp of air. "Yes mother I'm here. I'm on my way. Keep the phone next to you. Don't let him in until we get there."

"We?" her mother asked. "Who are you coming with?"

"I'll talk to you when I get there, Mom! Goodbye." Heidi hung up the phone and tossed it back in her purse. A deep feeling of regret filled Heidi as she thought about the phone call. She put both of her hands over her face and put her head down. Aaron tried to console her.

"Is everything okay, Heidi?" He asked.

"Yeah. It's just my mother's boyfriend. I can't stand his ass." Heidi raised her head. "She thinks he's cheatin' too." Heidi started sarcastically laughing to herself. "See what I'm saying? It's in y'all nature." Aaron decided not to take the bait. He quietly watched as Heidi started to pack her things and grab her jacket. "Well we can pick this up another time, sweetie," Heidi quietly said. Her mood was very gloomy. "I'm not busy tomorrow, maybe we can get together after work. I'm still moving my stuff out of the old apartment. So maybe we can have dinner or something after that."

"That's right. You're moving right?" Aaron asked. "So have you found a new place yet?"

"Yeah. I been renting out a room until my apartment is ready."

"I feel you." Aaron said. "If you need anything, just let me know. I don't want you roaming the streets with no place to stay."

A smile grew on Heidi's face as she looked over to Aaron. "Thanks. I'll be fine."

"Okay. Let me walk you to your car," Aaron suggested.

Heidi agreed and watched as Aaron paid for the drinks. They both put on their fall jackets and headed for the exit of the Cheesecake Factory Restaurant. The brisk November air made Heidi move with purpose to her car. Aaron was right with her. As they approached her car, Aaron started chuckling to himself. Heidi turned to him.

"What's so funny?" Heidi asked.

Aaron started shaking his head and pointed to her license plate. "That right there. I'm laughing at that." Aaron said.

Dashawn Taylor

Heidi looked at her license plate and laughed. "Yeah that's an inside joke between me and him."

"Your ex-fiancé?"

"Yes. He bought those for me trying to be funny. You don't know how many times I got pulled over for these damn vanity plates." Heidi started laughing.

"So why don't you change them?" Aaron asked.

"Nah. I have to keep them," Heidi quietly said as she stared at the rear plate. "These plates are the only things I got left that he ever gave to me." There was a brief silence in the parking lot. Heidi turned and gave Aaron a friendly hug. He returned the gesture.

"Goodnight, Princess," he whispered.

After a moment, Aaron watched Heidi get into her car and start the engine. He was slowly walking toward his car when she pulled out of her parking space and headed for the main road. She slowly passed him and blew the horn. Aaron smiled and watched her pass. He read the license plate one more time. What he read made him chuckle again and shake his head. The license plates simply read: SO HIGH.

Chapter 2

Thursday, November 1, 2007
Patterson, New Jersey

11:23 p.m.

*"W*here the fuck is my jacket?" Faith's voice was cracking as she tried her best to yell over the loud music. The flashing lights in the club made it hard for her to see. Faith rarely worked on her day off and something told her to stay home tonight. Three days of serving drinks to horny men and women down at Dirty Betty's Go-Go Bar was usually enough for Faith during the work week, but tonight she needed the extra money for a major problem she was dealing with back home. As she recklessly looked for her twelve-hundred-dollar chinchilla fur she couldn't believe another problem was waiting for her at the job.

"I hate to leave early but this bullshit is messin' up my money." Faith groaned as she frantically looked around. "Who the hell got my jacket?"

Faith was fuming. The commotion behind the bar started to draw a small crowd from the dance floor. The nosey patrons could tell by Faith's body language that something was terribly wrong. Her very attractive baby-face was twisted with anger and disgust. She started to leave the bar area when a demeaning male voice screamed from behind her. *Yeah bitch, you betta get the hell outta here*! Faith quickly turned around and noticed a familiar face emerging from the crowd. It was Jordan. He was bobbing his head heatedly and pointing at her. Faith instantly flared up.

Dashawn Taylor

"Oh my God nigga you funny," Faith yelled. "You wasn't sayin' that dumb shit when ya tongue was all in my asshole. You punk bitch!" Laughs and snickers came from the crowd seated at the bar. Jordan looked around and tried to defend himself. His girlfriend Maya was next to him wearing a confused and angry expression.

"Bitch, we only fucked once and it wasn't all like that and you know it!" Jordan yelled. "I can't believe you lying to my girl like that. Just tell the truth you goddamn liar."

Faith frowned at Jordan and turned to his girlfriend. Maya was close to tears as the details of Jordan's indiscretions were revealed by the argument. It took every bone in her petite body to fight back her true emotions. She didn't know who to be angrier with: her boyfriend of two years or her co-worker of ten months.

"Maya...I swear girl, this nigga told me that y'all broke up four months ago," Faith pleaded. She tried to ease her tone when she spoke to Maya. "That's why he stop coming to the club. Now all of a sudden he's coming to the club to check you out? Please! This nigga thought it was my day off so he knew it was safe to come through. I swear, Maya. You my girl! Why would I mess with him behind ya back like that?"

" 'Cause you a slut monkey. You nasty bitch!" Jordan yelled. His words seemed to cut brutally into Faith's ears like a broken bottle.

"Nigga, fuck you!" Faith screamed. She was pushed beyond the boiling point. Faith grabbed a martini glass from the bar and threw it at Jordan. The vodka flew everywhere as the glass hit Jordan in the chest. The small crowd backed up to avoid being sprayed by the drink. Maya went into attack mode. She rushed to the bar and tried to grab Faith's arm. She managed to get a hold of Faith's wrist with her left hand as she swiftly followed with a flailing right that connected on Faith's cheek. More club-goers gathered around the bar to watch the fight that seemed to explode in a matter of seconds. The two women were banging like total strangers. Jordan tried to pull his girlfriend away from the bar but her hands were tangled in Faith's extra-long hair. The bouncers noticed the commotion from across the room and rushed to the scene. As three bouncers grabbed Jordan and Maya another bouncer jumped over the bar and grabbed

Faith. The two women were still yelling insults and swinging as the bouncers separated them.

"Faith... chill baby. Chill! It's over. Let's go!" One bouncer yelled as he picked Faith up by her stomach and carried her away from the bar. The three bouncers hustled Jordan and Maya through the club. The standing-room-only crowd seemed to part like the Red Sea as Jordan, Maya, and the bouncers rushed through the club yelling and cursing. The DJ stopped the music and tried to calm everything down. It took less than a minute for more bouncers to rush over and force Jordan and Maya out of the front door. At the same time Faith was being forced into the back office of the club. "Stay in here Faith. I'll be right back," the bouncer instructed.

Faith humbly agreed with the bouncer and stayed in the office. The excitement and fear had her pacing back and forth. Her hands were still shaking as she looked in the mirror and noticed that her mouth was bleeding. She couldn't feel the pain but she knew Maya hit her with a few good shots before the bouncers got to her. Although she had a very bad temper, Faith was not a good fighter. She could talk her way out of most fights but when it came to defending herself, she needed a lot of work. As she checked to see if her tooth was loose Faith realized that her Tai Chi Chuan classes had been a total waste of money.

A loud crash from the office door startled Faith. She turned around expecting to see Maya coming through the door still in attack mode. To her surprise she saw a short and heavyset dark-skinned woman. The 238-pound lady was tawdrily draped in a black sleeveless dress topped off with a kimono duster. The costume jewelry on her wrist, neck, and fingers grossly failed to exude the desired classy appearance. Her middle-aged wrinkles and permanent pout made her face appear angry all the time. Her name was Bethany Stanford; also known as Dirty Betty.

"Child...I'm 'bout fed up with yo' hot ass. What's yo' problem?" Dirty Betty's tone was livid. Her croaky voice exposed her smoking addiction with every word. Faith looked at her in fear. She didn't know what to say. Dirty Betty was a powerful woman in her circle. She was close to celebrating her 55th birthday but she still maintained her ties to the street hustlers and young guns in northern New Jersey. They all frequented her Go-Go Bar and Betty took full advantage of every service they had to offer.

When the owner of another Gentlemen's Club tried to steal a few of her dancers, Dirty Betty called on those same young guns and paid them a handsome sum to correct the problem. Unfortunately for the owner of the other club, the job was carried out to perfection and he died from his injuries. Since then, people both respected and feared Dirty Betty. She didn't hesitate to use her resources to stay on top of her game. Now that she was approaching her winter years, Dirty Betty was becoming less tolerant and more ruthless. Tonight Faith was trying her best not to see Betty's ruthless side as she tried to explain herself.

"Betty...I didn't start that shit out there," Faith squealed. "That was Maya. She wasn't trying to hear shit I had to say." Dirty Betty's expression never changed. Her judging eyes seemed to read through Faith's weak explanation. Faith didn't give up. She was determined to tell her side of the story. "Look Betty, I'm sorry for what happened out there. You know me. She jumped on me. And she's a wild bitch. I couldn't even get her off of me. I was about to leave when her and her boyfriend flared up on me."

"So you still didn't answer the right question," Dirty Betty said. Faith sensed something dark about her tone.

"What question?" Faith asked. She was clearly confused.

Dirty Betty moved closer to Faith. "Did you fuck him?"

"Excuse me?"

"You heard me, Faith".

Dirty Betty was becoming more leery. "I said did you fuck him? Tell me the truth."

Faith couldn't figure out where this line of questioning was going. She decided to be honest with Betty to see where it would lead. "Yes. I did. I thought they broke up," Faith pleaded.

Dirty Betty started shaking her head. Her mood grew darker. "Godammit, Faith! Y'all bitches work together. That shit is just nasty. You got a lot to learn about boundaries, little girl."

Faith's mouth fell opened. She didn't know how to react as Dirty Betty continued to bash her. "You a wrap, Faith. I was

gonna keep you on but Maya is my best dancer and you fuckin'
her man like you own the place. I can always find another
bartender. But do you know how hard it is to find a girl that can
move like her?" Faith was frozen. She couldn't believe what
she was hearing. She was getting fired on her day off. And the
worse part was that she was being fired because of a man. Dirty
Betty walked by her and gave her a double take. "What are you
doin'?" Dirty Betty yelled at her. "Get the fuck out! Did I
stutter? You're fired!"

Faith was stunned. She stared at her boss in disbelief.
For a brief moment Faith felt the courage to fire back at Dirty
Betty, but decided not to pursue it. Her pride turned her around
and she headed for the door. As bad as she needed the job she
knew her boss had it out for her. It was just a matter of time
before Betty's animosity towards Faith would come to the
surface.

Faith stormed out the office and slammed the door
behind her. She was greeted by one of the bouncers from the
club. It was Rueben. He shot her an indifferent expression and
handed her the chinchilla fur she was looking for.

"Thanks Rue'." Faith's voice sounded defeated.

Rueben nodded and walked her out the club. He had
heard the entire argument through the door and knew Faith was
getting a raw deal. But he was scared of Dirty Betty, too, so he
kept his opinion to himself. Fearing that Maya and Jordan were
outside waiting for her, Rueben walked Faith all the way to the
car and shook her hand. Of all the bouncers in the club he was
the only gentleman. Faith didn't speak as she got in the car and
fired up the engine. She wiped a few tears away and watched
Rueben walk back into the bar. A quick flashback of the fight
with Maya made her jerk the car in gear and peel out of the
parking lot. She got about a half-mile down the road when she
heard a beeping sound come from her jacket pocket. It was her
cellphone. She quickly grabbed the jacket and pulled the phone
from her pocket. The name on the phone calmed her spirits.

1 Missed Call
Heidi

Dashawn Taylor

A befitting smirk rose on her face as she shook her head. She couldn't wait to return the call and tell her best friend what just went down at Dirty Betty's.

Chapter 3

Thursday, November 1, 2007
Irvington, NJ

11:48 pm

$\mathcal{A}$ couple towns over in the city of Irvington, New Jersey, the sound of a car horn echoed off an empty street. Shaheed Porter, a twenty-one-year-old street hustler, was sitting impatiently behind the wheel of his 2006 Dodge Charger. Shaheed had been blowing for over fifteen minutes now and there was still no sign of his older brother Robert. Shaheed poked his head out of the window and stared at the three-family house he was parked in front of. Shaheed was noticeably frustrated. He looked at his watch again and grabbed his cellphone.

"This muthafucka betta be dead!" Shaheed whispered to himself. He aggressively dialed ten numbers and pressed SEND. He let the phone ring a few times before Robert's voicemail picked up. A loud song came blaring out of the other end of the phone. Shaheed pulled the phone away from his ear in frustration. Shaheed secretly cursed his brother. *This fuckin nigga, I swear!* Shaheed waited for the beeping sound and started yelling into the phone. "Yo! Asshole! It's midnight! I'm outside. Come the fuck on!"

Shaheed hung up the phone and tossed it in the passenger seat. He looked at the house again and blew the horn. Still no sign of Robert. After a few seconds Shaheed's cellphone began to ring. Without a thought Shaheed flipped the phone open and started yelling again. "Yo, nigga, lets go!" Shaheed commanded. "If you make me miss this tonight, imma fuck you up!"

A female voice on the other end let out a loud gasp. "Shah', is that you?"

"Oh damn, Rhonda. I'm sorry bay, I thought you was my brother," Shaheed stuttered.

"What are you doin', you never called me back from earlier today," Rhonda said. She sounded worried.

"I told you I gotta work tonight. Let me call you back, okay?" Shaheed tried his best to rush his girlfriend off the phone. He didn't want to miss Robert's call. Rhonda realized this and tried her best to keep him on the phone.

"I'm not worried about me anymore, Shah." Rhonda said. Her voice was becoming sterner with every word. "I'm worried about you. I don't want you to do anything stupid."

Shaheed immediately flared up. "Imma call you back, Rhonda. I gotta go." Without warning Shaheed hung up the phone and tossed it back into the passenger seat. He blew the horn a few more times before he unlocked his door and got out the car. He decided to knock on Robert's door until he came outside. Shaheed was quickly reaching his boiling point tonight. Today had already been a very long day for Shaheed and his brother wasn't making things any better.

Shaheed was not the typical street hustler. In fact, Shaheed didn't hustle at all. He made most of his money as a middleman for a big time hustler from Harlem named Abdul. On the surface, Shaheed could pass for a regular young man living a normal life. His well-groomed appearance and fresh-face gave him a college boy look. But in the tri-state underworld Shaheed was best known for setting up major deals between drug crews from different cities. He always felt that it was safer never to touch the product. That was rule number one.

Rule number two was never to mix business with family. Tonight he was breaking that rule. But desperate times called for desperate measures. Shaheed's life was on the line. A few weeks back a major deal went wrong in Detroit. In a strange twist of fate, Shaheed's name came up in a conversation between a snitch and the Detroit Police Department. His boss Abdul found out the news and threatened to kill Shaheed and eliminate any links to him. The news scared Shaheed so much that he set up a meeting with Abdul's right-hand man Rafeek. Rafeek's instructions to Shaheed were clear and to the point:

Abdul doesn't wanna see you at all, Shaheed. He thinks you fucked him with the Detroit deal. He's expectin' $75,000 by next Friday and he wants you to leave Jersey. And if I was you, I would bounce down south or to the west coast or somethin'. Adbul's been known to eliminate smaller problems if you catch my drift! Trust me on this one, Shah', just do what he says and leave before next Friday.

Shaheed was not the type of person to scare easy. But he knew Abdul's reputation and he knew the threat against his life was serious. He was playing in a man's game and the circumstances quickly turned against him. Shaheed had been given ten days to come up with the money and pick up his things and go. He managed to raise close to $20,000 but tonight was his last opportunity to come up with the rest of the money. Although he was confident in his plan, Shaheed knew that he didn't have a minute to waste. If he could just get his brother Robert to cooperate everything would work out fine.

Shaheed banged on the front door of the three-family house. The sound was loud enough to cause a few dogs in the neighborhood to start barking. Despite the noise, Shaheed continued the banging. He paused for a second and looked through the window on the top of the door and noticed his brother jogging casually down the stairs. He stepped back and watched his brother open the door. As soon as the door swung open Shaheed immediately tore into Robert.

"Yo man, you can be so fuckin' ignorant at times!" Shaheed yelled.

Robert gave Shaheed an abrupt look. "So that means you want me to go back upstairs and get back in the bed then?" Robert snapped. "I told you, nigga, I'm not like you. I can't be stayin' up all night like you!" Shaheed stared at his older brother Robert and shook his head. He turned around and headed back to the car. Robert waved him off and followed him.

Robert and Shaheed were like oil and water. They were blood brothers but they had two totally different personalities.

Dashawn Taylor

Although Shaheed was four years younger than Rob, he was clearly more mature. Shaheed was a go-getter. His determination and hustle would always stand out in any crowd. His heart was made of steel and he was very intelligent. Shaheed hated the fact that Robert was the total opposite. Robert was more of a laidback person. He was less confrontational and borderline timid. Shaheed loved and respected his older brother but hated his cowardly ways. A few years back Robert's personality landed his younger brother Shaheed in a tight situation that shifted his life into another direction.

Before he entered into the world of drugs and money, Shaheed had another serious addiction: he was addicted to stealing cars. Before his sixteenth birthday Shaheed had stolen over a hundred cars and been arrested twice for joy riding. Some cars he stole for fun and others he stole to make money. He used to work with his older cousin Vegas who would sell the stolen cars to a chop shop in Hillside, New Jersey. Shaheed would make a couple of hundred dollars per car but most of the time he would steal cars just for the adrenaline rush. On his sixteenth birthday Shaheed decided to steal a car for himself. His plan was to steal the car, take it to the chop shop and replace the VIN. He was stalking a 1998 Honda Accord for nearly two months. The owner was careless with his vehicle and it was simple for Shaheed to steal it. It took about a week but Shaheed finally got the car from the chop shop, complete with the new VIN. Feeling proud of himself and eager to show off his new car, Shaheed decided to pick up his brother from his girlfriend's house one afternoon. It didn't take long for the questions to start from Robert once he got in the car with Shaheed.

"Baybro, whose car is this?" Robert asked as he gave the car a quick once-over. He focused his attention on the steering column to see if it was broken or if any wires were exposed. Robert was shocked to see a full set of keys in the ignition. Shaheed lowered his car seat and put one hand on the wheel. He started nodding to the imaginary music in his head as he sped away from the house.

"C'mon fam, this is my shit," Shaheed said confidently. He continued to nod even harder as he headed for the Garden State Parkway. "I told you I was making me some serious

money, man. So I went out and got me a little sumthin'
sumthin'." Robert shot him a dubious look. "You like it?"
Shaheed asked.

"Yeah, it's decent. Where's the paperwork?" Robert
asked cautiously.

"Man, you are one shook nigga. Relax, the paperwork is
in my name. Vegas hooked it all up for me. All I gotta do is pay
the insurance on it." Shaheed cracked a devilish smile. "If you
want one, Rob, just let me know and I'll go get it for you."

Robert shook his head emphatically. "Hell no, nigga. I
don't need no stolen cars parked in front of my girl's crib. She's
already bitchin' about my work schedule."

Shaheed quickly snapped his head and looked at his
brother. He closed his eyes and started shaking his head. "Rob,
you a sucker for love man. I don't know why you stay in those
dumbass relationships. You know what, I'm 'bout to take you
with me to one of my shorty's crib. She got a cousin that's a
straight up frizeek." Shaheed started laughing as he hugged the
on-ramp doing close to 40 mph. "Trust me man, you'll love her.
And she will definitely love you back!"

They both started laughing as Robert looked at Shaheed.
"Knowin' you dog she's probably a hood rat," Robert said. "I'm
good. Thanks for the offer."

Shaheed was doing about 80mph now. He was weaving
through the parkway traffic like a reckless ambulance. Robert
started to get worried and put on his seatbelt. Shaheed tried to
ignore him and turned up the music. He was doing close to 90
when he saw a speed trap ahead. He immediately tried to slow
down but his momentum forced him through the trap. Robert
turned around just in time to see the red and blue lights flashing
from the state trooper's vehicle. The police car came speeding
out of the trap and headed straight for the Honda.

"This is crazy," Robert said to himself as his heart
dropped into his stomach. "Goddamn. We gonna fuckin' go to
jail for this shit." Robert was yelling now. He frantically turned
around and stared at Shaheed who was now smiling. His brother
had a shifty look in his eyes and Robert didn't like it. "See, you
like this bullshit, Shah'," Robert yelled. "This shit ain't funny,
nigga."

Shaheed's mood suddenly changed as if he was coming

Dashawn Taylor

back to reality. He turned off the music and tried to calm Robert down. "Man, shut the fuck up," Shaheed snapped. "I ain't gonna run with yo scared ass in the car. Relax and sit back. I'll take care of this cracka. I told you I got all the paperwork on this thing so we good."

Shaheed started to pull the car over to the side of the road. His heart was racing but he stayed calm. The rush of adrenaline felt like a natural high to him. Shaheed cracked another slick smile and turned to his brother. Robert put his hand on his head and started mumbling to himself. Shaheed started nodding to more imaginary music as he reached over to grab his paperwork from the glove compartment. He patted Rob on the shoulder in an effort to reassure him. "C'mon man, trust me, we good. I been through this bullshit a million times," Shaheed bragged.

Robert didn't budge. Shaheed saw some movement in his rearview mirror and turned around. His smiled widened as he saw the state trooper cautiously approaching the driver side door. He lowered the window just as the trooper arrived to the door.

"License, registration, and insurance card, son." The trooper's voice was stern and arrogant. Shaheed made eye contact with the trooper and tried his best to appear relaxed and confident. He shuffled through his paperwork and pulled out a fake registration card and fake insurance card. Before he could give the trooper the credentials, Shaheed heard a loud commotion just over his right shoulder. The trooper quickly stepped back and ducked his head in the window. The sound startled Shaheed as he turned to see what was going on. His mouth fell open when he saw his brother fumbling to unlock the passenger door. Before Shaheed could react, his brother pushed the door wide open and jumped out of the car. The trooper reached for his gun and told Robert to freeze. Robert was too fast. He managed to make it out of the car in a split second. Robert darted down a steep hill just off the highway and out of site before the trooper could pursue him. Shaheed was shocked. He couldn't believe how fast his brother was running to get away from the scene. Shaheed started laughing. Knowing that there was nothing he could do, Shaheed shut off the engine and put his hands up. This would be the third charge he would catch for a

- 30 -

stolen car. This time he would spend nine months in the youth house instead of the normal sixty days.

Shaheed's life changed for the worse after his third arrest for grand larceny. He eventually dropped out of high school and started hustling on the streets of Newark. Shaheed never really blamed his brother for his situation. He had too much love and respect for him. It was that same love and respect that made him call on Robert tonight to help him out with his problem with Abdul. And although he was willing to come along for the ride, Robert began to feel an all-too-familiar uneasiness as Shaheed fired up the engine of the Dodge Charger and sped up the quiet street.

$Chapter$ 4

Friday, November 2, 2007
New Brunswick, New Jersey

12:18 a.m.

Twenty minutes later, in a semi-posh apartment in New Brunswick, a very attractive Melissa Davis was finding it hard to fall asleep. But this twenty-six-year-old professional type was seeking a different kind of satisfaction. Melissa slowly stood up from the queen size bed and gave her boyfriend Lamar a sensual smirk. Just a few moments ago, Lamar ordered her to stand up and come to him as he leisurely leaned against the adjacent wall. Melissa and Lamar were both stark naked and the anticipation of pleasure was heavy in the air. Melissa strolled over to her boyfriend like an evil temptress and slowly wrapped her long arms around his neck. Her skin tingled with excitement as she felt Lamar's hands grab her tightly around her naked hips. Melissa always became nervous before she made love to her boyfriend Lamar but something was very special about tonight.

"I swear to God, boy, if you drop me I'm gonna to kill you." The playful tone in Melissa's voice did not match the seriousness of her threat. Her heart jumped as Lamar quickly lifted her off of her feet and raised her in the air. She instinctively raised her long sexy legs and wrapped them tightly around Lamar's waist.

"Shut up M', you killin' my concentration," Lamar joked. "Let's do it like this."

"Boy, you can't last long when we layin' down." Melissa snickered as she gave Lamar another playful smile. "What's gonna happen to me when you cum? Huh?" Melissa giggled. "I just know you gonna drop me, nigga." They both laughed. Melissa slowly began to kiss Lamar on his lips.

"Come on, baby, lay me down," Melissa whispered. With both her hands she grabbed Lamar's face. "Let's do it regular first. After that, you can have me however you want me." Lamar gave Melissa a quick grin. He had to chuckle to himself as he thought about her request. Lamar knew that she was very frisky and down for whatever when it came to him. He could never last long the first time with her. Between her sexy curves and crazy facial expressions, Melissa would make him cum within minutes of penetrating her. So he agreed to move to the bed.

As Lamar began to carry her to the bed, Melissa's body language suddenly shifted. Her arms became more relaxed and she started to rub Lamar's back. She started kissing his lips again and released a sexual moan.

"I missed you so much, daddy," Melissa whispered. She rubbed her moist pussy against Lamar's washboard stomach in slow motion. Up and down. She felt Lamar's dick slowly rise again. He was walking slowly now, trying to maintain his balance. Lamar pulled her closer. His huge hands were gripped tightly around her naked ass and he lifted her higher. Melissa gritted her teeth and inhaled sharply as she felt the head of Lamar's throbbing dick graze her skin.

"Damn, baby," Lamar whispered.

"I know," Melissa moaned. "It feels like I haven't seen you in five years!"

Lamar laid Melissa down on the bed and slowly crawled on top of her. Before she could look down at Lamar he was licking the middle of her chest and working his way up to her neck. As she felt his warm tongue against her collarbone, a loud humming sound came from the other side of the room. It was his cell phone. Lamar started kissing Melissa's neck passionately, trying to ignore the sound. After a few seconds the humming stopped. Lamar grabbed Melissa's shoulders and slid up to her left ear. He started to nibble on it and she responded by raising her legs in the air and wrapping them higher around his waist. She noticed her lips were just inches away from his ear and she decided to take full advantage.

"What are you gonna do to me daddy?" Melissa whispered.

"What do you want me to do to you?" Lamar chuckled. He raised his head to look at Melissa. Her face grew more serious and Lamar could tell that she was getting more and more excited. She grabbed the back of his head and pulled him closer to her.

"I want you to say it, daddy."

"Say what, baby?" Lamar whispered. "That you want me to fuck you?"

"Yes! Say it, daddy, I miss hearing you—"

A loud ringing noise suddenly came blaring from the foot of the bed, interrupting Melissa. It was Lamar's house phone. His ringer was set on high and the sound caused Melissa's heart to race.

Lamar abruptly looked at his phone in discontent. "You gotta be shittin' me!"

Melissa quickly grabbed his face again. "Don't answer it, sweetie! Please don't, Lamar."

Lamar looked towards the phone and then back at Melissa. She was noticeably disappointed. "I got to." Lamar whispered. "I just came home. It could be anybody."

"Please, baby, we almost there." Lamar gave her a rueful look and turned to reach for his phone. Melissa grabbed his wrist and turned him around. "It's been eights months, Lamar. They can wait 'til we done." Melissa's face told the whole story. She didn't want Lamar to answer the phone. The last time she saw Lamar was in late February and she remembered the exact day as if it were yesterday.

Almost eight months ago on a cold winter night, the heavy snow and bad weather forced Lamar and Melissa to stay home. It was too cold to hang out at the club so Melissa decided to treat Lamar to a Japanese massage session. She was right in the middle of working his lower back when the phone rang. She pleaded for him not to answer but he said he had to. Within seconds of picking up the phone Lamar's mood changed. He tossed the phone against the wall, got dressed, and rushed out the door without saying a word. Melissa was devastated. She got a call two days later from the Middlesex County Correctional

Facility with Lamar on the line. He had been arrested for assault and strong armed robbery. He eventually pleaded down to a lesser charge and was sentenced to thirteen months for the assault.

Eight months later Lamar was now out of jail and back at his apartment in New Brunswick. But now Melissa was experiencing an eerie sense of déjà vu as Lamar seemed to be giving her the same look. As she gazed into his dark eyes she couldn't help but feel that she would soon be left alone and confused, again. Lamar looked at the house phone and then back at Melissa.

"I swear Melissa, if this is not important, I'm gonna make this up to you." He looked down at her sexy legs again and licked his lips. "And the last eight months, too."

Melissa was not convinced. She felt a knot suddenly form in her stomach as she watched Lamar walk over to pick up the phone. He grabbed the house phone but did not answer it immediately. He paused for a moment with the phone in his hand. After the seventh ring, Lamar walked over to his cellphone mounted on the charger. He was curious to know who could be calling him this late and so persistently. He picked up the cellular with his free hand and read the call log.

1 Missed Call
1 New Voicemail

Jesus Christ! Who is this? Lamar thought to himself. He couldn't imagine who it could be. The ninth ring of the house phone had Lamar cursing out loud. He was now in a rush to see who called his cellphone. He clicked on the view button and found the answer.

1 Missed Call
High (CellPhone)

Lamar cracked a nervous smirk. Melissa was still watching him and he didn't want her to see that his anger subsided. Lamar was almost excited to hear the eleventh ring on his house phone. He started to walk towards his window away from the bed when he answered the phone.

"Well, well, well...Ms. High? What's goin' on?" Lamar said with a pleasant tone.

"Stop calling me that!" Heidi snapped from the other line.

"No doubt. My bad." Lamar said. "Long time stranger. What's the deal?"

"Whatever! What are you doing right now?" Heidi's voice was filled with purpose and Lamar could tell she was not in the mood for small talk.

"I'm watering my lawn!" Lamar joked.

"Is she cute at least?" Heidi snapped.

Lamar's smile widened. "Yes. And it definitely needs some trimming." Lamar said. His voice was lower now.

"Well, you have to put your weed wacker away, nigga. I need to talk to you. It's about Rick."

Lamar looked over his shoulder at Melissa who was sitting impatiently on the edge of the bed. "Don't do this to me, High. Not now," Lamar whispered.

"That's not my name, dammit!" Heidi was getting angry now. "I'm going to Mom's house now and I want you to meet me over there. Don't say "no" either Lamar. I really need you to be there. She just called me and told me that he's not home but he's comin' there soon. He's such an asshole and I'm ready to put him in his place!"

There was a long silence. Lamar grabbed the phone with both hands and began to poke the antenna gently against his forehead. He felt stressed now.

"You still there?" Heidi yelled. "Lamar? Hello?"

Lamar could hear Heidi's voice cutting through the quiet air in his bedroom. He was hesitant to come back to the phone. He hated to rush to Heidi's aid all the time. And although they were first cousins, Lamar loved Heidi like a sister. They were born only ten days apart and both grew up in the same house together as kids. Lamar's mother and father died in a car crash when he was only four and Heidi's mom took Lamar in as her own son. Heidi didn't have any real brothers or sisters so Lamar was like her only sibling. His role as Heidi's protector began many years ago when they both were kids.

Dashawn Taylor

Lamar and Heidi attended the same grammar school. One day when they both were in the fourth grade Heidi came home crying. Because her young body began developing at a very early age, all the boys used to tease Heidi about her chest. Names like *Double Deez* and *Betty Boop* seemed to follow Heidi around like a lost puppy. One older boy even took the teasing a step further and grabbed Heidi's chest during gym class. When she confronted the boy he pushed her down and stepped on her ankle. Heidi was scared to tell the teacher so she went home and told Lamar. Lamar was also big for his age and he always had his father's temper. The next day Lamar waited after school and Heidi pointed the boy out to him. The fifth grader's name was Tyrone. Tyrone didn't get six steps outside of the doors before Lamar ran up and swung at him. *Bam!* From afar it looked as if Lamar knocked Tyrone out with his bare fist. But when they got home Heidi saw that Lamar swung a sock at Tyrone with two d-sized batteries in it. None of the kids ever messed with Heidi again until she got into high school. Lamar protected Heidi his whole life and never apologized for his love for her. But tonight something didn't feel right about Heidi's request.

Instead of getting angry and protective like he did in the past, Lamar tried to calm his temper. He decided to listen to everything she said. He put the phone back to his ear and continued his conversation with Heidi.

"What time are you gonna be at Mom's house?" Lamar whispered.

"I'm passing Trenton now so I should be there around 1:30 or so."

"Goddamn, High." Lamar was fuming. He was gritting his teeth now trying to control his anger. "I just came home!"

"So what the fuck does that mean, Lamar?" she snapped.

"What does that mean?" Lamar barked. "That means that my dick is harder than a stick of dynamite and I'm ready to take care of this shit."

"Aww, nigga, fall back," Heidi snapped as she interrupted Lamar. "You can take care of that shit tomorrow. I wouldn't ask you to do this tonight if I didn't think it was important, man. She's not only my mother, Lamar. She is yours too! Or did you forget that?"

"What the fuck?" Lamar whispered as he looked at his clock on the wall and turned back to Melissa. She stood up angrily and put her clothes back on. It took her less than a minute to get dressed. Melissa was pissed. Lamar motioned to her, but Melissa waved him off and grabbed her jacket. Lamar turned around and whispered into the phone.

"This better not be another false alarm, High." Lamar said. "Give me like forty-five minutes and I'll be there." Lamar watched Melissa as she put on her jacket and reached for her car keys. He shook his head in disgust and put his hand over the phone. He didn't want Melissa to hear the rest of his conversation. "Heidi, you better be at Mom's house when I get there and we better make this quick," Lamar angrily whispered. "Don't make me wait like last time. I wanna get back over this way in less than two hours."

Lamar walked over to his nightstand and slammed the phone down. He noticed Melissa was headed to the door and tried to stop her. "Melissa, I know you mad but I have to do this," Lamar pleaded. Melissa continued to the door, deciding not to turn around. "Melissa, you just gonna leave like that?" Lamar asked.

"I'm so tired of competing with that bitch," Melissa yelled. "If you get locked up this time, don't fuckin' call me again."

Lamar rushed over to Melissa and grabbed her arm. "Don't call her a *bitch*," Lamar snapped as he turned Melissa around. He noticed for the first time that her eyes were filling with tears. She was more frustrated than sad. Lamar decided to lower his voice as he continued to plead with her. "What do you want me to do, Melissa?" Lamar said. "She's my sister."

"She's ya cousin, nigga! And she doesn't care about you all like that!" Melissa barked. A few tears slid down her face as she blasted Lamar. "We talked about this crap before, Lamar. She only cares about the shit you can do for her. You're gonna go over there, she's gonna get what she wants, and that's it." Melissa pulled her arm away from Lamar and backed up towards the door. "Eight months Lamar? She never came to see you. No letters, no notes, no pictures, nothing. Why not? Ask her that. You ain't been home twelve hours and you gotta run to her aid? Fuck that! Blood sister or kissing cousin, she is playin' you in the worst way and you don't even see it."

Lamar tried to calm her down. "Melissa listen to me-"

"No, Lamar, listen to me," Melissa yelled, cutting him off. "Since I've met you, you been on this *blood is thicker than Kool-Aid* shit. But that shit is tired, nigga. She's miserable! Can't you see that? She has no man, no life, and just waits around for people to bail her out of shit all the time. You know that, Lamar. I love you and I hate to see you acting so weak. And to be honest, if it were up to me, I would've smacked that bitch a long time ago."

Lamar tittered and turned away from Melissa. He hated to hear her talk like that. Melissa was a very preppy girl from Pittsburg, Pennsylvania. She was half Black and half Arubian but she was always mistaken for being half Asian because of her very fair skin and slightly chinky eyes. Lamar was always fond of overly–ghetto girls. The bigger the backside and the bigger the attitude the better the chance a woman had of grabbing Lamar's attention. Lamar rarely dated preppy girls, and Melissa was as preppy as they came. She was beautiful, affluent and too busy to deal with frivolous drama. Lamar always joked that Melissa's nose was so far in the air that she could smell what God was eating. But he loved her. And although Melissa came from a rich family, she was very down to earth when it came to dealing with Lamar. But in Melissa's eyes Heidi was threatening her happiness with Lamar. She hated the fact that Heidi had so much control over his emotions. And tonight she saw exactly what kind of power Heidi had over him. As Melissa stared into her boyfriend's eyes, a strange feeling came over her. She knew that she would lose another piece of Lamar once she left the apartment that night.

"I really mean it, Lamar," Melissa whispered. "This is not anger or jealousy talking. This is some real shit, sweetie. I really can't stand that bitch. Leave my man out there like that? No calls, no visits, no "*I'm sorries*"? Fuck that! She's the only reason you in this pile of shit you're in right now. If she was really in your corner, she wouldn't be puttin' so much pressure on you."

Melissa had a lot of conviction in her voice and Lamar could hear it. He quickly became angry as he listened to her. Lamar knew most of the things she was trying to tell him were true but he didn't want to hear them from her. Lamar tried to calm her down and reached out to hug her, but again she backed away. Melissa was so upset that her hands were twitching slightly.

"I tell you what, Lamar, go see her tonight. Do what you got to do. But please do me a favor. Ask her why she didn't come see you while you were locked up. Ask her where she was and what she was doing. And I bet you a hundred over fifty that the answer will tell you a lot about your so-called sister."

Lamar looked at Melissa. She gave him a last look over and walked out the door. He didn't stop her. He closed the door behind her and walked over to his closet to get dressed. The stress began to mount. He had too much to think about in one day. Just hours ago he was walking out of the steel doors of the Middlesex County Lockup and now he was dealing with an old beef between his girlfriend and his sister. Lamar got dressed and grabbed his keys. He noticed Melissa left her diamond studs on the table next to his wallet. He reached for the house phone to call her before she got too far. When he turned the phone around to dial, he noticed the red light was still lit on his cordless phone. *I didn't hang up the phone?* Lamar thought to himself. Lamar quickly put the phone to his ear.

"Hello?" Lamar blurted. There was no answer. Lamar couldn't hear a sound. He waited for a few moments and hung up the phone. He quickly dialed Melissa.

On I-95 North, Heidi was looking at her cellphone when the indicator switched to CALL ENDED. She was staring into space for the longest time as she secretly listened to the argument between Lamar and Melissa. She couldn't believe the things she heard Melissa saying about her. Heidi tried to calm herself as she felt a sharp sensation of rage go through her body. Her speedometer was quickly approaching 87 mph now as Heidi contemplated ways to confront her beef with Melissa.

❖

Chapter 5

Friday, November 2, 2007
New Jersey Turnpike

12:41 a.m.

A resentful feeling came over Heidi as she passed exit 8A on the New Jersey Turnpike. She was so caught up in listening to Melissa and Lamar's argument that she didn't realize how fast she was traveling. She was about forty minutes away from her mother's house and making good time. Heidi turned away from her dashboard clock as she thought about her problems with Melissa. She was trying to figure out how to handle the situation when her cellphone started buzzing on her lap. It was her best friend Faith. Heidi smiled. She couldn't wait to tell her about Melissa's threats. Heidi answered the phone with a playful attitude.

"Hey chick, where you at?" Heidi joked. "I tried to call you like a hour ago."

"Yeah I know I just saw your missed call," Faith mumbled. Her voice didn't sound right. She was still shaken by the fight at Dirty Betty's club. "I'm sorry I missed the call," Faith continued. "I went to the club tonight to put in a few hours."

"Tonight? On your day off?" Heidi asked. "Damn bitch, you need to give me a loan. You makin' all that money over there." Heidi started laughing. She was alone. Faith didn't find the comment funny. Her silence set off Heidi's alarm. "So you okay, Faith? You don't sound good. What's goin' on, honey?" Heidi was concerned. She could tell that something was wrong with her best friend.

"I'm just so sick of this shit, High." Faith blurted. She sounded frustrated. "I must've pissed somebody off up there. I keep getting the bullshit handed to me."

"What do you mean, sweetie?" Heidi asked. "What happened?"

"Listen okay, you know me," Faith muttered. "I try to do everything right. I mean, am I a bad person? What part of this shit am I not getting?"

Heidi was confused. She'd heard Faith upset before, but never like this. "Wait, Faith, slow down. What happened?" Heidi tried to calm down her best friend.

"Girl, I went to the bar tonight to make me some extra money. Now I know it's my day off but I wasn't doing shit. So I figured I would try to make a quick two or three hundred dollars to put to the side for next month. Something told me to stay my ass home and study but I went anyway thinkin' shit was gonna go smooth. Why would I think that right?"

"Right!" Heidi agreed. Her ear was glued to the phone.

"So I get to the club about eleven o'clock or so. Girl, I wasn't there for no more than a half hour when I ran into Jordan. You remember I told you about him right?"

"From Asbury Park right?" Heidi asked.

"Yeah. This fool was at the club tonight. So peep this shit right. You know I was seeing him for a minute now. But it's nothing crazy like that. Just some *jumpoff* shit. So when he gets to the club he sees me walking behind the bar and decides to come over and say *hi*. So I don't think nothin' of it. I walk over and hug the nigga or whatever...you know like it's nothin'."

"Uh huh, right," Heidi groaned.

"So we huggin' and I'm like *how you*? I haven't seen him in a couple of days so I'm trying to be nice. So this nigga is all drunk and shit and tried to grab on me in the club. Now...any other day I'm like whatever, we cool like that. He can get that. But today I knew his ex-girlfriend was working and-"

Heidi interrupted her. "Wait, so his ex-girlfriend is a bartender at the club?"

"Nah, she's a dancer," Faith answered. "I told you that. Remember?"

Heidi's mood changed slightly. "Nah, girl," Heidi said. "You didn't tell me that y'all worked together. But go 'head, finish."

"Anyway, listen," Faith snapped. "Don't nobody at the club know we was kickin' it like that and I didn't want to start no rumors tonight. So I'm trying to push Jordan's hands away and make it to the bar so I can make that money. Long story short, he actin' all stupid and loud and gonna say some stupid shit like *'yeah I guess we can save the rough stuff for later on.'* I'm like *what the fuck?* Now I'm pissed. I look over and all the other bartenders are lookin' at me and smilin' and shit. Now I know I should 'a left that drama right there and went home. But for some stupid reason I decided to stay and work my shift. Girl, about two hours later here come Maya."

Heidi interjected. "Wait, which one is Maya? Is that the small one with that headstand shit?" Heidi joked.

Faith chuckled a little. She was still upset, but the image of Maya bouncing upside down half naked made her giggle.

"Yea, High, …..wait…listen. I'm telling you this bitch must have eyes like a hawk 'cause here she come with the mouth. *'What the fuck is wrong with you, bitch grabbing on my man like that. You fuckin' slut this and you fuckin' whore that and blah blah blah.'* Now first off, High, you know I don't like bein' called a bitch by them fuckin' hoes. Second of all, I'm like *'well who the fuck is ya man because I know you can't be talking about Jordan.'* Now at this point we screamin' back and forth at each other. After a while I told her straight to her face that me and Jordan had been fuckin' for over two months now and she's the dumb bitch if she thinks they're still together."

"Oh my God, Faith." Heidi yelled. "Please tell me that you wasn't fuckin' that girl's man."

"Huh? What do you mean?" Faith asked. "He told me that they broke up in July. So we dated a few times and yes, we slept together."

"Jesus, Faith. You never told me that." Heidi sounded disappointed.

"Yes I did," Faith insisted. "I told you I was seeing the guy in Asbury Park again and that it was some casual shit."

"If you told me that, Faith, I must've forgot. But go 'head with the story."

"What's wrong with you, High?" Faith snapped. "Are you gonna judge me today, too? Jordan told me that he broke up with Maya and then we hooked up. If I would've known they were still together trust me, I definitely would've never slept with the nigga." Faith was growing angrier with every breath. Heidi could sense her frustration and decided not to pursue it.

"Nah, sweetie. I'm sorry. Finish the story," Heidi said. "I didn't mean it like that. I just was trying to figure out who the guy Jordan was. But go 'head. So what happened when Maya tried to curse you out?"

Faith took a deep breath and tried to calm her tone. "To be honest I couldn't hear everything she was saying because the music was loud in there," Faith continued. "But while I was arguing with her, Jordan walked over and tried to defend her. Can you believe that shit?"

"Are you serious?" Heidi asked.

"High, he came over to me yelling, talking 'bout I need to get the fuck outta the club and shit. Like he owned the place! Then next thing I know Maya is rushing up to the bar and swinging at me. "

"Holy shit!" Heidi yelled. "Oh my God. Really?"

"Hell yeah!" Faith said. "She hit me right in my mouth with all them rings on. But that's the only hit she got in because after that I fucked her little ass up. I must 'a hit this wild bitch with about seven good hits. I broke her nose and everything."

"Wow, girl." Heidi gasped. "I can't believe you was fightin' in the club like that. So you good? Are you okay?"

"I'm okay," Faith said. "Just upset. But that's not even the end of the story. So it took like three bouncers to get me off her ass. By the time they got to us, Maya was crying and shit and begging them to get me off of her. And then....you are not gonna believe this shit.. . . after they pulled me off of her, I went to the back office and tried to find my jacket. Do you know my boss had a nerve to fire me? On my day off. This bitch fired me!"

"Oh no, Faith. Really?" Heidi was shocked. "She fired you on some emotional shit? No suspension or nothing?"

"Girl, Betty told me to get the fuck out of her club," Faith said. "She was pissed at me."

"Wow. I didn't expect that. That's crazy girl. So what are you gonna do?"

"I don't know. It just happened not too long ago. I'm just upset right now. It feels like I keep getting kicked in the head by life. And I always knew Betty didn't like me. She was always sayin' slick shit to me and behind my back. And I told her that I didn't fuck her boyfriend-"

Heidi interrupted her again. "Wait....what? Fucked whose boyfriend?" Heidi asked. "Maya's boyfriend? Wait, I thought you said they broke up."

"No, Heidi, pay attention." Faith snapped. "What are you doing?"

"Driving to my mother's."

"For what?"

"Long story, girl." Heidi said. "I'll tell you about it. Finish telling me. So who's boyfriend?"

"Dirty Betty's boyfriend," Faith continued. "She was dating some hustler from Boston last year when I first started. Now this nigga was funny. He would give me ridiculous tips when he came to the club and was always flirting with me. But come on, I didn't sleep with the dude or nothing like that. She was just paranoid 'cause he was eying me. Acting like he wanted to hop over the bar and take it to me. But since then she never acted the same towards me. And it got worse this summer. She started cuttin' my hours and giving me the bullshit schedule. But it's cool. She just mad 'cause she ugly. So whatever! I don't know what Imma do now. I really need to get this money together. I gotta take care of this shit next month."

There was an uncomfortable silence on the phone. *Next month* was quickly becoming a touchy subject. Heidi didn't want to state the obvious because she knew exactly why Faith was stressing so much.

****

Three Months Earlier
1:14a.m.

Faith woke up in a cold sweat. She thought she heard a noise in her apartment but it was a headache pounding on the side of her head. A knot in her throat made her jump up and rush to the bathroom. Before she could make it to the toilet a thick stream of water, blood, and vomit poured out of Faith's mouth. Her stomach contracted again causing another large stream to spill all over her sink and bathroom floor. Her heart started racing and she felt lightheaded. A sudden rush of tears came to Faith's eyes. The ugly sight and horrific smell of the vomit made her throw up again. This time she managed to make it to her bathtub. After a few minutes there was nothing more to release but blood. Faith was scared now. The first thought that came to mind was that she was pregnant. Her second thought was maybe it was something she ate. Either way, Faith needed to get to a hospital, quick. Only one person came to mind who would be willing to take her this late without a word: her best friend Heidi.

When Heidi got the call from Faith, she rushed right over to her apartment and picked her up. By the time they both arrived at Hackensack University Hospital, Faith was doubled over in pain. She was complaining of massive stomach aches and a sharp burning feeling in her chest. All initial tests, including her pregnancy test, came back negative. Faith spent the next three days in the hospital. After a number of tests and subsequent negative results, Faith received the worse news of her life. She was diagnosed with gastric cancer. Heidi was right there in the hospital room when she received the devastating news. Faith couldn't believe it. She was only thirty-six and the medical doctors were giving her five to seven years to live without any corrective surgery. Her only option to beat the cancer was to undergo a partial gastrectomy to remove the tumor. To ensure the full removal she had to follow the procedure with a number of chemotherapy sessions. Heidi felt bad for Faith. She knew Faith had basic medical insurance and the procedure could cost close to $80,000 and even more for the chemo. Things were definitely looking dark for Faith. However, Heidi always knew that her best friend was a fighter. Three months later, Faith found herself in a better position. She managed to raise close to $30,000 and was working on a few grants and loans for her surgery. Faith was not going to give up and Heidi vowed to help her in any way she could. Losing her job tonight was a major blow to her confidence. Now Faith was forced to go back to the drawing board and develop a new plan.

****

(present time)

"So what are you gonna do, Faith?" Heidi asked. "You know I'm here for you, right?" Heidi was still very much concerned for Faith. The silence between the two gave Heidi another uneasy feeling.

"Girl, I don't know. I think I just need to sleep," Faith said. "I'm so fucking tired of this bullshit. Sometimes I feel like *what's the use*? Feel me? You live this life and try to make the best and every day somethin' comes in and rips ya heart out. I don't know. I swear I don't know." Faith was close to tears. The drama of the past few months was catching up to her. Heidi tried her best to console her.

"Don't give up, Faith. I got you." Heidi lowered her tone. "I'm here. We'll figure something out. You not giving up on me, are you?"

Faith was silent.

"Faith?" Heidi yelled

"Yea, girl, I'm here. I'm just tired." Faith's voice sounded defeated. "I'm not giving up. I got too many things to do. I just need to go home and get some rest. Imma get up early tomorrow morning and figure this thing out."

"That sounds like a good idea. You should do that," Heidi said. "Get some rest and I'll come by tomorrow and cook. We'll work this thing out together, okay?"

"Sounds good to me." She was happy Heidi was there for her. "Before you get off the phone, girl, what's goin' on at your mother's house?"

"This nigga Rick is trippin' again," Heidi said. "Don't worry about it. You got enough on your plate. I called my brother and he's gonna meet me over there."

"Oh, okay. Call me tomorrow." Faith said. "I'll be home all day."

"Okay, sweetie. Don't stress. I'm in your corner."

"Thanks, High. I'll talk to you tomorrow."

"Okay, baby. Goodnight."

Dashawn Taylor

"Goodnight."

Heidi hung up the phone and took a deep breath. An ugly feeling came over her as she thought about the conversation she just had with Faith. Being ashamed of her best friend's sexual behavior was an understatement. Heidi was beyond disgusted with the news that she was sleeping with a co-worker's boyfriend. *That's just nasty.* Heidi thought to herself. She couldn't shake the feeling. She sat back in her car seat as her SUV sped up the New Jersey Turnpike. Heidi began to shake her head again as she thought about the drama at Dirty Betty's. She took a deep breath and slowly exhaled. Faith's behavior made Heidi think of the first day she realized her boyfriend Jayson was cheating on her.

****

Friday, October 20, 2006
Newark, New Jersey

11:27 a.m.

The corporate tower located at 744 Broad Street in Newark was buzzing with movement as the hectic work week was winding to a close. The thirty five-story skyscraper seemed to pulsate as phones, fax machines, and network servers echoed throughout the building. Friday was always a busy day in the high-rise. This particular Friday was no different. Jayson was standing near the window of his new office and admiring the amazing view of the largest city in New Jersey. A heavy feeling of pride and triumph came over him as he imagined how a young black boy from the inner-city could elevate so quickly up the corporate ladder. Now at the tender age of 29, Jayson became the youngest V.P. of Communications in the history of Datakorp.Com. The news sent shockwaves throughout the industry. Jayson's new corner office was a pleasant reminder of how all of his hard work and perseverance was beginning to pay off for him. He was deep in thought when the chirping sound of his office phone interrupted him. Jayson turned away from the beautiful skyline and headed for his desk. He answered the phone.

"Jayson Carter here, how can I help you?" he said.

A sensual yet professional female voice answered from the other line. It was Judith Smith, the executive assistant to his department. Her voice sounded mischievous as she responded to Jayson. "Good afternoon, birthday boy." Judith uttered.

Jayson smiled as he corrected her. "It's not my birthday yet, Judith. I told you. It's October the 22nd. You have to remember that. 1-0-2-2, it's just that simple."

"Well, you know I won't see you this weekend," Judith said. "So I thought I would give you a nice birthday wish before your big day."

"Well thank you, Ms. Smith. I really appreciate that," Jayson playfully said.

"No problem, Mr. Carter," Judith sarcastically replied. "You have a couple of messages that came in this morning while you were in your meetings. The first one was from Mr. Thomas McEernst from the purchasing department of Prudential and you have another one from a Ms. Heidi. She didn't leave her last name."

The news of the second caller brought a frown to Jayson's face. He couldn't imagine why his fiancée Heidi would be calling him at the office. He reached down to grab his cellphone. He quickly noticed the phone was not on his hip. It didn't take long for him to remember that he had left his cellphone in the car. Jayson tried to gather more information from his secretary.

"Do you have a full message from Ms. Heidi? Is there anything else she said?" Jayson asked.

Judith immediately sensed the concern in his voice. "No sir. She simply left her number. She did say to call her immediately. She said it was an emergency and to call her as soon as you can." There was a short silence on the phone. Jayson was trying to figure out what the emergency could be. Before he knew it, he hung up on Judith and was dialing Heidi's cell phone. The phone rang twice before a low voice answered on the other end. It was Heidi.

"Honey, where have you been?" Heidi somberly asked. "I been trying to reach you all morning, sweetie."

"I was in meetings all morning, High. What happened?" Jayson was overly concerned. His voice was trembling with anticipation.

"We gotta talk, Jay, right now. This is getting out of hand." Heidi's tone quickly went from somber to stern. Jayson was stunned on the other line. He looked down at the office phone with his mouth opened. He didn't know what to say. "Jayson, are you there?" Heidi snapped.

"Yea...I'm here....what happened, High?" Jayson lowered his voice. He tried to keep his cool. "What do we have to talk about? Is it something I did?"

"I'll talk to you when I get there!" Heidi said.

"What? Wait....High, what are you talking about....you coming here?" Jayson stood up behind his desk. "What time are you coming? Do you want me to meet you in the parking lot?"

Heidi's tone was very firm from the other line. "No, Jayson, just stay there," Heidi snapped. "I'm not close at all. I will call you in a few to let you know when I'm close to you." Before Jayson could say another word, he heard a subtle click on the other line. Heidi hung up the phone. Jayson slowly sat down in his chair. Dozens of thoughts began to race through his mind at once. No matter how hard he tried, Jayson could not figure out why his fiancée was on her way to his office to talk to him. He began to think about his cellphone. He rushed to check his cellphone messages to see if his affairs were in order. All six messages were from Heidi. *Nothing unusual there*, Jayson thought to himself. He sat back in his chair and glanced at the ceiling. He seemed to drift into a short trance as he tried to brace himself for a possible argument with Heidi.

Ten minutes later, Heidi was downstairs marching through the main lobby of 744 Broad Street. With little time to waste, Heidi moved with purpose as she passed the fine marble walls of the impressive office tower. The sound of her Matisse-Cannes tall boots echoed throughout the lobby and forced a crew of daytime security guards to gawk at her presence. She totally ignored the men on duty and headed for the elevator. Within a few minutes, Heidi was on the 22nd floor of the building and heading straight for Datakorp.Com. Ignoring all protocol, Heidi confidently walked into the offices without checking in. Her mood began to grow more determined as she moved quickly through the busy office floor. When she reached Jayson's office, she was greeted by Judith Smith.

"Hello, ma'am, how can I help you today?" Judith politely asked.

"Heidi Carter," Heidi quickly snapped. "My name is Heidi Carter and I'm here to speak with Jayson Carter."

Judith was immediately taken aback by Heidi's tone. She tried to keep things professional and decided to probe. "Okay, Ms. Carter." Judith said. "And do you have an appointment today?"

"Mrs. Carter," Heidi snapped again. Her face began to show her lack of patience with Judith. "My name is Mrs. Carter and it's a domestic matter."

Judith decided not to pry and quickly dialed Jayson's extension. He answered on the first ring. "Hello, Judith." Jayson said.

"Hello, Mr. Carter. You have a visitor sir." Judith said. "There is a Mrs. Heidi Carter requesting to see you."

Jayson took a moment to think and let out a loud gasp on the other line. Judith could hear paperwork being shuffled aside as Jayson tried to straighten his desk. "Okay, Judith, let her in and hold all of my calls." Jayson stammered. He couldn't believe Heidi was outside of his office. He leaned back in his chair and put his fingers on his chin. He expected to see Heidi come through the door with a fiery attitude. Jayson braced himself for the drama. The glass door to his office opened up and Heidi slowly walked in.

Jayson was amazed at the sight of his fiancée. His eyes widen as he watched Heidi glide into the office like a runway model. The first sight of her suede boots and matching trench coat made Jayson realize that she was well overdressed for an argument. Heidi closed the Venetian blinds and locked his office door. She wanted total privacy for what the two were about to discuss. Heidi turned around and leaned on the door. Her foreign expression confused Jayson. "What's wrong with you, High?" Jayson aggressively asked.

Before Jayson could say another word, Heidi suddenly put her finger over her mouth. "Shhhhhhh. Don't say a word, Jay," Heidi whispered.

Something about the way she was acting changed the mood in the office. She smiled at Jayson and shot him a seductive glare. Although he was at work, Jayson couldn't help but pick up on her vibe. Butterflies started to bounce in his stomach as a nervous feeling came over him. Heidi took a deep breath and started to walk over to his desk. With every tantalizing step Heidi was slowly transforming into a totally different person. Like a patient predator, Heidi locked her target in sight and was moving in for the kill. Jayson seemed to freeze in his chair as he stared into her beautiful brown eyes. He was mesmerized.

"You know you've been avoiding me for too long, Jayson," Heidi whispered. "You can't run today, boy. We definitely got some things to discuss."

Jayson's heart started to race faster. Heidi's passionate voice sent a warm sensation through him. He decided to remain quiet and see where this would lead. Heidi walked to the front of his desk. She pushed a few papers to the side and placed her palms on the flat surface. As she leaned over to get closer to him, Jayson noticed for the first time that she wasn't mad at him at all. Heidi had other plans in mind for him. Jayson opened his mouth to speak again but Heidi slowly waved her finger to stop him.

"I don't wanna hear it, Jay." Heidi smiled at him. "You brought this on yourself." Jayson chuckled at her playful tone. Heidi returned the gesture. "Push your chair back away from the desk, sweetie." Heidi commanded. "I wanna show you something."

Jayson obeyed. He casually pushed his chair against the wall and created some space between him and the desk. Things were getting interesting. Heidi slowly walked around the desk. She headed over to Jayson who was staring hungrily at her. She looked good. From her well-manicured fingers to her $400 weave, Heidi was made-up like she belonged on somebody's red carpet. Her silken brown skin meshed perfectly with her light brown Brisa mink that covered her entire body. Jayson couldn't help but smile at the incredible sight. Heidi walked in front of Jayson as he sat in his office chair. Jayson was still frozen. Heidi stood directly in front of him for a moment and admired her handsome fiancé. After six long years, she was still very attracted to his incredible features. From his deep dark skin and well built body to his serious yet engaging beautiful brown eyes, Heidi loved everything about him. She slowly licked her top lip as she gazed at him. It didn't take long for Jayson to shoot her that sexy–crooked smile that she liked so much. Heidi's heart started to race as the mood in the room grew more seductive. She playfully looked down at her long mink.

"Open it," Heidi whispered. She shot Jayson a devilish smirk. "Go 'head, baby.... don't be afraid. Open it."

Jayson reached for her coat. He slowly pulled apart the hook-and-eye clips to reveal another secret she was hiding. Heidi was completely naked under the soft fur. Another rush of adrenaline ran through Jayson as he exposed his fiancée's nude body. The sight of her curvy hips and perfectly round breasts caused nature to take control of his body. Jayson was instantly aroused. Heidi noticed his manhood bulging through the slacks and chuckled to herself. She knew total pleasure was just moments away. Before she could react, Jayson's lips were pressing gently against her stomach. He couldn't take it anymore. Jayson slowly ran his soft tongue from the middle of her chest to her belly button. She tasted so good. He missed her. Heidi let out a sensuous moan and grabbed the back of Jayson's head. She pulled his head away from her stomach and knelt down in front of him. They began to kiss, passionately. Heidi could barely speak without breaking Jayson's rhythm but she managed to *squeak-out* her peace to him.

"Jayson, don't ever make me wait so long to have you again. You hear me?" Heidi whispered.

Jayson was taking off his jacket and unbuttoning his shirt when he answered Heidi. "I won't, baby. I'm so sorry. Work has just been so crazy."

Suddenly, in one motion, Heidi backed away from Jayson. She stood up and dropped her coat to the floor. Now dressed in nothing but boots, her naked body was exposed to the office. Jayson thought about his co-workers and peered toward the door. The fear of getting caught only excited him more. He fumbled with his belt until the clip unlatched. Heidi leaned over him and pulled his slacks down to his ankles. As she stared at his swollen penis, Heidi let out a loud gasp and shook her head.

"Boy, you just might get fired today," Heidi joked.

Jayson smiled and pulled her by the arm. "No I won't. Just promise me you won't wake the neighbors."

Heidi laughed. She slowly placed her arms around Jayson's broad shoulders and carefully straddled him. A severe feeling of pleasure gushed from her body as Jayson entered her and took her to ecstasy.

Sixteen minutes later the sex was over. Heidi was playfully gasping for air. The intensity of the lovemaking took her breath away. Jayson was also out of breath. A faint smile emerged on his exhausted face when he noticed the sweet smell of their over-sexed bodies still lingering in the office.

"That was incredible, Jayson," Heidi moaned.

"Oh my God... you ain't never lied," Jayson concurred. "That was insane. So, what do I have to do to get you over to the office more often and greet me like this?"

Heidi slowly raised her head from his chest and looked into his eyes. "Have a birthday everyday and I'll be here everyday," she playfully said. Heidi kissed him on the cheek and stood up. Not wanting to ruin a great time with Jayson, she decided to leave the office right away. Jayson picked up on the vibe and they both quickly got dressed.

"Baby, thanks for playing along with me. I love you," Heidi said as she walked over to Jayson."

"Love you too, babe." Jayson whispered.

"I have to get things ready for this weekend," Heidi said. "I'll see you when you get home tonight."

"Okay."

Heidi kissed him on the forehead and turned around. All Jayson could do was shake his head as he watched his lovely fiancée gracefully leave his office.

As Heidi closed the door she was immediately greeted once again by Judith Smith. An uneasy feeling came over Heidi as she tried to read Judith's peculiar expression. *Did she hear us*? Heidi thought to herself. Before Heidi could gather her thoughts, Judith was standing up and approaching her.

"Hey, Mrs. Carter you have perfect timing," she said gleefully. "Your package for Mr. Carter just arrived."

A confused looked flashed onto Heidi's face. "What package?" Heidi asked.

"The flowers. For Mr. Carter. They just got here while you were in the office," Judith said. She walked Heidi to the front of the desk where a massive bouquet of roses was waiting.

"Here they are, Mrs. Carter. I figured you wanted to surprise him with the flowers so I waited for you to come back out."

Heidi was still confused. She hadn't ordered the flowers for her fiancé. As she approached the flowers, a stiff anger overpowered her feeling of confusion. Heidi decided to play it cool.

"You know Judith, I'm so sorry. I must 'a forgot that I ordered these flowers for him." Heidi calmly said. "I've been so busy lately." Heidi reached for the card that was attached to the bouquet. "Let me make sure they got the message correct this time." Heidi opened the card and read it. Her mouth fell open at the sight.

> Happy Birthday Jayson
> I was hoping you didn't forget about me,
> And all the things I have in store for you!
> I Look Forward To Seeing You On The Big Day.
>
> -PS
> "Don't forget the number: 862-487-8537"

Heidi instantly felt sick. She couldn't believe that someone had sent flowers to her fiancé. Heidi's face began to twist with anger. Judith immediately sensed something was wrong and moved closer to Heidi.

"Is everything okay, Mrs. Carter?" Judith asked.

"Umm….yes…I'm sorry….yeah ummm…they ummm." Heidi was flustered. She tried her best to regain her composure. "I have to take these back, Judith. They misspelled too many things." Heidi put the card in her coat pocket. "I hate when they do this." Judith suspiciously nodded her head as Heidi continued to speak. "Would you do me a favor, hun? Please don't tell Mr. Carter about his surprise. I want to surprise him the right way."

"Okay, Mrs. Carter. No problem. My lips are sealed." Before Judith could ask any other questions, Heidi snatched the bouquet from her desk and stormed to the elevator. It took every inch of her body to hold back the tears in her eyes. Heidi read the birthday note again and committed the phone number to memory. She couldn't wait to call the number and find out who could be sending flowers to her fiancé.

****

(present time)
1:05 a.m.

Heidi was still thinking about that unforgettable day when she passed exit 14 on the New Jersey Turnpike. She reached in her jacket pocket and pulled out the birthday card that was sent to Jayson's office. The ink on the card was fading away but she could still see the writing. Heidi gripped the card tightly and then returned it to her pocket. Feeling the stress of the evening, Heidi took another quick sip of her wine and punched the gas. Tonight was quickly becoming a long night for her and she was ready to get it over with. Heidi turned her music up as she darted down the dark highway.

Chapter 6

*C*linton Avenue connects two of the wildest and most notorious cities in New Jersey, the city of Newark and the city of Irvington. Like an angry stream joining two raging rivers, Clinton Avenue is frequently traveled by Drug Dealers, Deacons, Students, Strippers, Police, Pimps, Governors and Gangsters. You can find everything on this three-mile drag, from schools to restaurants to underground casinos to churches to the political headquarters of both Mayors. The never-ending power struggle between Good and Evil plays itself out everyday on this track. Whether it's the corner of Sanford, Ellis, Bergen, Irving Turner or MLK; many problems are created and solved right here on Clinton Avenue. Tonight, this deleterious street would play matchmaker for another underworld connection between Shaheed and his older cousin Vegas.

A 1999 Classic Mercedes Benz quickly pulled up to the ExxonMobile on the corner of Clinton and Elizabeth Avenue. The coppery paint on the CL-500 reflected all available light on the dimly lit corner. The streets were uncomfortably empty tonight. A fresh-faced young man peered through the crack of the tinted windows and scanned the area. His hawk-like eyes seemed to survey the entire perimeter within seconds. There were no bums asking for money, no tricks asking for dates, and no cops harassing the locals. It was all too perfect. The young man went against his instincts and turned off the V-8 engine as a middle-aged Nigerian man walked slowly out of the convenience store and headed for the Mercedes Benz. The young man rolled his window down and greeted the worker.

"Waddup, doe. Fill it up with premium, daddy," The young man said as he confidently handed the gas attendant a Visa Gold card. The attendant took the card and nodded to himself. The young man gave the attendant a suspicious look but decided not to pursue it. He just closed the window and sat back in his leather seat, knowing he was lucky to find a gas station open this late. He was running out of gas and Newark was not the place to leave your car at one o'clock in the morning. The young man reached into his pocket, pulled out a roll of fifties, and started counting. A seductive smile emerged on his face as he counted over $1,600. The young man was in love with his money, and even more in love with spending it. Feeling cocky and above the world, he unlocked his doors and jumped out. The gas attendant watched as the young man confidently strolled toward the convenience store. Getting closer to the door, he started walking very fast; too fast to notice a concrete brick flying towards him from behind a dumpster near the entrance. The young man never saw what hit him. The six-inch brick smashed into the right side of his head with an immense force that threw him sideways to the ground. The gas attendant let out a gasp as he watched a dark silhouette walk slowly from behind the dumpster. As the silhouette moved closer to his unconscious prey, the street lights presented a very tall yet husky man wearing a heavy hood and black baseball cap. His facial expression was cold and emotionless as he looked down at the young man and then at the gas attendant. His grayish eyes were piercing and controlling. His shadowy beard couldn't hide the scars and welts on his face that reflected years of pain and triumph. His name was Vince Galloway, also known as Vegas.

The gas attendant watched cautiously as Vegas walked over to the young man. Vegas patted the young man's pockets until he heard a jingle come from his limp body. The blood from the young man's head began to flow over like a backed up sink. But Vegas was not fazed by the horrific scene. He shuffled through the man's pockets and pulled out the car keys. A loud *click* came from the gas pump, startling the gas attendant. Vegas stared at the Mercedes and then looked back at the young man's peaceful face. He leaned over his victim until he was intimately close to his ear.

"Thanks for the ride, faggot," Vegas whispered.

The gas attendant watched as Vegas got up and walked toward him. His body tensed up; he didn't know what to expect. Vegas turned off the alarm and jumped into the car. He started the engine and rolled down the tinted window, his eyes fixed on the attendant.

"How much is that?" Vegas asked. The attendant shot Vegas a dumb look. "How much is that, man?" Vegas pointed to the pump. "The gas?"

"Oh shit. Um.....it's...um, $68.34," the attendant stammered.

"Okay. Where do I sign?"

The attendant shot him another dumb look and then fumbled to grab the charge card. He quickly snatched a pen from his pocket and placed the receipt on the clipboard. Vegas grabbed the clipboard and signed the receipt. He threw the charge card in the passenger seat and handed the clipboard back to the attendant. His rough face seemed to crack like glass as he smiled at the attendant. "You be careful out here. I heard they car jackin' niggas tonight!" Vegas barked as he started laughing. He quickly rolled up the window and sped away from the gas station.

Vegas was twenty-seven now. He was a long way from popping ignitions and using dental floss to unlock car doors. These days, Vegas was getting high off of a new drug: strong armed robbery. He not only enjoyed the rush of stealing expensive cars but as an added bonus, he was just mesmerized by the sight of other people in pain. If there was a car he wanted he didn't hesitate. Vegas would simply walk up to the car and take it violently, even if it meant hurting the driver. And in some cases the passengers, too.

The V-8 engine roared as Vegas punched the gas pedal. The empty streets seemed to part for the Mercedes as it blew through all the red lights on Clinton Ave. A loud buzzing came from Vegas's hip. He grabbed the phone and looked at the display. What he read caused a smirk to rise on his face.

INCOMING CALL
Shaheed (Cellphone)

Vegas slowed the car while he answered the phone. "Waddup, nigga?" Vegas asked. "What happened? Don't tell me you punked out on the job?"

Shaheed laughed on the other end of the phone. "Nah, fam. You know how Robert is, man," Shaheed said. "That nigga's gonna be late to his own funeral. Where you at? I tried to hit you about a half hour ago."

"I was car shopping," Vegas joked. Some lame ass nigga called hisself tryna get a late night snack on 'lizabeth Ave."

"Oh shit. Say no more, my nigga. What was it? A Lexus?" Shaheed asked.

"A CL!"

Shaheed raised his fist to his mouth. "Aww shit, cousin. That's crazy, nigga. That nigga deserved that shit. Can't be sleeping on these streets.

Vegas pictured the young man lying in the gas station parking lot and laughed at the irony of Shaheed's statement. He decided to keep the joke to himself. "So what's good, Sha'?" Vegas asked. "It's kinda late, homie. You still wanna do that?"

"I got to, cousin. This nigga Abdul is comin' for my head for real. My back is square against the wall now. You still in?"

"Hell yeah. Where you want to meet at?" Vegas asked.

There was a brief silence as Shaheed thought. "I'm passing through Irvington now. Are you still up top?"

"Yeah man, I'm headed up Clinton Ave now." Vegas said.

"Cool. Meet me in front of Irvington High. Imma be there in five minutes."

"I'll be there in two minutes." Vegas hung up the phone and tossed it in the passenger seat. He floored the pedal again and the sound of the engine echoed off of the empty street.

❖

Chapter 7

Friday, November 2, 2007
East Orange, New Jersey

1:23 a.m.

*B*ack in East Orange, New Jersey it didn't take long for Heidi to make it safely to her mother's house. The combination of loud music and her imagination made the ride virtually painless. But when Heidi turned down her mother's street she felt a rush of nervousness come over her.

It was always hard for Heidi to return to the house where she grew up. Most of her childhood memories were disturbing and seeing her old home reminded her of so much pain and stress. The front of her mother's house seemed to be extremely dark tonight. The two street lamps that usually illuminate the front of the house were shorted out. If it weren't for her headlights beaming off of the front porch, Heidi wouldn't have seen the 8-pound possum scampering to avoid her 4runner. She curiously looked at her watch and noticed that it was a little before 1:30am. A creepy feeling came over her, a feeling that was all too familiar. The last time she was at her mother's house was just over eight months ago.

****

February, 28, 2007
1:02 a.m.

Heidi's mother called her around one o'clock that morning and told her that her boyfriend Rick was hitting on her. She told Heidi that she was stuck in the bathroom and scared to come out. Hearing this news, Heidi's temper immediately kicked in. She jumped in her jeep and rushed over to her mother's house. When she got there her mother's front door was wide opened and Rick's car was still running in the driveway. Heidi cautiously approached the house, expecting to see Rick sitting in the car but he wasn't there. She heard her mother scream from inside the house and rushed to locate her before Rick could do any more harm.

Heidi was in the living room when she heard screams coming from the basement, but it wasn't her mother. Two men were arguing downstairs. It was Lamar and Rick. Heidi's mother started screaming louder from the bathroom upstairs. Heidi hit the steps with lightning speed and rushed upstairs to her. She knocked on the bathroom door.

"Mom, open the door! It's me!" Heidi yelled.

Heidi's mom was on the other side of the door, terrified. She did not want to open the door. "Where is he, High?" Her mother moaned. "Is he out there with you?"

"No, Mom, open the door. What happened?" Heidi twisted the doorknob in a failed attempt to open it.

"I'm coming, High. I'm so sorry." Heidi's mother was crying now. Heidi could hear her sobbing through the door. "High, I'm so sorry about this," her mother whimpered.

"Sorry about what? Open the door, Mom." Heidi continued to try the doorknob. Still locked. "Mom, do I have to bust the door down?" There was no answer from the bathroom. Heidi put her ear to the door but she couldn't hear a thing. "Mom? Open the door!" Heidi was becoming enraged. She rushed to her mother's bedroom and snatched a screwdriver from the closet. She yelled for her mother again. No answer.

"Goddammit!" Heidi banged on the door one last time before she shoved the screwdriver into the keyhole of the doorknob. This lock had been broken numerous times since she was a kid. All she had to do was get the screwdriver deep enough. Heidi got a good grip on the makeshift key and opened the door. Heidi's jaw dropped at the sight of her mother battered and bruised. She instantly fell to her knees and started crying.

****

(present time)

Now, just eight months later, Heidi felt herself getting emotional as she sat in the car, flashing back to that night eight months ago. Heidi prayed that this wouldn't be a repeat. She cautiously looked around but was unable to find Rick's car. She got out of her SUV and surveyed the street. No sign of his car. She grabbed her cellphone and called her mother, praying that nothing had happened to her. The phone rang four times before her mother answered it.

"I'm downstairs, Mom."

"Okay, sweetie. "I'm on my way down."

Her mother's voice sounded a lot calmer than before, tired but still alert. Heidi turned off the truck engine and walked to the front door. She put her cellphone in her jacket pocket. A nervousness stirred in her stomach as she waited for her mother. Before Heidi could calm herself she heard the deadbolt locks turn. Heidi pursed her lips as her mother cracked the door and walked away. Any other night this would've been strange, but Heidi decided to dismiss the gesture. Heidi pushed the door opened and walked into the house. Her mother walked slowly into the living room, heading for the sofa and Heidi locked the door and followed her.

Heidi's mother was quiet. When she reached the sofa she slowly turned around and sat down. Her face was showing a mix of fatigue and concern. Heidi's mother was four years away from celebrating her 60th birthday. Her strong features and deep brown skin were a direct contrast to Heidi's more subtle features and lighter skin. And although her face showed decades of experience and pain, Heidi's mother was still a very attractive woman. She was very petite, standing at just five feet and two inches. But what she lacked in height she made up in looks. Her name was Pearl. Heidi would joke all the time about how her mother was a precious jewel who gave birth to a diamond. Tonight Heidi had to be tough as a diamond to help her mother through a very rough time with Rick. She sat down next to Pearl and grabbed her hand.

"You okay, Mom?" Heidi whispered.

Pearl looked away and nodded towards the kitchen. "I'm okay, sweetie. You want me to make you some coffee or something?"

"No, I'm good, Mom. So what happened? Rick didn't call or nothing?"

"Child, this man is crazy." Pearl's voice was calm but direct. "I don't know why the hell I'm still in this house with him."

"When was the last time you seen him?"

"This morning when he left out to go to work."

"Did he call from his job?" Heidi's voice sounded less concerned.

"No he didn't," Pearl answered.

A loud ring came from Heidi's jacket pocket. She stood up and walked to the other side of the room. When she looked at the phone she cracked a wide smile. It was her friend Aaron on the other line. Heidi quickly answered the phone.

"Hey, Aaron. Is everything okay?"

"I was just calling to ask you that." Aaron said from the other end of the phone.

"Yeah, everything is good so far," Heidi nervously answered. "I just got to my mother's house."

"Okay. I was just calling to check up on you. I was a little worried. Do you need anything?"

Heidi turned around and quickly surveyed her mother's mood. "Nah, I think we straight," Heidi whispered. "Thanks for calling me though."

"No problem. Call me if you need me."

Heidi cracked a childish smirk as she listened to Aaron's concern. "Okay, I will." Heidi softly said. "I'll call you later."

"Okay, Goodnight, Princess."

"Bye." Heidi hung up the phone and tried to contain her momentary excitement. The sound of Aaron's voice seemed to calm her mood. It had been a long time since a man was genuinely concerned about Heidi and the thought made her feel good. Heidi slowly turned back to her mother and walked back over to sit with her.

"I'm sorry about that," Heidi apologized. "So, Mom, what exactly is goin' on with you and Rick?"

"Child, we have been arguing like crazy over here the last few days?"

"Why?" Heidi asked.

"Well, one thing I know is that Rick's been stressin' hard for the last month. Always talking about money. I think he is in some kind of trouble because he stays out late like he's scared to come home or somethin'. I don't even know if he went to work these last few days."

"Really?"

"Eight years, I have never known that man to stay away from the house or the job like this."

"So you didn't talk to Rick all day?"

"Absolutely not." Pearl answered. "Last night he didn't come to bed until three o'clock in the morning. He was up talking on the phone and watching TV all night, sittin' right there where you sittin'. When he finally came to bed I asked him what was wrong and he said *nothing*. So I don't know what to think. The last time he did this, he came in the house drunk and pissed off. I just don't want him coming home and tryin' to kick my ass. I can't have that bullshit."

"Mom!" Heidi raised her voice. "Do you have to talk like that?"

"Child, I keep telling you that you are not my mother. You may look older than me but you still my child." Pearl rolled her eyes at her daughter.

Heidi waved her mother off and turned back around. "Whatever, Mom. I told you that you sound like a damn bartender when you talk like that."

"Well I asked you if you wanted something to drink and you said *no*, so I'm definitely not no goddamn bartender," Pearl snapped.

"There you go with the mouth again." Heidi shook her head. "So how are you holdin' up? The house looks really nice. When did you change the living room around?"

"About two months ago. I had a few people over, so I decided to add another end table. You like it?" Pearl asked.

"I do," Heidi answered. She felt bad about not coming around to her mother's more often. The photos on the wall made her think of her early days in the house growing up with Lamar. Pearl watched as Heidi stared at a few photos on the wall.

"So where have you been, child?" Pearl asked sarcastically. "You don't call as much as you should, Heidi".

"I know, Mom. I been so busy with the new job now. I may become a senior executive over there if everything goes right."

Pearl ignored the last part of Heidi's statement. "Busy, huh?" Pearl snarled. "Too busy to call the person who raised you? You know I'm not a spring chicken anymore. Women are dyin' a lot younger these days from all kinds of shit, Heidi. We might not have a lot of time together."

Heidi gave her mother a cynical look. She knew what her mother was up to. Ever since Heidi was a teenager her mother would play on her emotions to get her attention.

"Why do you do this to me, Mom?"

"Do what?"

"You know what you doin'? I told you that I have been busy at work." Heidi was getting a bit angry now. "Stop trying to make me feel bad about not seein' you more often." Heidi continued to look at the pictures.

"I'm not doing anything to you." Pearl was getting angry with Heidi but tried her best not to show it. "I asked you where you been. Now if you feel guilty about not seeing the only person that really cares about you in this world then that's on you."

"Goddamit, Mom! That is not fair," Heidi snapped as she turned to Pearl.

"And you talk about my mouth, child?" Pearl smiled.

"You are a true asshole, Mom, I swear. You knew what you were doin' from the beginning. You called me over here just because you wanted to see me? I hate when you do that, Mom. Why did you lie to me?"

"Calm down, Heidi. I didn't lie to you. I was scared so I called you." Pearl stood up and began to walk to her kitchen. Heidi could hear Pearl's voice become angrier as she yelled from the hall. "You really changed, child. I'm hurt that you would think I would call you this early in the morning to see you and make up some stupid shit about Rick. What kind of person do you think I am? I don't need your goddamn attention."

Heidi didn't respond. She looked toward the photos again. Pearl started banging pots together in the kitchen. She was about to make some coffee when she heard a loud knock at her back door. Her heart started pounding. Heidi rushed into the kitchen from the living room. She saw her mother frozen solid staring at the back door. She was terrified. There was another knock on the door. This time it was louder.

"I know this asshole is drunk." Pearl's voice was filled with fear. Her hands were shaking nervously as she put the small pot back on the counter. Heidi started looking around the kitchen for a weapon. Finally she rushed over to a tall cabinet and pulled out a wooden broomstick. She stepped on its end and snapped the bristles off. Pearl looked over to Heidi. "What the hell are you doing, girl?" Pearl whispered. "You just broke my broom!"

"Mom, open the door. I'm going to stand right here and if he comes in on some slick shit imma take his head off." Pearl gave her daughter a peculiar look and walked over to the door. Another loud knock came from the door and Pearl jumped back. She could feel her heart pounding through her chest. She was very scared now. She looked back to Heidi who was positioned in a serious Barry Bonds-like stance. Another knock came from the door.

"Okay, I'm comin'!" Pearl yelled.

"Go 'head, Mom. Open the door." Heidi said. "I'm right here." Pearl slowly inched toward the door and grabbed the knob. She gave Heidi one last look before she opened the door. She twisted the knob, pulled the door back as hard as she could, and stood back. Heidi cocked back the broomstick, waiting for a confrontation. But instead of Rick, Heidi and Pearl were surprised to see a fresh-faced young man at the back door. It was Lamar.

"Jesus Christ, Lamar, you scared the piss out of us!" Heidi yelled.

"What the hell is goin' on in here?" Lamar stammered as he walked into the house and headed toward Heidi. "Damn girl, what was you gonna do with that?" Lamar started laughing.

"Shut up Lamar, I thought you was Rick." Heidi said. "And for your information I was gonna go Babe Ruth on his ass if he started trippin'." Heidi threw down the broomstick and gave Lamar a long hug. It wasn't until that moment that Heidi realized how much she missed her brother. She looked him over and smiled. It was good to see him back in the real world.

"Somebody wants to see you even more than me, Lamar." Heidi turned Lamar around.

"Lamar baby, I'm so glad it's you," Pearl whispered. In all the commotion, Lamar hadn't realized that Pearl was behind the door.

"Mom, I didn't even see you. How are you doing?" He walked over to his mother and gave her a big hug. "Are you okay? I take it that Rick didn't come home yet?"

"Oh baby, it's so good to see you." Pearl said. "I didn't know you were comin' home this soon."

"Yea Mom, it was a piece of cake," Lamar offered. "You know I'm strong, Mom. I can do that time standin' on my head."

Heidi smiled at the sight of her mother and Lamar talking. She turned around and headed back to the living room and left them alone. Pearl gave Lamar a quick pat on his chest and headed back over to the stove.

"No, Rick didn't come home yet," Pearl whispered. "Didn't even call. You want some coffee or somethin'? I was about to make me a cup before you came in."

"Yea Mom, I'll take a cup. I'm sorry for coming to the back door. I thought I saw Rick's car around the corner and thought he might be in the backyard or somethin'."

"No, honey. What time you got?" Pearl asked.

"It's a little after one thirty." Lamar said.

"Yeah, I'm sure that he's out doing God knows what with God knows who. He's never stayed out this late on a work night." Pearl's voice was calming down now. "But I'm sure he'll be home soon. All drunk and shit."

"I hope not," Lamar added. "He betta not come in here talkin' that bullshit."

"I doubt it, baby. He won't act out if y'all here. You can believe that." Pearl pulled two coffee mugs from the cabinet and set them on the table. "So how have you been, Lamar? I never got to say this to you before, but I'm so sorry about the last time you were here."

Lamar cut her off. "Don't worry about it, Mom. It's cool. I don't really want to talk about it. It's in the past and I put the work in. So love is love."

Pearl looked at Lamar and nodded to him. She felt bad about the fact that Lamar and Rick didn't get along. She wanted to continue the conversation but Heidi re-entered the kitchen with a photo in her hand. She sat down at the kitchen table in front of the two coffee mugs Pearl set out. Lamar watched Heidi but didn't say a word. He sat down directly across from her and tried to figure out what the picture was all about. Pearl grabbed the coffee pot off of the counter and poured herself a cup. She waited for a second and poured Lamar a cup.

"What is that you got, High?" Pearl asked. Heidi didn't answer. "Child do you hear me talking to you?"

"Mom, how many times I have to tell you. That is not my name." Heidi was still looking at the photo. "My name is *Heidi*, not *High*."

Pearl frowned. "What are you talking about, *Heidi*? You never had a problem with it before."

Lamar sat back in his chair and stared at Heidi. He was taken aback by Heidi's tone.

"Well, that's not my name, Mom," Heidi snapped, focused on the photo in her hand.

"What the hell is up your ass tonight, girl?" Pearl barked. "I'm tryin' to have a decent conversation with you and you're acting like I'm some stranger on the street. Now if I pour this hot coffee on you I would be wrong right?"

Heidi stood up so fast her chair slammed to the ground. She backed away from the table and stared at her mother.

"What the fuck is that suppose to mean, Mom?" Heidi yelled. Why would you say some cruel shit like that to me?" Her mother said nothing. Lamar jumped up and rushed over to Heidi.

"Calm down, Heidi." Lamar said. "What are you doin'? This is your mom. She didn't mean it like that." Lamar raised his voice but he could tell that he was not getting through to her. Heidi's quick temper completely took control of her. She was staring at her mother now with an uncontrollable intensity. Pearl was noticeably nervous. She balled up her lip and her eyes began to tear. There was an uncomfortable silence in the kitchen; the women did not say a word, they just stared at each other. Lamar grabbed Heidi by the shoulders and tried to turn her around.

"C'mon Heidi, lets go outside." Lamar ordered. "You need to cool off."

Heidi didn't acknowledge Lamar at all. He started pushing her harder and forcing her to turn around. He managed to turn her body around but her eyes stayed fixated on her mother. "Heidi, let's go." Lamar yelled. "Stop this. You know she didn't mean it in that way. It's not like that anymore. Let's go."

As they made their way to the living room, Lamar started pushing Heidi harder. He grabbed her jacket from the couch and tossed it to her. Heidi was still angry. She unlocked the deadbolts on the front door and walked outside on the porch. Lamar followed. He watched as she sat on the top step of the porch and put her head down. She was breathing heavy but tried to calm herself. Lamar stood behind her and gave her a minute to relax.

Back in the kitchen, Pearl managed to calm herself quickly. The rush of emotions immediately drained her and she took a seat at the table. She felt bad for making her daughter so angry. She wiped her face with both hands and stared over where Heidi was sitting. She noticed that the photo Heidi had been looking at was still on the table. Pearl picked it up. A rush of emotions filled Pearl's body. The picture made her look up from the table and stare toward the front of the house where her daughter was trying her best to calm down.

Chapter 8

Friday, November 2, 2007
Irvington, New Jersey

1:48 a.m.

*W*hen Vegas arrived at Irvington High School, he was shocked to see Shaheed and his brother Robert parked in front of the school. He blew through every possible red light on Clinton Ave and still managed to move slower than his baby cousin. As Vegas pulled up to the school Shaheed watched the sparkling Mercedes coast to a stop on the opposite side of the street. When he noticed it was his cousin Vegas, he gave him a confirming nod. Shaheed chuckled to himself as he watched his 300-pound cousin emerge from the luxury coup. The site reminded him of a circus clown getting out of a miniature car. Shaheed and Robert jumped out of the Dodge Charger and headed over to Vegas. Robert was noticeably nervous. And like the predator he was, Vegas sensed Robert's fear the minute he arrived across the street.

"What's good, Rob? You look like you could use some toilet time," Vegas joked. "You lookin' all shook-up and shit."

Rob was not amused. "Fuck you, nigga." He snapped.

"Nah, no thanks," Vegas fired back. "I'll leave all the nigga-fuckin' to you, pink boy."

Shaheed felt the vibe getting tense and decided to calm the air. "Go 'head, Vegas man. Leave him alone," Shaheed ordered. "What's good with you?"

Vegas totally ignored the question as he stared at his cousin Robert. He had a laundry list of reasons for not liking him. For most of his life, Vegas had been the type of person who preyed on other people. He had a knack for reading people in a matter of seconds and taking advantage of their weaknesses. From the time they all became teenagers, Vegas could tell that Robert was a weak person. Vegas never forgave him for being part of the reason why Shaheed went back to jail when they were younger. He also felt that Robert was not a strong example for his little brother. Shaheed was Vegas' favorite cousin. They had similar personalities and Vegas was always fond of people who had no fear. So when Shaheed called on Vegas to help him out with his problem with Abdul, Vegas was more than happy to come to his aid. Now the only thing left for Shaheed to do was to get Vegas to calm down so they could get down to business.

Shaheed walked over to Vegas and gave him a handshake and a hug. "Relax, homie." Shaheed said. "Don't get yourself all worked up yet. Imma need all that aggression tonight for this thing."

Vegas looked down at this favorite cousin and nodded his head. "Of course. Just give me the word," Vegas snarled. "I'm puttin' niggas on they back tonight."

Rob looked away from Vegas. He couldn't believe he'd agreed to go through with this. The sound of screeching tires interrupted the family discussion in front of the high school. Shaheed quickly turned his head to investigate the noise. It didn't take long for him to notice a 1996 Camry hugging the corner of Stuyvesant and Clinton Avenues. The dark colored Camry was doing close to 40 mph down Clinton Ave. but managed to stop on a dime right behind Shaheed's car, startling the group.

"What the fuck is this?" Vegas shouted as he reached for his gun that was tucked neatly below his beltline.

Shaheed grabbed Vegas' wrist and stopped him. "Chill dog, this is my nigga Troy," Shaheed said.

They all watched as a short and stocky young man jumped out of the Toyota. He was about five-feet-two-inches and barely looked taller than the car. From the minute he saw him, Vegas didn't like Troy. He was dressed in brown corduroy slacks and a dark grey pea coat. His glasses made him look extremely studious and borderline nerdy. He looked as if he had just got off of work from a call center job. From the time that he opened his mouth Vegas knew his suspicions were correct. Troy was definitely not a street person. But what Vegas couldn't tell from looking at him was the fact that Troy was behind a very lucrative credit scam last year.

For Troy, working in the Human Resources Department of Equifax had its advantages. Before Troy moved back to New Jersey he worked in the main office of Equifax back in Atlanta, Georgia. A self-proclaimed credit savior, Troy charged his clients close to fifty dollars per line to erase negative information on their credit reports. Troy was always a good salesman and he was vicious with his research. After a couple of months in the business he decided to create a network of employees from the other credit agencies. In a little under twenty-four months, Troy made over six figures running the network. However, he lost it all after being arrested and charged with identity theft. Troy skipped bail and ran north to avoid prosecution. He decided to set up shop in Newark, New Jersey and lay low until he raised enough money to fight the case. Tonight, Shaheed was not the only person with high stakes in this stunt. Troy was just as excited about pulling off the job tonight.

Troy's face seemed to light up as he jogged across the empty Clinton Avenue to meet the rest of the crew. When he saw Shaheed his smiled widened.

"Fellas, I'm sorry that I'm late," Troy said. His excitement and the short run made him sound a little out of breath. "I had to wait until his light went out before I left." Robert and Vegas both looked puzzled. Shaheed walked over to Troy and shook his hand.

"Waddup T. Don't sweat it." Shaheed offered. "We just got here not too long ago. I didn't tell them anything yet. I just wanted you to explain it to them."

"Sounds good to me." Troy sounded ready to do whatever the night called for in order to get the job done. But Vegas was not giving off a comfortable vibe and Shaheed immediately picked up on it. He knew his cousin well enough to know that Vegas was not going to open up to Troy for some time. Shaheed tried to break the ice with some introductions. He pointed to his Vegas first.

"Troy, this is my cousin Vegas. He will be handling the muscle for tonight's activities." Shaheed smiled as Vegas gave Troy a cold nod. "And this is my brother Rob. He will be doing the driving." Rob nodded to Troy and then looked back to his brother. Robert was still unclear as to what his role would be tonight. He waited patiently for an explanation. Shaheed pointed back to Troy. "And fellas, this is my man Troy. I officially met this dude twice." Shaheed gave a sly grin as he explained himself. "The first time I met this dude was in the Fulton County bullpen a few years back. And then I met him again up this way swiping fake credit cards for niggas." Shaheed and Troy laughed. "So this slick muthafucka definitely got some serious dirt on him."

Vegas hit Troy with a skeptical look as he still wasn't convinced. "So what's the plan, Troy?" Vegas calmly asked.

The smile on Troy's face was immediately erased by Vegas' tone. He stiffened up, preparing to answer the question.

"Have you fellas ever heard of the *Gifting Parties*?" Troy asked. There were no answers, only bollixed looks from Robert and Vegas. "Okay, let me go through this slow for the slow people," Troy laughed. He was alone. "I'm joking, fellas. Lighten up. This is gonna to be fun. Anyway, a couple of years ago this guy named Steve LaCon from Baltimore started a pyramid scheme called the Gifting Board. Basically it was a quick and easy way to raise money for his business. LaCon modeled the scheme after a real business. Imagine this. One guy hires two people and places them under him. He calls his new employees Presidents. Now the job of the two Presidents is to hire two Vice-Presidents each. Keep in mind that there is no money being exchanged yet. The hustle has just begun." Troy couldn't help but let out a hellish giggle. He was really enjoying his audience. All three men were listening attentively to him. He continued to explain the process. "So now the job of the Vice-Presidents is to bring in two Managers each. But at this point, in order for the Manager to officially become a part of the organization they have to bring $200 to the table. No checks or money orders either. Straight cash."

Vegas' eyes lit up. "So who gets the money? The Vice Presidents?" Vegas quickly asked.

Troy shook his head. "Not exactly. Patience, big man. I'm getting to the meat." Troy raised his hand. "So now you have Steve LaCon who is the CEO of this fake business. He has two Presidents who went out and hired four Vice Presidents who went out and hired eight Managers. When all of the Managers bring their money to the Vice Presidents you have what is called the *Cash-Out.* Imagine a pyramid in your mind right now. At the top you have Mr. LaCon. On the next level below him you have the two Presidents. And below them you have the four Vice Presidents. And at the bottom of the Pyramid you have the eight managers who are all waiting with $200 each to buy into the company. That's $1,600." Shaheed started nodding his head and rubbing his palms together. Troy continued to explain the hustle.

"This is where it gets tricky. When you have all fifteen people to complete the pyramid this is how the money gets made. The eight managers on the bottom have to give the money directly to the CEO. That money cashes out Steve LaCon and the pyramid splits into two different boards." Troy put up both of his hands to illustrate the two boards. "Now that the pyramid is split in two, both Presidents who were brought in by LaCon now have a chance to get cashed out. The Presidents become CEOs of their own boards and everyone involved in the Pyramid moves up. In order for them to cash out, the Managers have to bring in two more Managers and the money is given to the CEO's. After those CEOs are cashed out, the Pyramid moves up until everyone involved gets a chance to cash out."

Before he could continue, Rob interrupted. "Wait a minute. This sounds like bullshit," Robert groaned. "How did LaCon keep makin' money if he cashed out once? This don't make sense. What? He made a couple of g's and that's it?"

Troy started laughing. "I know it's crazy. And I know where you coming from. It took me some time to catch onto the concept, too. Let me break it down like this." Troy pulled out a crispy $20 bill. "Let's say this *twenty dollar bill* is the first board. Steve LaCon owns this bill. He starts the first pyramid off from this bill. After he cashed out the first time the board splits in two." Without warning, Troy swiftly ripped the bill in two.

"Now you have two boards. When the two presidents move up to CEO and cash out, now you have four boards." Troy put the two halves together and ripped them. He took three pieces and handed them to the three men.

"Now let's say that we are now the four Vice Presidents. Rip the piece you have into two pieces." Everyone ripped their piece and held up the two parts. "Now these pieces represent the smaller pyramids that will form as a result of more people coming into the business with $200. When the money comes in it comes goes straight to the top. And eventually every Manager that comes in will become a CEO and *Cash Out* for $1,600."

Shaheed started nodding his head again. "Troy, tell them the best part." Shaheed said. He sounded excited. Troy obliged.

"Rip the two pieces in half again," Troy said. "Now we all should have four pieces each. That makes sixteen pyramids. This is how LaCon makes his money. He charges every other CEO two hundred dollars to be a part of the big business. So every time somebody cashes out he gets the money from them." Troy could see an imaginary light bulb flash over Vegas' head as his face lit up.

"Awww man, I heard of this dumb shit before," Vegas yelled. "My goddamn barber tried to get me with this shit. He kept tellin' me to get two people and they get two people and they get two people. Talkin' 'bout we can all get money. Remember I came to you about that shit, Shah'?"

Shaheed started shaking his head. "Hell yeah I remember, my nigga. Them niggas was doing that shit down at Rutgers a couple of years back. Them niggas was makin' some serious paper, too."

Vegas was still not excited. He started shaking his head in disbelief. "Nah, nigga. I don't remember nothin' about niggas cakin'. I remember niggas dyin'. Remember that bitch got killed at the Days Inn in Somerset over that shit?"

"True." Shaheed's mood changed. "True, that was over that Giftin' shit."

Vegas quickly turned back to Troy who was still wearing his nefarious smirk. "So this is how we gonna get money?" Vegas skeptically asked. "That shit ain't gonna work. That shit is dead ain't it?"

"Hold on Vegas, I'm getting to it." Troy said. "I haven't told y'all the best part. So now you know of the concept. You know that LaCon started the whole shit. What y'all don't know is that he is up here in Jersey doing this shit. But he left that $200 shit alone. He is now doing it for bigger money. Way bigger money!" Troy's face began to glow as he noticed the men were quiet and listening. "Every Thursday night he does that shit at a hotel in Parsippany. This nigga is charging every Manager $2,000 to get on the boards. Do the math. That is $16,000 for every CEO that cashes out. LaCon found a way to keep it legal too. This nigga got doctors, lawyers, rappers and even cops from everywhere coming through there to cash out. It's crazy. And the best part, for him at least, is that he takes $2,000 off every cashout for the house." Vegas put his hand on his chin. Troy could see the dollar signs in his eyes. "Yes. On every cashout he's walking away with $2,000. And there are at least seventy-five cashouts per night. This is big business. And it's all legal."

Robert was on the side doing the math. It didn't take him long to tally the total. "So you mean to tell me this cat is pulling close to a $150,000 per night?" Robert asked.

Troy nodded his head in agreement. "Sometimes more," Troy answered. "But he always do at least one hundred even. Trust me, this has been going on for years up here. He keeps it secret. The *cash out house* only got changed once. And he told the whole room that the only way they could keep getting money was to keep the shit quiet. Trust me, when it's money involved people will do whatever it takes. Shit, look at us tonight."

There was a short silence. The men were thinking of all the ways they could use $100,000 per week. Troy broke up the daydreaming session.

"So now this is where y'all come in at," Troy said. "LaCon hosted a special Gifting Party tonight. He's going out of town next week so he did a two-for-one tonight. He did over one hundred cashouts. He killed them tonight. From what I'm hearing he took home at least $120,000 after he paid everybody off." Troy began to lower his voice as if someone was listening to him from afar. "Now what a lot of people don't know is that LaCon doesn't know how to drive that good so he uses a driver. He tries to stay low-key so he keeps his money on him for a couple of days before he takes it to his bank. Now I got the access code for the alarm to his crib and I can tell you how his house is laid out. The only thing I can't tell you is where he puts the money."

Vegas began to get overly suspicious. "Whoa. Hold up, nigga," Vegas barked. "Back up. How the fuck do you know all of his access codes and shit?"

Troy smiled at all three men as he revealed his big secret. "I'm the driver," Troy confidently said. "LaCon is my uncle."

Robert smiled for the first time tonight. For a split second he felt as if the job might be easier than he thought. Vegas nodded his head. The plan started to sound good to him.

"I've been working for him for almost six months now," Troy said. "He gave me the codes about three weeks ago when I moved in with him."

"So you live with him?" Robert asked emphatically.

"Yeah, how else did you think y'all were getting in?" Troy joked. "This can go really easy. Before I left, I told him that I was going out with a girl and I'd be right back. I waited until he went to sleep and headed out. Now all y'all got to do is give me about an hour head start. I will go back to his house and chill in the living room. Y'all come in, break me up a little and go up to his room and do the same. Trust me, the minute he realizes it's a home invasion he will tell you where the money is without a problem. And that's it."

Shaheed looked at his cousin. "Easy enough right, Vegas?" Shaheed asked.

"Too easy," Vegas added. "Let me ask you this, Troy. Why you doing this? If that's really yo' uncle you should be good right? What? Your rich uncle don't pay you enough?"

Troy did not like Vegas' tone but he was too scared to confront him. He decided his best defense would be honesty.

"I got a case back home in Atlanta I need to face," Troy said. "Identity theft and fraud by deception. I don't know if you heard about the south, but you do not want to do time down there. They got niggers working on the chain gang down there. Still!" Troy and Vegas started laughing. "Yes. So I need something extra in my Christmas stocking this year. Which brings me to my next question. How are we splitting this, Shah'?"

Before Shaheed could answer the question, Vegas cut him off. "Nah man, chill. We can talk about that shit after it's over. Just do yo' part Troy."

There was something about Vegas' statement that didn't sit well with Troy. He decided to drop the conversation. "Okay, no problem. You're the boss Vegas," Troy said cautiously. "We can talk about that later. I'm out of here. It's about 2 a.m. now. Give me until like 3 or so before y'all come through." Troy motioned to Shaheed. "You got the address, right?" Shaheed nodded to him. "Okay…don't forget Shah. The code to the back door is 4-4-6-8. Please don't forget it." Troy looked at all three men one last time. Robert grabbed his phone and saved the code. Vegas tapped his temple with his index finger.

"I got it," Vegas said.

"Okay, fellas. Good luck. I'll be in the living room waiting for y'all." Troy grabbed his keys and headed for his car. He picked up his cellphone as he got into the car. The sound of the ignition broke up the silence.

Shaheed watched as the Camry tore down the street in a loud roar. He turned around and walked toward Vegas. "So what you think, man. This should be a cake walk, right?" Shaheed asked. "We go in there, bend these niggas up, and get the money. Twenty minutes tops." Vegas didn't say anything. He was still thinking about the plan. "Right?" Shaheed asked. "Simple enough, right?"

"Oh yeah," Vegas answered. "I just don't like that coward shit, man." Vegas said. Shaheed looked confused as he turned to Vegas. "Troy man." Vegas said. He was now visibly upset. "Why he doing his family like that? That shit is corny."

Shaheed tried to bring him back to reality. "Man fuck that moral shit. These niggas is food right now." Shaheed put his hand out to give Vegas a pound. "Let's eat, my nigga. Fuck that!"

Vegas gave Shaheed a pound and nodded his head. "That's what it is. Let's eat," Vegas said. The three young men jumped in Shaheed's car and sped away. Shaheed drove halfway down the block before he turned to Vegas who was in the backseat.

"Damn yo, what about the CL?" Shaheed asked.

Vegas handed Shaheed the keys from the backseat. "Consider it a going away present, my nigga." Vegas joked. They both laughed as Shaheed punched the engine and headed up Clinton Avenue on their way to South Orange.

Chapter 9

Friday, November 2, 2007
East Orange, New Jersey

2:06 a.m.

$\mathscr{B}$ack at Pearl's house, Heidi was still sitting on her mother's porch when she heard the loud ringing of Lamar's cellphone behind her. Although the sound momentarily startled her, she was still concentrating on calming down. She could hear Lamar behind her fumbling to answer it. The ring was loud enough to wake the neighbors and Lamar didn't want to draw too much attention. He finally found the phone in his pocket and answered it. It was Melissa.

"Hey, is everything okay?" Lamar asked.

"Yes but I'm still mad at you," Melissa snapped from the other end of the phone. "Is your mother okay? There's nothing crazy going on over there is it?"

"No Mel, everything's good," Lamar said. "We just waitin' for him now. He wasn't here when I got here so Imma stick around and wait for him."

"Did you talk to your sister about what we talked about?" Melissa asked.

Lamar walked to the edge of the porch away from Heidi. He lowered his voice so she couldn't hear him.

"Why are you asking me that now Melissa?" Lamar whispered. "I'm going to take care of it." Lamar didn't do a good job of lowering his voice. His voice was too deep to hide. She couldn't make out every word but Heidi knew he was on the phone with Melissa. "This is really not a good time to talk about this right now Mel."

"Okay. I'm not going to argue with you," Melissa said. "I know you are at your mother's. But you betta ask that bitch why she didn't come see you. If you don't ask her anything else tonight, please ask her that. Don't be afraid to check her, Lamar." Lamar didn't say anything in response. It was silent on the phone. "Okay, Lamar," Melissa said. "Call me in the morning. I'm going to bed now. If something happens call me." Lamar didn't say anything. "Okay?" Melissa yelled.

"Yeah, I will. I'll call you as soon as I leave here," Lamar said. His voice sounded frustrated.

"Okay, baby. I love you."

"Love you too." Lamar hung up the phone. Heidi cracked a sarcastic smile to herself. She always joked that Lamar open for his girlfriend, but Melissa would take Lamar on an emotional ride anytime she felt like it. Melissa had a sweet way of manipulating the men in her life from her father to her brothers and now Lamar.

"Trouble on the home front, Lamar?" Heidi joked.

Lamar walked over to where Heidi was sitting and took a seat next to her. "What's going on with you, sis? Real talk." Lamar said. "Why you in there talkin' to your mother like she is some chicken head or something?" Lamar's voice was very direct.

Heidi looked away from Lamar. "I don't know why she thinks it's cool to joke with me about shit." Heidi said. "You don't know what it's like, Lamar. I still have nightmares about that."

"I know you do." Lamar lowered his voice. "But you can't believe she meant it to be mean do you?"

"It doesn't matter," Heidi snapped. "She knows that I'm getting my life back together and she just wants to aggravate me and try to piss me off. I don't know why you take up for her all the time, Lamar."

"I'm not the enemy here, High." Lamar fired back. "I'm here to help." Heidi waved him off. "This is all I'm saying, you only get one mother, Heidi. You know what I'm sayin'?"

Heidi looked over to Lamar. She grew concerned. She knew exactly what Lamar was driving at. Lamar's parents died when he was only four. He never got to know his mother so he looked to Pearl as his own. Although Pearl loved him like her only son, Lamar never knew what it felt like to confide in a real mother. He grew envious of Heidi as they grew up together. Every time Heidi got mad at her mother or they got into an argument, Lamar would always take Pearl's side. He felt like every older woman in his life deserved respect because he truly believed that his mother would want him to act like that.

"Do you feel what I'm saying?" Lamar sternly asked again.

"You know I do," Heidi said reluctantly. "I just don't want to hear it from her. And even if she's not trying to do it purposely, she has to know that she *is* hurting me. Just because she didn't mean to do doesn't make it right."

Lamar nodded his head in agreement. He knew Heidi was in a tough situation. Her quick temper would always get the best of her no matter who got hurt. Unfortunately, tonight she unconsciously released her temper on her mother. Heidi started to feel remorseful about the incident. Lamar sat quietly next to her on the porch. He remained quiet and gave Heidi a moment to herself. He looked at her truck and laughed to himself.

"What's so funny?" Heidi asked as she turned to him.

"Those damn license plates!" Lamar snapped as he continued to titter. "SO HIGH? Now that's funny. And you wonder why people still call you *High*." Lamar joked. "When are you goin' to change those plates?"

"You the second person that asked me that tonight," Heidi said. "I don't know. These plates came from him. So I don't want to get rid of them." Lamar was silent again. He didn't have to ask who gave the plates to her. From her tone, he guessed that it was her late fiancé Jayson.

Heidi's mood suddenly changed as she turned to her brother. "I gotta show you something, Lamar, and you can't tell Mom about this."

Lamar looked over to Heidi. "Okay, what's on your mind, sis?"

"I want you to take a look at this." Heidi reached in her jacket pocket and pulled out a small bottle of pills. She handed it to Lamar. Lamar grabbed the plastic bottle and read it. It was a bottle of *ZOLOFT* pills.

"What's this for?" Lamar sharply asked.

"It's an anti-depressant. My therapist prescribed it for me."

"Therapist?"

"Yup," Heidi somberly answered. "I only went to her a few times. And to be honest I didn't even start taking the pills yet. But I keep having these nightmares about Jayson and they are starting to really bother me."

Lamar was confused. "Sis', I know I didn't ask you this before, but you never told me what happened that night between you and Jayson."

Heidi instantly dropped her head as she thought about that night last year. "I know, Lamar. It's so tough to talk about."

"I can only imagine."

Heidi slowly shook her head as she reminisced about her last night with Jayson. Lamar had no idea what type of secrets she was harboring about that infamous night exactly one year ago.

"Me and Jayson had a big fight that night," Heidi whispered as she turned to her brother. "I don't know how it started exactly. I remember it was a Tuesday night and I went out with this guy from my job. Me and Jayson was having stupid problems at the house. Like sleeping in different rooms and arguing about stupid shit. So I could tell things were changing between us. So when this guy from work asked me out, I went."

"Did you cheat on Jayson?" Lamar quickly asked.

"Absolutely not," Heidi snapped. "I loved Jayson. Now, don't get me wrong. I thought about it a few times, but I never did. But Jayson thought I was cheating on him anyway. It was crazy."

"So who burned the house down?" Lamar asked.

"He did!" Heidi said as she raised her voice. "Listen, Jayson went berserk that night. He was drunk as shit first off. Then when I got home he totally blacked out on me. I mean, Lamar, he kicked my ass from one end of that house to the other."

"Goddamn," Lamar blurted as he twisted his face at the news. He was growing angrier just thinking about a man touching his sister. "So what the fuck was his problem?"

"See that's the thing, I just don't know. He kept saying somebody told him things about me. But I swear to you, I was not cheating on him."

There was a brief silence between the two. Heidi was staring out into the quiet street and thinking about her ex-fiancé. Before Lamar could say another word, Heidi began to reach into her jacket pocket. She pulled out a small index card and handed it to her brother. He shot her a confused look as he cautiously took it from her hands.

"What's this?" Lamar asked.

"Read it and let me know what you think." Lamar unfolded the white index card. The words on the card made his face twist as he slowly began to read the contents.

Happy Birthday Jayson
I was hoping you didn't forget about me,
And all the things I have in store for you!
I Look Forward To Seeing You On The Big Day.

-PS
"Don't forget the number: 862-487-8537"

Lamar quickly read the card again and passed it back to Heidi. "So what is that?" he asked.

"Somebody sent that card to Jayson's job with a bouquet of flowers last year for his birthday," Heidi explained. Her tone grew very dark. "See the phone number at the bottom? I called it and some chick answered. So you tell me what you think it is."

A disappointed expression grew on Lamar's face. He was beyond upset. "So Jayson was cheating on you then?" Lamar somberly asked.

Heidi slowly nodded her head. "Hell yes, he was," she snapped. "And I knew something was different with him. I just don't know who it is. I called the number a few times but this bitch keeps hanging up on me."

There was a silence on the porch. Lamar was reflecting on Heidi's shocking news. He was, again, at a loss for words. He turned to Heidi and watched her as she seemed to boil over with emotion. Her eyes were filling now and Lamar noticed that it was becoming harder and harder for her to fight back her disappointment. Before he could reach out and comfort her, Heidi blurted out an even more troubling revelation.

"You know Lamar, sometimes when I'm alone in that apartment and thinkin' about Jayson I can't help but think that phone number has something to do with his death. I just don't know why I feel like that, but I do."

"Really?" Lamar asked.

Heidi could no longer hold back her tears. They began slowly to trickle down her flustered face. "I'm so lonely at night without him," Heidi whispered, "and it hurts to know that he will never come back to me. Ever."

Heidi tried to wipe her tears but they continued to flow. Her emotions were out of control and Lamar helplessly watched her as she battled with her thoughts. She continued to vent.

"Every time this bitch picks up the phone I just want to reach through the receiver and choke the shit out of her. And I just don't understand why she won't tell me somethin'. I hate being in the dark like this. Of course I'm not sure if he cheated on me. But why did she send him flowers. And what *Big Day* was she talkin' about. I hate this. I just want to go over there and smash her windows out until she tells me somethin'!"

Lamar could hear the aggravation in her voice and tried his best to console her. "Sis', don't act like that." he said. "You don't know for sure if he cheated so don't let it fuck with you right now. I mean, he's not here right? There has to be a better way to confront her then blowin' up her phone-"

Before Jayson could finish his sentence he heard the front door open behind him. It was his mother Pearl walking through the door. She inched onto the porch with caution. She didn't know if her daughter was still in attack mode. She asked Heidi to turn around.

"I think you owe me an apology, Heidi." Pearl said as Heidi jumped up from the porch and stared at her. Lamar stood up on cue and positioned himself between the ladies once again.

"Wait a minute, Heidi. What did we just talk about?" Lamar said.

"You gotta be outta ya goddamn mind if you think imma apologize to you, Mom. Are you kidding me?" she yelled. Her voice now echoed throughout the quiet neighborhood. "After

- 88 -

that slick shit you said to me in the kitchen?" She quickly wiped the tears from her eyes and stared at her mother. Pearl raised her voice even louder to match Heidi's. She was not going to back down to the only daughter she had.

"Listen, you evil bitch," Pearl screamed, "I'm sick and tired of you coming in my goddamn house and disrespecting me! I don't care what I said to you. You not gonna keep getting' up in my face like I didn't carry your stankin' ass for nine months. Now if you don't feel like you owe me an apology then I think it's time for you to get your disrespectful ass off my porch and out of my sight."

Heidi didn't say a word. For the first time in her life she felt mad enough to raise her hands against her mother and she felt almost ashamed of letting the thought enter her mind. Lamar could sense that things were quickly getting out of control. He tried his best to keep this from escalating.

"Mom, go back in the house for a second," Lamar said. "I'm going to finish talkin' to her and we'll be inside in a minute." Pearl didn't budge. "Mom, did you hear me?!" Lamar raised his voice. He was getting more and more frustrated by the minute. "Please Mom, just go back inside and let us talk. We'll be back inside in a minute." Pearl continued to stare at her daughter. She was not afraid. She turned around slowly and walked back inside the house and Lamar slammed the door behind her.

"I'm leaving, Lamar." Heidi said as she turned around and headed to her truck. Lamar trotted down the steps and caught up to her.

"Hold on, Heidi, don't leave yet! I don't know what's going on with you and why you are so angry with her, but all you have to do is apologize. Even if you think she is wrong."

"Hell no. Fuck that! I don't have to apologize to her or anybody else. She knows that I'm goin' through a tough time right now and she wants to keep baiting me into an argument. I'm leaving. She just wants to aggravate me. I don't care if Rick comes home and tears this place to shreds. Fuck it." Heidi wiped the angry tears from her eyes. She shut off her car alarm and jumped in her truck. Lamar chased after her.

"Wait, High! Don't leave!" Lamar said. "I don't think you should drive right now. Not in the condition you in. You all liquored up. And you mad as hell too. Maybe you should just hang out here and shit."

Heidi turned her lip up at Lamar. "I'm a grown-ass woman, Lamar. I'll be fine." Heidi fired up the engine. "I'll call you tomorrow."

As much as Lamar wanted to stop her, he didn't. She seemed to be possessed with anger and frustration. He decided to let her go. Lamar cautiously watched as Heidi backed her truck out of the driveway and sped away down the quiet street.

Chapter 10

South Orange, New Jersey sits royally atop both Irvington and Newark. Constructed on a mountainside almost one and a half centuries ago, this very affluent suburb is only minutes from the violence and madness of both inner cities. The gentle neighborhoods and rich atmosphere seem to subdue anyone passing through town. But tonight, this Mayberry-style community was sending a different sort of vibe through Shaheed and his crew. The men were silently admiring the large homes and luxury cars as Shaheed slowly pulled up to Stonehill Road and turned off the engine.

"Okay, this is it," Shaheed proclaimed. "LaCon lives a block over on Harding Street."

"So are we all going in?" Robert asked. He was visibly nervous.

"Nah." Vegas answered. "Imma go to the house first and look around outside. If these nosey crackers see this car driving around in circles they gonna get suspicious." Vegas sounded confident. "Shah', what's the address?"

Shaheed turned around to face his cousin. "The address is 144 Harding Street. Troy said it's a white house with a blue Tahoe in the driveway."

"Cool. I'll be right back," Vegas said as he unlocked the car door. "Give me a couple of minutes."

Vegas jumped out of the car and slowly pushed the door closed to avoid any unwanted attention. Robert watched him as he cautiously walked down the peaceful street.

"Goddamn man, look at these houses. This shit is crazy," Robert said with envy in his voice. "I bet these crackers be into all types of shit. Beatin' on they wives and molestin' they own kids and everything."

Shaheed looked over to Robert. "What the hell are you talkin' about?" Shaheed sharply asked.

"I'm talking about rich white people man. They be the ones in the news for killin' they own family over the inheritance money and makin' little Billy touch his baby sister in private places."

They both started laughing. "Nigga, somethin's wrong with you. You crazy," Shaheed joked. "I think a lot of black people live out here too now. I heard Lauryn Hill gotta house out here."

"The singer?" Robert asked. "She gotta house in South Orange?"

"Yea. If not her, I know her peoples stay out here. But I feel you, these are some nice ass houses. Man, I can't wait to finally get my money right."

There was a steady silence in the car. Both brothers were privately surveying the neighborhood in amazement. The half-a-million dollar homes towered over the brothers like castles. The combination of well-kept lawns and showroom-style cars gave the street a storybook feel. Shaheed was gazing at a Jaguar XKR when a premonition came to him.

"Yo Robert, man," Shaheed whispered. "This is my last job. I don't want to do this shit no more." Robert turned to look at his brother. "I couldn't tell you this shit before, but these niggas is runnin' me out of town." Shaheed said. "That's why I gotta get this money tonight. My name is all in the newspapers out in Detroit for some old shit and it blew up in my face." Shaheed's voice was grim. "I don't even fuck with Abdul like that anymore. So I gotta be out by the end of the week comin' up. I was thinkin' 'bout headin' down to Houston or something like that."

Robert shot his brother a baffled look. "What the hell you gonna do in Houston?" Shaheed asked.

"Start over," Shaheed answered. "It can't be no worse then Jersey right? I got a few dollars saved. Hopefully tonight I can buy the bounty off my head and keep it movin'. Take a couple of racks down there with Rhonda and get a job or somethin'. Imma hate to do it but, I don't know what else to do."

"Damn, nigga. I wish you would've told me this earlier. How much you owe? I got some money saved myself."

"Seventy five." Shaheed answered.

"Hundred? And how much you short?" Robert asked.

Shaheed started laughing and shaking his head. "Nah, bro. Thousand. I owe seventy five racks." Shaheed revealed with a nervous grin.

Robert was stunned. In a matter of seconds another weight was instantly piled onto Robert's shoulders. For the first time tonight, he understood his brother's reasons for doing this job.

"Damn, Shah." Robert sounded disappointed. He turned around and stared out the window. His heart was beating faster as he weighed the consequences of what they were all about to do. Although he was nervous and clearly playing a game he had no knowledge of, Robert understood that something had to be done now that he knew his brother's life was on the line. "Fuck it. Let's take everything this nigga got in here," Robert said confidently. "From what Troy was saying earlier, LaCon probably got more than enough to make it happen for you."

Shaheed turned to his brother and nodded his head. "No doubt, Rob. Let's eat." Shaheed was feeling more confident with every minute. His confidence was building even more now that he and his older brother were on the same page. Shaheed had spent the last week preparing for tonight. If this turned out to be a success, Shaheed would have more than enough money to pay off Abdul and make his move. What Shaheed failed to tell his brother was the fact that he was planning to relocate for nearly a full year. The city of Houston was the perfect place for Shaheed. His girlfriend Rhonda was originally from Houston and her family were willing to take them in. It was perfect.

"Thanks for coming, dog." Shaheed said. "I really didn't have nobody else to call."

Robert turned back to his brother. "Man, it's all good" he said. "You my brother, dog. Fuck it." Shaheed started nodding his head as he smiled at his brother.

A loud banging on the window startled Robert and Shaheed. It was Vegas. He motioned for Robert to open the back door. Shaheed was anxious to hear the news.

"How does it look over there?" Shaheed quickly asked.

"It's quiet." Vegas answered as he peered through the backseat windows. "Ain't no lights on at the house. I can't really tell if he sleep or not."

"Troy said the backdoor would be opened. We just need to shut off the alarm," Shaheed reminded him.

Vegas nodded his head. "Okay, so that's what it is then. If it's just LaCon and Troy in the house then we can do this in less then ten minutes. If we in the house longer than that, it might not be worth it."

Robert turned around to his cousin. "What do you mean? Ten minutes?" Robert asked.

"I did this shit a few times," Vegas said. "You don't want to be in nobody's crib fa' no more than ten minutes." He had a demonic tone in his voice. "After that, too much shit can go wrong. Muthafuckas wanna turn into heroes and shit. Fuck that. Let's just get in and get out."

Shaheed agreed with Vegas. "Ten minutes?" Shaheed pondered. "Okay that sounds good. So what's the plan, big man?"

"We go in through the back door and shut off the alarm," Vegas said. "We find Troy and find out where LaCon's room is. Hopefully we don't have to break him up too much and we can get the money quick. That's it. You got anything in the trunk, Shaheed?"

"What you mean? A pistol?"

"Nah, I got mine. I just wanna grab some duct tape or something."

Shaheed shot Vegas a confused look. "I don't know if I got some in the trunk but I'll pop it for you." Vegas jumped out the car and headed to the trunk. It didn't take long for him to slam the trunk closed and come back with a hammer and two Timberland boot strings. Shaheed looked at his hands and started laughing.

"What the fuck you gonna do with those?" Shaheed asked. "Lace this nigga boots up?" Robert started laughing. Vegas wasn't smiling.

"Shah', how else we gonna hold this nigga down?" Vegas asked.

"With this!" Shaheed pulled out a pitch black handgun.

A sly smirk grew on Vegas' face as he analyzed the Glock 17 Pistol. "I feel you. But put it on safety, Shah'." Vegas said. "We can't be shootin' in here. If these motherfuckas hear that shit you gonna be the one lacin' niggas' boots...in Rahway."

Shaheed started laughing. "No doubt, cuzzo. Let's go. I'm ready to eat." All three men jumped out the car. Shaheed grabbed a ski mask from his pocket and tossed it to Vegas. Robert raised his hand expecting to catch another ski mask coming from Shaheed. "Nah, Robert," Shaheed whispered as he walked toward his brother. "I need you to stay here and keep the car running. We might come blazin' out of that crib and need to get a head start."

Robert was clearly upset. He gave his brother an indifferent expression. "Shah, you brought me all the way up here to be the goddamn driver?" Robert barked.

"C'mon Rob, you know it's not like even like that. You my only brother, man. If somethin' happened to you up in here, I would kill one of these niggas." Shaheed put his arm around Robert's shoulders and walked away from Vegas. He lowered his voice as he moved closer to the front of the car. "I need you to do this for me tonight. Swallow that pride homeboy. We 'bout to get a lot of money tonight. All you gotta do is make sure we get out of here in one piece. Cool?"

Robert didn't say a word. He had mixed feelings about Shaheed's decision. He wanted to go inside the house with Vegas and Shaheed. He wanted to feel the rush of the robbery and the excitement of the job. But another side of him was relieved that he could remain in the car and wait for them to return. Robert nodded his head and proceeded to the driver side of the car. He never said a word.

"Okay Rob, good lookin'," Shaheed whispered as he headed off. "Don't forget, we'll be back in ten minutes. Leave the engine running." Rob nodded and Shaheed motioned to Vegas. They walked quietly down the dark street. Rob was

Dashawn Taylor

trying to stay calm as he watched his cousin and his younger brother disappear into the darkness.

Chapter 11

Friday, November 2, 2007
East Orange, New Jersey

3:05 a.m.

*P*earl's house seemed to be extra quiet now that Heidi had gone. Lamar walked into the kitchen expecting to see his mother but she was nowhere to be found. He yelled for her a few times before she yelled back from the bedroom. She told Lamar she'd be down in a while, after she took a quick nap. Lamar could tell she was tired from the way her eyes looked earlier. It was now a little after three in the morning and Rick still hadn't shown up. Lamar wasn't going to take any chances that he would surprise them so he locked the front and back doors and decided to put the chain on both of them. If Rick wanted to get into the house he was going to have to make a lot of noise doing it.

After putting the chain on the back door Lamar put the coffee pot back on the stove and turned on the burner. He noticed the photo Heidi had been looking at was still on the table. He picked it up. It was a photo of Pearl and Rick sitting at a bar a few years back. He turned the photo around and read the writing.

Pearl and Rick
-Our First Date-
(Saturday 9-21-02)

Lamar turned the photo back around, and felt himself getting angrier as he stared at it. Lamar sat down at the kitchen table and put his hand on his chin. He started to rub a four-inch scar on his neck as he reflected on the photo. Lamar and Rick had a long history. In fact, their story began long before Rick and Pearl started dating.

****

December 1997

The winter of 1997 was cold for many reasons in Camden, New Jersey. Snow storms and drug wars dominated the streets that year. Lamar was fresh out of high school and looking for a new direction in his life. He'd outgrown East Orange and Pearl's house long before he turned eighteen. And even though he didn't want to leave Heidi, Lamar decided to move down to South Jersey with his friend Bobby, who was a small time hustler at the time. Bobby told Lamar that he needed a driver and offered him $500 a week to drive him around. Lamar quickly accepted and relocated to South Jersey. The job lasted about five months before Bobby got locked up for fourteen years and Lamar lost his job. In desperate need of money and a new place to live, Lamar started hustling for himself. It didn't take long for Lamar to get back on his feet and stack some serious money. He was making close to $1,500 a week, and this was more than enough for him. But in the fall of 1998 Lamar had a conversation that would change his life forever.

For his 19th birthday Lamar went to Gotham Nightclub in Philly to blow off some steam. While waiting in line, he was approached by a young man. Lamar immediately sensed a problem and reached into his pocket.

"Wait, hold up, Lamar," the man said. "There's no beef. I'm reaching out to you 'cause of a mutual friend we got."

Lamar kept his hands in his pockets and stared at the man. "A mutual friend? Keep talking."

The man extended his hand to Lamar. "I'm Quinton. My bunkie told me to find you when I touched down," the man said. "His name is Bobby. He said you used to work for him."

Lamar cracked a smirk. He hadn't heard from Bobby since he went inside. Lamar sent him a letter but Bobby said it would be safer to never write or visit just in case his beef ever came from behind the wall. Lamar shook Quinton's hand. "So what happened?" Lamar asked. "How's that nigga holdin' up in there?"

"He's good. That's a strong dude. Time's gonna fly for him," Quinton said. "But you know we gotta deal with the livin' right now."

"The livin'? Yeah right." Lamar cautiously surveyed his surroundings. "And what's that gotta do with me?" Lamar asked. He was getting a bit anxious because he didn't know Quinton. He had never seen him around and never heard his name in the streets.

"I'm getting' my own thing back together and I need a driver," Quinton offered. "Bobby said you used to drive for him and you'd be perfect for the job."

Lamar shot Quinton a piercing stare. "So you found me to offer me a job?" Lamar asked. His voice sounded extra skeptical.

"Hell yeah! Trust me, this is serious money. And it's easy." Quinton said.

Lamar started to laugh out loud. "Tell you what, give me your number, dog. I got a photogenic memory so I'll remember it. I'll call you if I need a job. Cool?"

Quinton smiled and handed Lamar an orange pager. "Nah. I tell you what," Quinton said. "I'll give you a week to think about it. The job pays five figures a week for three days of work. That's it. I'll page you next week and see what your decision is." Quinton was very serious and his tone was certain. Lamar could tell he wasn't playing. He took the pager from Quinton and nodded to him.

"Okay Quinton. A week? I got it," Lamar said. Quinton gave Lamar a pound and left. Lamar looked down at the brand new pager. It still had the plastic on the display screen. Lamar decided not to go into the club and headed back to Camden. He had a lot of things to think about, especially about his future and that five-figure job.

For a full week Lamar contemplated the offer. He trusted Bobby enough to consider it but he still had to do major research on Quinton. Most of the news that came back on Quinton was positive. He found out that Quinton was only twenty-six and was making Wall Street dollars with his own thing. With each passing day the offer seemed more and more attractive. That following week the orange pager started beeping. Lamar's heart started racing as he considered his options. He could ignore the pager and stick to his own thing or he could call the number back and start making some serious money. He took a deep breath and headed to the nearest pay phone. The offer was too enticing to pass up. He called the number expecting to hear Quinton's voice. Instead, he reached an answering machine.

"Lamar, don't hang up, you know who this is. And if you're hearing this message then that means you're interested in the job. I guess you don't need a pen with that photogenic memory right? Well here's your chance to put it to use. I have some instructions for you. This Saturday at 11a.m. I want you to go to the 30th Street Station in Philadelphia. Don't be late. 11a.m. Head over to the lost and found and tell the girl you are coming to retrieve a lost Elmo book bag. She won't give you no problems. There'll be a key in the bag. Take the key to the passenger lockers near the baggage claim area. Your package is in box 387. And Lamar, please don't get slick with that package because I will be watching. Peace."

The recording stopped and Lamar heard a long beeping sound. He hung up the phone. The message excited and scared Lamar at the same time. He smiled to himself and nodded his head. He knew the job was real and it was time to make some Wall Street dollars.

The job was simple. Quinton hired Lamar to run guns for him. Every Friday, Lamar would pick up a set of keys and an envelope from the passenger locker. He would then be instructed to use the keys to pick up a cargo van and head down I-95 south to Durham, North Carolina. Here he picked up his package and traded the envelope with his supplier for another envelope which contained a list of drop off spots. Then he returned to the 30th Street Station and Lamar simply returned the key and picked up his money out of the same locker. Every Sunday, without fail, Lamar was making close to $12,000 just to complete the deliveries. Lamar was on cloud nine with all the money he was making.

After a full year and a couple of close calls with the state troopers, Lamar decided that he was taking too much of a risk being the front man. He decided to flip the script and rob Quinton. After finding out the packages had a street value of almost $300,000, Lamar wanted a bigger piece of that, and in March of 1999 Lamar made his move on Quinton.

He headed to the 30th Street Station just as planned. He took the van and headed down to Durham. When he reached Durham he played everything cool and picked up the guns, but instead of heading to Durham, North Carolina, Lamar made a quick detour and headed to Virginia Beach where $400,000 was waiting for him. He remembered having conversations with Bobby about some *lay-low* spots down there. So after the deal was made, Lamar stayed in Chesapeake, Virginia for a couple of weeks before he contacted Quinton. He ended up telling his boss that he was kidnapped and robbed by some stick-up kids at a rest stop, but Quinton wasn't buying it. He told Lamar everything was cool and told him to come back to New Jersey so they could start the train moving again. Lamar was cautious but he headed back home anyway. Before leaving, Lamar hid the money in Chesapeake. He didn't want to take any chances with bringing the money back to Jersey.

Everything was cool for a couple of months. Again, Quinton embraced Lamar and he never made a big deal of the incident. But in a strange twist of fate Quinton was murdered in a drive-by shooting in Baltimore, and Lamar lost his job. After hearing the news of Quinton, Lamar decided it was time to quit the business all together. He jumped on a bus to Virginia to pick up his money and brought it back to New Jersey.

Friday the 13th was always bad luck for Lamar. Friday August 13, 1999 was no different. That was the night Lamar returned to his apartment in Camden after making his final run to Virginia. He was extremely tired from the drive and couldn't wait to pack his things and leave the apartment. Lamar got a strange feeling when he pulled up to his block but he ignored the feeling. He figured he was just tired and needed to get some rest, but he couldn't sleep until he'd grabbed the rest of his things and left town. Not wanting to waste any time, Lamar left his bags in the car and rushed into his building. He barely even noticed the homeless person outside of his building asking him for money as he made a dash for the front door.

Taking two steps at a time, Lamar made it upstairs to his apartment in record time. He took a quick pause as he caught his breath, put his key in the door, and twisted the knob. The first thing Lamar noticed when he opened the door was how dark it was in his living room. He couldn't see a thing. He reached over to turn on the lights. *Click.* The lights didn't come on. Lamar quickly looked over to the light switch and tried it again. *Click, click.* Nothing happen. An instant feeling of aggravation came over Lamar. He walked into the apartment and let the door close behind him. Before he could turn around and try the switch again he felt an incredible weight striking him square on the back of his head. He was immediately knocked unconscious. Lamar fell like a pine tree to his living room floor. His face hit the floor so hard that it woke him up. Lamar couldn't figure out what was going on as he tried to open his eyes. Blood started pouring from the back of his head and onto his neck. He tried his best to reach for something to brace himself. He felt his body being turned around but he couldn't react, he was too weak. Lamar was lying on his back when he saw a shiny gun barrel emerging slowly out of the darkness and moving closer to his face. Lamar slowly closed his eyes and turned his head to the side. He knew it was his time to die. And there was nothing he could do.

"Wake up, nigga, you ain't dead. Wake the fuck up!" Lamar didn't react. "Wake ya punk ass up, faggot." A low voice commanded. "I didn't even get a good grip on that one."

Lamar could hear the voice but he couldn't open his eyes. He could feel the pain from the back of his head along with a few piercing smacks on the side of his face. It felt like he was in a bad dream and couldn't wake up. If it wasn't for the sudden strikes to his face, Lamar could've sworn he was sleeping back at the hotel in Chesapeake.

All of a sudden a bright light forced Lamar to open his eyes. He saw the silhouette of two men. One man was standing in the doorway watching another man lean over Lamar's limp body.

"Yo G, you makin' too much noise up here. Goddamn dog, you tryin' to get a nigga locked up?" the man near the doorway said.

"Nigga, shut the fuck up and close the door asshole," the second man barked. "You always bitchin'. We good. Come here. I need to put this nigga on the couch."

The combination of time and fear was helping Lamar to regain consciousness. He was still dizzy but he felt his eyesight slowly returning to normal. The men grabbed him by both arms and pulled him to the couch. They turned him around and the second man pulled up a chair and sat next to him. Lamar leaned back on the couch and tried to focus his eyes. All the lights were now on in his apartment. The man near the door was visibly shaken by the whole ordeal. He kept pacing back and forth while the second man continued to stare into Lamar's eyes.

"Yo nigga, can you hear me?" the second man whispered sarcastically. "I ain't got all day so you better tell me what I want to hear."

Lamar could barely think let alone speak. He struggled to lift his head as he looked at the second man. He fixed his mouth to ask a question, but before he could get one word out of his mouth the back of the second man's hand hit him flush on the jaw. Lamar's head shifted violently to the right and his eyes rolled into the back of his head. The pain was so excruciating that Lamar let out a painful grunt.

"Before you say a fuckin' word I want you to know that I'm not here to play no fuckin' games with you, nigga. Now we worked for the same nigga, so I know the whole story." Lamar wiped his mouth and managed to turn to face the second man. He could taste the blood flowing into his mouth from his lower lip. The man continued to lecture Lamar.

"Now don't tell me you don't know where the money is. Don't tell me you lost it and don't tell me some fuckin' stick-up kids robbed you at a rest stop." Lamar gave the man a peculiar look. "Yeah nigga, I know the whole story." The man smiled. "Who do you think Quinton hired to find yo stupid ass?"

The man by the door started to pace a bit faster now. Lamar looked over to him. He got a quick glimpse of the man's face and their eyes met. A quick flashback of the homeless man downstairs flashed into his mind. Lamar couldn't believe it was the same man dressed as a homeless person. Lamar slowly closed his eyes and shook his head. He couldn't believe he fell for such an old trick.

"Open yo eyes, boy. Look at me!" The second man's voice startled Lamar and brought him back to reality. His time was running short and he could feel it. The moment of truth was upon him. He opened his eyes and looked at the second man who was still holding the pistol. He finally mustered up the strength to talk.

"What do you want to know?" Lamar asked. The feeling in his jaw made him grimace in pain.

The man looked back at his partner and then back at Lamar. "So you a soldier, huh?" the man whispered. "Don't worry man, I'm not gonna hurt you no more. I just wanted to get ya attention. Just tell us where the money is and we outta here."

The man by the door started pacing again. Lamar put his head down. He felt defeated. He took a deep breath and let out an exacerbated gasp. "The money's in the trunk of my car. I put it in the spare tire. You can't miss it." Lamar said.

The man near the door shot outside of the apartment. Lamar could hear his loud footsteps clear the hallway in a matter of seconds. Lamar began to get very nervous sitting on the couch. He thought about running for the door but he knew he would be shot before he even stood up. He had fully regained his consciousness now and started contemplating different ways to escape. The second man was still sitting across from him. Lamar looked at him and looked down at his gun again. He noticed the man had a tattoo on his left hand. It took a few seconds but Lamar did manage read the tattoo.

D-V-8

It didn't take long for Lamar to figure out who he was dealing with. The D-V-8 or *Deviate* Crew was a hustling crew out of Trenton, New Jersey. Since the crack money was slowing down everywhere, a lot of crews had to find other ways to make money. Richer crews would hire smaller crews to enforce orders, make deliveries and even track deviants. That's why this particular crew was in Lamar's apartment tonight. Quinton hired them to find him. Lamar was starting to figure it all out. He began to make small talk to buy some time.

"So how did you find me?" Lamar asked.

The man looked at Lamar. He found it amusing that Lamar wanted to know. He cracked a devilish smile. "Your boyfriend Bobby likes to pillow talk at night." The man started laughing. Lamar didn't bother to pursue it any further. He tried to change the subject.

"And what about Quinton?" Lamar asked.

"What about him? He's dead. Fuck him. I'm just coming to collect the rest of the bounty." The man's voice was cold and emotionless. Lamar started to feel that there was no reasoning with him. Lamar was about to ask another question when the man's partner came stumbling through the door. He had two duffle bags of money in his hands and an unmistakable smile on his face.

"We straight, man!" He was elated.

The second man glanced over to his partner. "Is it all there?"

"Hell yea, gee," the man announced. Lamar looked at the man with a confused expression. The man near Lamar turned from his partner and stared back at him. Lamar didn't recognize the man's expression. It was close to a blank stare and it scared Lamar. The man stood up over him. Lamar watched as the man raised his arm and pointed the pistol at him.

The man near the door yelled, "What are you doing, man? You don't have to kill him now. He gave us the money." Lamar's heart was racing. Those words sent a razor sharp chill through Lamar's body. His hands began to shake uncontrollably.

"I'm sorry, gee, I can't take no chances," the man whispered. Lamar sensed that things were about to escalate and raised his hands in an attempt to protect his face. His nerves made him fall back into the couch as the man fired two shots. The loud bangs echoed off the hollow walls of the apartment. The first bullet completely missed Lamar, but the second struck his neck. The man near the door dropped the bags and dove on top his partner to stop the shooting. Lamar bounced off the back of the couch and fell to the ground. His eyes filled with tears and he felt the blood leak from the open wound in his neck. While

Dashawn Taylor

Lamar tried to crawl out of the room, there was a tussle in the middle of the floor. The two men were struggling over the gun.

"What the fuck are you doin', nigga? Don't kill this one. We are good. I told you that," one man yelled.

"I'm not going to jail for this asshole. Fuck that! Get off of me," the second man yelled

"Nah gee, you are acting crazy now. We don't have to go out like this."

Lamar could hear the two men arguing and fighting for the gun. He tried his best to regain his motor skills and flee the scene. His fear and the site of his own blood made his body feel like a ton of bricks. He couldn't bring himself to stand up and so he continued to crawl out of the living room. After a few seconds Lamar heard another gunshot and everything went black.

Lamar survived the attack. He woke up three days later in hospital with a four-inch scar on his neck. Lamar was lucky the bullet didn't do more damage to his body. He was released a few days later. After being robbed and nearly murdered, Lamar felt it was time to rethink his steps. The whole ordeal scared him enough to make him change his life around. With the help of Heidi and his new girlfriend Melissa, he did just that. Lamar went back to school for computer science and got a job with the City of Camden. The money was slower than the street money but Lamar felt he was making the right move. Still, the memory of that night continued to haunt Lamar. He was forced to relive that horrific night four years later while visiting his mother in East Orange.

May 14, 2003
East Orange, New Jersey

Pearl called Lamar one evening in the spring of 2003 and asked him to come up to her house to have dinner. She told Lamar that she had a surprise for him. She asked him to bring Melissa so they could make it a family affair. Lamar agreed and headed up to his mother's house that following weekend. He didn't think anything of the surprise before he pulled up into her driveway. But when he saw Heidi's car Lamar cracked a smile.

He figured she would be there with her boyfriend Jayson and they were going to have a pleasant dinner.

Lamar and Melissa went into the house and were greeted by Heidi and her boyfriend Jayson. After exchanging a few pleasantries Lamar headed to the dining room to find his mother.

Instead of seeing his mom, Lamar saw the man he had been trying to find for the past four years. The older man was sitting patiently at the dining room table waiting on Pearl. He was neatly dressed and presentable. His 5'6" frame was awkwardly thin for a man of his age and his salt and pepper beard seemed to be a result of years of hard living. His name was Rick.

When he saw Lamar a look of terror flashed over Rick's face. A sharp feeling of rage came over Lamar and he instantly shifted into attack mode. He grabbed a drink glass that was on the table and hurled it. Rick ducked out of the way and the glass shattered just behind him against the wall. Heidi and Melissa heard the commotion and rushed into the other room. By the time they reached the dining room, Lamar was on top of Rick and pounding his head into the wood floor and screaming at him. Heidi tried to grab Lamar and get him off of Rick but he was too strong. Melissa screamed. Pearl heard the yelling and rushed downstairs to see what was going on. When she got downstairs she saw her son fighting her new boyfriend and screamed in horror.

"What the hell is going on down here?" Pearl yelled. No one answered Pearl. Rick was trying to get out of Lamar's grip but he couldn't. He was taking major punishment when Heidi's boyfriend Jayson decided to help out. He grabbed Lamar's arms and attempted to break up the fight. "What the hell happened?!" Pearl yelled as she tried her best to break up the commotion.

"I don't know, Ms. Pearl," Melissa said. She was almost in tears at the sight of Lamar fighting. "Who is that?"

"That's my goddamn boyfriend!" Pearl snapped. Jayson managed to grab Lamar by the waist and pulled him off of Rick. Lamar was still screaming at him. "Lamar what the devil has gotten into you, boy? I know you are not upset that I have a boyfriend." Pearl said. She grabbed Rick and helped him to the other side of the dining room. Melissa, Heidi, and Jayson were

Dashawn Taylor

all holding Lamar back. He was still pushing and shoving them, trying to get back at Rick.

"Wait Lamar, calm down. Please. What the hell is going on?" Heidi asked.

"What the fuck is he doin' here, Mom?!" Lamar yelled.

Pearl was confused. "What? What the hell is that supposed to mean?" Pearl snapped. "He's here to see me. This is my boyfriend." Pearl was furious with Lamar. "Are you mad because I'm dating again?"

Lamar tried to catch his breath. He was still angry. "No Mom, I got beef with this nigga. This is the muthafucka that shot me! Remember I told you I was robbed. This is him. This is the mutherfucka that did it!"

The room fell silent. Pearl looked at her boyfriend. She didn't know what to think. "Rick, is that true?" Pearl was angry and almost in tears.

Rick was shaking his head nervously. He was in pain from all the punches he took from Lamar. "No, Pearl. No, baby. Hell no. He got it wrong," Rick pleaded. He put his hands up as if he were surrendering. "He got it all wrong. I tried to stop the person that shot him. I swear to God. Honestly."

"You a goddamn liar, nigga!" Lamar shouted.

Pearl started to back away from Rick. "Is that true Rick?" Pearl asked. Tears started flowing from her eyes. She tried to hold them back but she couldn't control herself. Rick started to get nervous. He noticed that the situation was leaving him. In a desperate plea he tried to appeal to Lamar.

"Listen Lamar, think back to that night. It was two of us, right?" Rick pleaded. Heidi, Jayson, and Melissa all looked at each other. "Think about it, Lamar. That was my partner Corey that shot you," Rick continued to plead. "You sent me downstairs to look inside ya trunk for the money. Remember?" Rick's voice was trembling at this point. He was very scared, but Lamar was listening. "Lamar, I swear man, as God is my witness." Rick said. "Quinton hired us to come get you but I never thought it was gonna go haywire like that. Look!" Rick reached for his waist and grabbed the bottom of his shirt.

"Whoa nigga, slow down!" Lamar yelled. At this point everyone in the room was focused on Rick. Lamar and Jayson moved closer to him. "Don't make no sudden moves, faggot.

- 108 -

You not out of the woods that fast." Lamar continued to stare at Rick while Pearl covered her mouth, trying unsuccessfully to fight back tears. She couldn't believe what she was hearing.

Rick put up his hands again. "No man, trust me, I ain't got no problem with you." Slowly he lifted his shirt and exposed a bullet wound on the right side of his stomach. "Man, I took a bullet for you that night. Cory was acting crazy and kept trying to shoot you and I stopped him. He shot me by mistake and we hauled-ass up outta there." Rick dropped his shirt. "Look man, if you don't believe me just think about that night. Who you think called the ambulance to come pick you up? You know nobody in that neighborhood was gonna call them for you!" Rick continued to plead to Lamar's reason.

Lamar looked over to his mom as he thought about that night. Although the assault had happened almost four years ago the pain was still fresh in his mind. He did, however, remember Rick having been the person he sent downstairs.

"So where's your partner?" Lamar asked.

Pearl threw her hands in the air. She was totally lost. "Wait, what the hell is going on?" she yelled in desperation. "Can somebody tell me something?"

"Hold on, Mom. Not now." Lamar pleaded for his mother to stay out of it. He was already confused enough. He turned back to Pearl's boyfriend. "Rick, where is he?"

"Man, I'm not gonna to lie to you. Cory fucked me royally that night." Rick put his head down and started to shake his head. Lamar was not the only one feeling pain from that night. "I was bleeding so bad that night that I thought I was gonna die. I kept telling him to take me to the hospital but he wouldn't. He waited 'til we got to a red light and then pushed me out the fuckin' car onto the street. Can you believe that shit? I was leaking right there on the street. Dying! And this faggot-ass nigga left me there for dead."

Lamar balled up his lip. "So you don't know where he is?"

"Oh Cory's dead," Rick answered as everybody in the room looked up. "Yeah, he got locked up and somebody killed him inside. And I never got a dime of that money. I couldn't find his ass. The only reason why I knew he died was because my cousin was inside with him. Trust me Lamar, if I got my cut of that money I would be on the other side of the world right now."

Lamar had mixed feelings. He knew that Rick was the only reason he was standing there that day. He started shaking his head and looked back at Heidi. She shot him a confused look, but Lamar didn't have any answers. He looked over to Pearl who was wiping tears from her eyes.

"Man, this is fuckin' stupid," Lamar gasped. He started walking out of the dining room toward the front door. The room was cemetery silent. He walked over to his mom and gave her a hug. "I'm sorry, Mom. I'm outta here." Lamar said as he motioned to Melissa and told her to meet him in the car.

Pearl tried her best to get his attention. "Lamar, what's going on? You just gonna leave like that?" Lamar didn't say a word. He let Melissa walk in front of him and she opened the door and headed out. Lamar was getting ready to head out when Pearl yelled at him. "Lamar!"

Lamar slowly turned around and looked his mother in the eyes. She could sense that there was a lot going on and that Lamar was obviously confused, hurt and angry all at the same time. She felt remorseful for him.

"What do you want me to say, Mom?" Lamar gave her one last look and gazed over to Rick. "He saved my life." Lamar turned around and headed to the door.

Lamar and Rick have always had a peculiar relationship. Lamar couldn't help but feel like he owed Rick something and it seemed that Rick was ready to take advantage of that. Because his mother loved Rick there were certain boundaries Lamar could not cross when it came to handling him. Still, Lamar didn't trust Rick. Even tonight as he waited for him to return home, he felt that Rick could flip the script at any moment.

❖

Chapter 12

Friday, November 2, 2007
South Orange, New Jersey

3:11 a.m.

J don't know if you know this, but Jesus promised us in Luke 6:38. Give and it shall be given unto you; good measure, pressed down, and shaken together, and running over, shall men give unto your bosom. For with the same measure that ye mete withal it shall be measured to you again.

The commanding voice of Reverend Robert Tilton blared from the sixty-three inch television and echoed throughout the quiet living room at 144 Harding Street. Unknowingly, Troy had fallen asleep watching BET Networks and never acknowledged the TV evangelist asking for his thousand-dollar-vow. The noise from the television seemed to bounce off every wall on the ground floor of LaCon's luxurious bi-level dwelling. New visitors to the LaCon residence would immediately recognize his expensive taste. Original paintings by Henry O. Tanner were gracefully hanging from his oyster-colored-walls as miniature sculptures handcrafted by Sargent Johnson were regally displayed within his marble cases. The imported Italian leather sofas, glass end tables and even the 19th century grandfather clock that sat atop a custom-expanded Persian carpet instantly impressed most of his houseguests. What his houseguests didn't know, was that LaCon secretly hated for anyone to sleep on his sofas. Troy was unwittingly breaking that rule tonight. But the long day had managed to catch up with Troy as he nodded off.

A sudden noise from outside the house caused Troy to quickly open his eyes. It took a few moments for him to realize that he was lying on the couch in his uncle's living room. A second thump startled Troy and made his heart race. A quick glance at the clock made him realize that he had been sleeping for almost thirty minutes. He stood up and rushed to the front door. There was no one there. Troy quickly wiped his eyes to take a closer look outside. Relief washed over him as he noticed the sprinklers in the front lawn sprouting up one at a time.

Having identified the mysterious sound, Troy smiled to himself and headed back to the sofa. He was extremely tired but he knew he couldn't fall asleep again. A twisting rumble in his stomach forced him to make a b-line to the kitchen. Troy was walking through the dining room when his left eye started jumping rapidly. Troy's heart started racing again. A heavy feeling of déjà vu made him turn around and stare at the front door. Something about this moment was eerily familiar to him. Troy stared at the door expecting someone to walk through it, but no one appeared. The déjà vu fizzled away and Troy cautiously looked around. He thought about looking outside again but decided not to pursue it. Instead, he turned around and headed to the kitchen.

The cold floor had Troy moving with a purpose. Without a thought, he headed for the refrigerator and opened the door. Troy always kept his snacks on the bottom shelf and tonight was no different. He grabbed a bag of chips and a Red Bull. When he closed the refrigerator door a large image appeared to his left. Troy quickly turned towards the image and dropped his snacks. His heart fell to his knees when he realized it was a man standing next to him, a man close to six-and-a-half feet tall and wearing a black ski mask. Troy was fixated on the man's grayish eyes. He never noticed the gun barrel pointing directly at his stomach. Troy's mouth fell open but he couldn't say a word. He was petrified.

"Where's his room at?" the man asked. His voice was too deep to whisper. Troy's emotion never changed. He was still frozen.

"Don't make me use this," the man forcefully suggested. His tone grew less tolerant. Troy looked down at the man's hands. He noticed the barrel of the pistol and quickly looked away.

"Who….umm...my uncle? Yea…okay….he is…umm, his room….the bedroom is…upstairs." Troy was noticeably shaken. He never had a gun pointed at him before and his reaction proved it. He continued to ramble. "The bedroom is…..at the top…on the…okay wait….on the right….go to the right ….it's next to the bathroom."

The man shot Troy a frustrated look. "Nigga, calm down." The man's eyes seemed to yell from behind the ski mask. "Don't have me go up here to the wrong room. Now slow the fuck down and tell me where his room is."

Troy nodded his head and took a deep breath. "True. Okay." Troy took a moment. "Okay…go upstairs and his room is on the right….it's on the other side of the bathroom. His room is the one with the white double doors."

"Is he alone?" the man asked.

"Yes," Troy nervously answered. The man shot Troy a piercing look. Something about the look was familiar to Troy. He peered closer at the man's grayish eyes. An innocent smile grew on Troy's face as he identified the man. "Vegas, is that you?" Troy asked.

The question set off an infuriating trigger in the man. He quickly raised the handgun and swung it at Troy. The four-pound stainless metal felt like a ton of bricks crashing over Troy's head. A splatter of blood shot from the gash initiated by the pistol. With this impact, Troy's knees buckled. He was seconds from unconsciousness but managed to shoot the masked-man a stunned expression. The man raised the pistol again in an attempt to finish the job. Before he could swing again, Troy's knees completely gave out on him and he collapsed to the kitchen floor. A second man rushed from the other side of the kitchen to investigate the sound. He was also wearing a black ski mask. He managed to make it to the refrigerator just in time to watch Troy's eyes roll into the back of his head as he drifted off to sleep. The man pulled up the ski mask to take a closer look. It was Shaheed. He quickly turned to his partner who was seductively watching his victim slip into unconsciousness.

"Vegas, what the fuck is wrong with you?" Shaheed whispered angrily. "Why the fuck did you just do that?"

Vegas was still watching Troy's peaceful face. "I told you Shah, no heroes. He already told me where his punk-ass uncle was. That nigga said LaCon's room is the one with the white double doors." Vegas turned to Shaheed. "You ready, nigga? Let's go eat."

Shaheed moved closer to Vegas. He was clearly worried. "Nigga, I'm not going back to jail," Shaheed whispered. His voice grew overly concerned. "You hear me? Five minutes with this asshole LaCon. That's it. Don't get up here and turn into the fuckin' chainsaw massacre on me. You hear me?"

A satanic grin appeared through Vegas' ski mask. He chuckled under his breath and nodded his head. "No doubt, cuzzo. Five minutes. We are in and out," Vegas assured.

Shaheed pulled his ski mask down over his face. He looked down to Troy one last time and motioned to the living room. "Okay Vee, you take the point. I'll back you up," Shaheed said.

"Sounds good. Let's go," Vegas answered as he nodded his head.

Vegas stepped over Troy's body and headed out of the kitchen. As they moved closer to the steps, Vegas heard a voice coming from the living room. *Send your thousand-dollar vow in today and I will guarantee you the blessings of the Lord will come to you in abundance.* Between the loud telecast and the thick carpet, Vegas realized he and Shaheed would have no problem making it upstairs undetected. As he moved carefully by the glass tables, Vegas took a quick glance at the television. He smiled to himself as he listened to the *Success 'N Life* broadcast. He motioned for Shaheed to move closer to him. When Shaheed got close enough, Vegas jokingly pointed to the television.

"See, my nigga. We not the only ones up this early in the mornin' trying to get this money." Vegas laughed quietly. Shaheed was not amused. He shook his head.

"C'mon man, stop playin'," Shaheed whispered.

Vegas nodded his head again and headed for the stairs. His eyes were wide open as he examined every corner of the dark stairway. Shaheed was following close behind. The darkness made it difficult to maneuver but Vegas managed to find LaCon's room on the second floor. They both stared at the white double doors. A sudden feeling of anxiety came over Shaheed. His fear began to overpower his logic as he imagined what was waiting for him on the other side of the doors. He quickly grabbed his gun from his waist. His heart was pounding uncontrollably as he watched Vegas grab for the doorknob. Vegas turned around and nodded to Shaheed. Although he was noticeably shaken, Shaheed gave his cousin a reaffirming nod. Vegas cautiously twisted the doorknob and Shaheed took a deep breath and tried to prepare himself for what was about to unfold.

****

South Orange, New Jersey
3:19 a.m.

Back in the Dodge Charger, Robert was impatiently waiting for his brother to return. The pressure of the evening was building rapidly in his chest and stomach. He was clearly stressed. The soothing R&B music on the radio proved ineffective against his fear. After a few minutes, Robert reached for the only thing that could calm his nerves right now; a Newport cigarette.

Robert was never a big smoker. On average, he smoked two packs per year. He only smoked to calm his nerves in tight situations, and tonight was undoubtedly one of those. Robert pulled a fresh stogy from his pocket. He looked around one last time before he set fire to the tip. Robert took a long pull and sat back in his seat, letting the warm smoke chase the stress from his stomach. Watching the gray haze, he reminisced about the last time he felt smoke in his lungs. It was two months ago.

September 5, 2007
10:54 a.m.

Robert was sitting in the parking lot of the Atlantic Federal Credit Union. He was working on his second cigarette as he weighed the consequences of entering the bank. There was no turning back now. All of his hard work and patience came down to this final transaction. Robert took one last long pull of the cigarette and jumped out of the car. He strolled confidently into the bank. With nothing to lose, he emphatically requested to speak with the manager and after a few moments a lanky Middle Eastern man emerged from the rear office. He cautiously approached Robert who was standing near the door with his hands in his pockets. As he got closer to Robert the bank manager noticed his mood was suddenly changing. Without warning Robert slowly removed his right hand from his jacket pocket. A nervous smirk grew on the manager's face as Robert extended an empty hand to him. The manager politely returned the gesture and the two men shook hands.

"I'm sorry I'm late, Mr. Asher," Robert stammered as he shook the manager's hand. "I was actually a bit nervous about coming inside so I was sitting in the car with my fingers crossed."

Mr. Asher shot Robert a reassuring smile. "Don't worry, Mr. Moses. We are very excited to have you here today." The manager patted Robert on the back as they both walked toward his office. Robert felt butterflies stirring in his stomach as he admired the prominent layout of the community bank. A company slogan mounted on the wall made him crack a smile. *Welcome to Atlantic Federal! A Place Where Dreams Are Made And Financed*! Robert confidently nodded to himself. He was beginning to feel like he had made the right decision.

"Okay, Mr. Moses. Have a seat." Mr. Asher's voice was polite yet imperious. "Now before we start the paperwork, I have to tell you that your initial scores did force us to bend some of our rules here." Robert quietly sat across from the bank manager. He didn't say a word. "I pulled your credit scores and they didn't look good," Mr. Asher said as he started rubbing his chin. He flipped through a stack of papers. "We usually put a lot of weight on the credit but I added a few more lines to the agreement to bypass the report." Robert was confused. He didn't know whether he was being told good or bad news. Mr. Asher opened up Robert's file on his desk. "So Robert, umm, can I call you Robert?" Mr. Asher asked.

"Yes. Oh yes, you can," Robert answered. The words barely squeezed by the knot lodged in his throat. With every second Robert was getting more nervous.

"Robert, let me ask you this, why do you want to go to film school? Why not a trade academy? Why not learn how to work on cars or attend a barber school?"

Robert was taken aback by the question. He hesitated to answer. "Well, to be honest Mr. Asher, my passion is for movies. I want to write and direct movies and I think the New York Film Academy will give me my best shot."

Mr. Asher dismissively nodded his head. "I understand the passion." Mr. Asher said. "But what about the money?"

Robert shot Mr. Asher a confused look. "The money to go to school?" Robert asked. "That's why I'm here. I figured if-"

Mr. Asher cut him off. "No. I'm referring to the money in the field. There are steady jobs in mechanics. You can make a lot of money working on cars or something of that nature. No offense, Mr. Moses, but there's a lot of people that fail in the movie business. That road is congested with people that didn't realize the hard work that they would have to put in. They get half-way to the finish line and give up or get distracted. Are you sure you want to travel down that path?" The men exchanged uncomfortable stares. Robert was almost insulted by the mere mention of giving up on his dream. He decided to keep a level-head and respond to Mr. Asher professionally.

"With all due respect, Mr. Asher, I am not those other people." Robert's voice started to gain confidence. "I've been dreaming of working in the movie industry since I was a kid. I do understand that my credit scores are not the best. And I have no collateral. But I will not quit. I will finish the job."

There was a loud silence in the room. The bank manager looked down at the paperwork. As he nonchalantly flipped through each page of the loan application, Robert began to feel less confident about the outcome. Sensing that this was his last chance, Robert decided to make one final appeal.

"Mr. Asher," Robert said. Something about Robert's voice made the bank manager raise his head. He noticed that Robert's mood had changed. Robert continued to speak. "Mr. Asher, my mother died when I was just eight years old. I don't remember much about her. Her face sometimes from pictures that my grandmother gave to me . . . but I do remember one thing about her. She gave me the best advice about life." Robert looked away and started to reminisce. "We were walking to school one day. My mother walked me to school everyday when I was in first grade. This particular day we were about four blocks away from the school. My mother was sad that day. I never knew why she was sad. She just didn't look right that day. She looked down and saw a single dandelion growing on the sidewalk. It was growing through a crack in the concrete. My mother stopped me and knelt down. She pointed at the yellow flower and made me look at it. I still remember her voice. She said, *Robert, that's you. Look at it. That's you, honey. You are that flower. That flower managed to move all that hard concrete to the side and grow above it. That's how you are, Robert. It's gonna take years of pain and struggle. But you are gonna move that concrete. And you are gonna grow to be successful. You can't give up. Even when that concrete gets heavy. You can never give up.*" Robert turned back to the manager, who seemed to be moved by the story. "So you see Mr. Asher, no matter how heavy that concrete gets out there, I'm not giving up. I will make it."

The bank manager nodded his head, closed the file, and pulled out a yellow sheet of paper from his desk. He started writing notes on the sheet and passed it to Robert.

"Mr. Moses, I've always prided myself on knowing good people. In my business sometimes you have to make a judgment call that goes beyond the numbers on paper." The manager watched as Robert read the contract. "Not too many young men your age are as focused and determined to make something of themselves. Because of that, I'm going to process the loan for you. I have a good feeling about you."

Robert let out a gasp of air. He was excited; a feeling of triumph shot through his entire body. "Thank you, Mr. Asher."

"No, thank you, Robert. I'm so happy to see that you are excited about this opportunity. I'm going to approve the loan for $6,000. That should be enough to help you complete your courses and get your materials."

Robert was excited. Despite trying his best, he could not hide his emotions. "Thank you very much. Trust me, Mr. Asher, you will not be disappointed." Robert was overjoyed. He signed the paperwork and returned it to the manager. "This is great news for me. You just don't know."

Both men stood up in the office and shook hands. The manager nodded to Robert as he walked him out of the bank.

"Good luck out there," Mr. Asher said. "Don't forget, when you film your first major movie, I want you to cast me, okay? I'd be great in a bank scene."

Both men laughed as Robert left. Things were beginning to look up for Robert. He now had the money for school and was set to pursue his dreams of becoming a major film director.

(present time)

Back in the Dodge Charger, Robert took another long pull of the cigarette as he thought about that day in the bank with Mr. Asher. He smiled at the thought of the $6,000 sitting in his account waiting for him to start school. For the past sixty days, Robert had managed to ignore the money. Tonight was the first time he imagined giving his younger brother a portion of the money to pay off his debt. But if Vegas and Shaheed could successfully get the money from LaCon, his school loan would remain in his account and he could start his life over again. Robert looked out the window one last time. He took another long pull of the cigarette and tried to calm his nerves. An eerie feeling came over him as he looked down the quiet street. Robert said a quick prayer to himself. *Please God let everything work itself out tonight. I really need this break.*

****

3:28 a.m.

Back at 144 Harding Street, a different kind of prayer was being said. An exhausted Steve LaCon was staring at his own reflection in the bathroom mirror when he quietly begged for his God to ease his piercing headache. He was in pain. This marked the third consecutive sleepless night that LaCon had suffered due to a sinus infection. Tomorrow was a big day for him and he was determined to get as much sleep as possible. He took one last look at his tired eyes and shook his head. *There's*

Dashawn Taylor

gotta be somethin' in here that can knock this headache out.
LaCon was growing desperate. He frantically opened the
frameless medicine cabinet to find a few Tylenol and Bayer
packets on his middle shelf. He waived them off. LaCon needed
something stronger. After pushing a few band-aids and nail-
clippers aside, LaCon finally found what he was looking for, his
Excedrin. He quickly snatched the blue box from the medicine
cabinet and like a starving squirrel trying to crack his nut
opened, LaCon fumbled with the child-proof container until the
lid popped off. The little white caplets flew everywhere. LaCon
instantly grew more frustrated. *Shit!* He slammed the empty
Excedrin bottle on the sink with disgust and stared at the pills
scattered about his floor. LaCon shook his head again. Without
a thought, he grabbed two small white pills from the floor and
tossed them to the back of his throat. With the help of a handful
of water, LaCon swallowed the pills and waited for the results.

The Excedrin started working immediately. LaCon felt
the pressure dissipate as he looked around the bathroom. A tiny
smirk grew on his face as he visualized the pills flying all over
the room. Although he was extremely tired, LaCon was too
much of a neat-freak to leave the pills scattered in his bathroom.
He imagined a small bristled broom and dustpan in his kitchen
and decided to go get them.

A chilling emotion came over LaCon as he walked out
of the bathroom. With every step he felt as though his entire
bedroom was spinning in slow motion. He stopped in his tracks
and cautiously noticing his digital clock. The red numbers on
the digital clock read 3:35. LaCon slowly wiped his mouth and
glanced around the room. His mind was racing. *Jesus Christ,
this feels like this happened before.* A few goose bumps rose up
on his arms and on the back of his neck. LaCon was determined
to shake the feeling. He was tempted to walk back to the
bathroom but decided to ignore the notion. After a moment the
feeling had fizzled away and LaCon slowly headed for the white
double-doors in his bedroom.

The short walk from his bathroom to the bedroom doors
seemed an eternity. He was touched by a strange and heavy
nostalgia, but decided not to dwell on it. LaCon was rubbing out
the goose bumps on his arm when he reached for the brass
handles on the bedroom doors. The first pull on the lever didn't

work. LaCon was confused. It seemed to be jammed. LaCon aggressively pulled the lever again and the bedroom door swung open toward him. In that instant, LaCon heard a loud bang. A blinding yellow light startled him. Before he could focus on the light, it was gone. The sharp flash seemed to blind him temporarily. He tried to cover his eyes but, oddly, he couldn't feel his arms. LaCon quickly realized something was wrong. A loud ringing was cutting through his ears like a sharp ice pick.

He opened his eyes. LaCon was surprised to find himself staring at the ceiling. He was now lying on his back. A blistering hot pain shot from his abdomen through his entire body. LaCon tried to yell but he could barely breathe and his heart pounded out of his chest. He couldn't understand what had happened to him. He noticed a body hovering over him like a black cloud. It didn't take long for him to realize that this was a very large man in a ski mask. Another rush of fear shot through LaCon. The adrenaline caused his vision to blur as his body started shaking without warning. Fearing that the worse was just on the horizon, he closed his eyes. The sound of two male voices could be heard just above his head. Weak and unable to respond, LaCon tried his best to listen to what was being said.

"What the fuck is wrong with you, nigga? Why the fuck did you just do that?"

"He scared me, Shah'. What the fuck? He opened the door right in front of me."

"So you shot him?"

"What? Hell yes! I think he knew we was out here, man. I didn't fuckin' know. For real, I thought he had a gun or somethin', the way he opened the door."

"Yo man, we goin' to jail over this stupid shit! Damn, nigga, you fucked us up with this dog. For real. We are fuckin' food now."

"Wait a minute, Shah. Relax-"

"What the hell you mean relax, Vee? He got a fuckin' bullet in his stomach right now. A bullet from ya gun, and this asshole is leakin' all over the place. How the fuck we gonna get the money now? You killed us, nigga. For real, for real, you killed us!"

"Wait hold up. We not done yet, wait. This nigga ain't dead. Look at him. He still breathin'."

Dashawn Taylor

LaCon's body felt funny. An ice-cold chill ran through him as he learned that he had just been shot. He closed his eyes tighter and tried to endure the pain from his stomach. A heavy smack on his left cheek made him quickly open his eyes. A large man was leaning over him and pointing a gun in his face. It was Vegas. LaCon didn't know what scared him more; the gun barrel or Vegas' piercing gray eyes. Vegas got closer to LaCon and spoke to him in a very even yet devious tone.

"Listen, asshole, you can still make it through this," Vegas said. "Just tell us where the money is and Imma call the ambulance for you." LaCon was weak. The chilling words sent shockwaves through his body. LaCon had never been shot before. He couldn't feel the bullet but he started to feel the thick blood leak from his stomach. Vegas continued to speak to him. "LaCon, wake up. Don't fall asleep on me, nigga." Vegas raised his voice. "You can't fuckin' die yet. Where's the money? I told you that I was gonna call the ambulance for you. But you gotta tell me where the money is first."

LaCon was very weak. He softly began to answer Vegas. "My wallet is next.....next to the bed in my pants."

Vegas was getting angry. He waved the gun in front of LaCon's face again. "Don't try to be a fuckin' hero, nigga," Vegas barked. "You know what money I'm talkin' 'bout. I don't wanna use this again, but I will. Just tell us where the real money is." More fear rushed into LaCon's already very limp body. After a few moments, LaCon mustered the strength to raise his head and nod toward his closet in the bedroom. Vegas shot him an interested look through the ski mask. "So the money is in the closet?" Vegas sternly questioned. LaCon closed his eyes and nodded. "Okay that's wassup," Vegas said. "The money is in the closet then."

Vegas turned around and anxiously stared at the wicker closet doors. He noticed that one of the doors was partially cracked but he could barely see inside. Before he could turn around, Shaheed was stepping over LaCon's body and heading for the closet himself. He moved through the dimly lit room with purpose. Vegas watched as his cousin cautiously peeked inside the closet. He still couldn't see a thing. Before he reached for the door handle, Shaheed put a tighter grip on his pistol and adjusted his focus. He grabbed the levers and pulled the doors opened. A soft ivory light illuminated the closet. Vegas' eyes grew wide. Shaheed was stunned at the sight. They both stared inside the closet in amazement. The wicker doors were concealing much more than LaCon's Zegna suits and Prada shoes.

LaCon's walk-in closet was twice the size of his bedroom. Sixteen wood cases were deeply embedded into the walls. The eight-foot structures were all of equal length and height and covered the walls completely. Shaheed slowly walked inside the closet. The room felt slightly cooler than the master bedroom. As he made his way around the closet Shaheed decided to peer into a few of the cases. He marveled at the racks of expensive dress shirts, jackets and suit pants draping from the stainless steal hangers. Each wood case featured a different style of dress, from corporate to urban to athletic. As he continued to walk about the closet, Shaheed felt like he was browsing through a new-age department store. He examined each case as he passed them. Shaheed arrived in the middle of the room where he began to notice that the expensive clothes and shoes were only the tip of the iceberg. LaCon was selling more than $16,000 dreams. He was also an antique dealer. Ageless wines and priceless paintings sat patiently waiting for a buyer. Signed baseball bats and eighty-year-old comic books were also in the cases. Shaheed was shaking his head in frustration when he turned around and headed back to the entrance of the closet.

"Yo man, ask that nigga where the money is," Shaheed barked. He was clearly angry. "It's like twenty cases in here and I don't see the money."

Vegas nodded his head and turned to LaCon. "Hey, LaCon! Where's the money, nigga?" Vegas snapped. "You are runnin' out of time, Stevie."

LaCon turned to Vegas who was a lot closer to his face than he wanted him to be. LaCon was still weak but decided to cooperate with the criminals.

"Tell him to go to the air conditioner on the wall," LaCon said as his voice cracked with fear and fatigue. He tried his best to raise his voice but the pain from his stomach was intensifying. "Tell him to pull off the cover and he'll see the money's in the case. The money is in the case."

"In the air conditioner?" Vegas quickly snapped.

"Yes, the air conditioner isn't real," LaCon whispered.

A demonic smirk expanded across Vegas' face. He chuckled to himself. "Keep the money in the fake air conditioner? I like you already. My type of hustler," Vegas joked. He turned to Shaheed who was standing in the doorway. "Pull the cover off the air conditioner. The money's in there. The air conditioner is not real." Vegas watched as Shaheed turned around and headed back inside the closet. He turned back to LaCon, noticing that he was having trouble breathing. The bullet was causing more damage to LaCon with every passing second. Vegas moved closer to LaCon's ear and started to whisper to him. "Don't worry, man, we not gonna let you die," Vegas whispered. "Soon as we get the money Imma call them boys for you. Trust me."

LaCon didn't respond to Vegas. Something about Vegas' tone was causing anxiety in LaCon. Vegas continued to whisper in his ear.

"While we got this time alone, I wanna talk to you for a minute, my dude." Vegas took a deep breath and started talking again. "I used to rob niggas down in Kentucky a few years ago. I was down there for like six months cleaning up the bullshit jobs that nobody would take. You know, the pimps, the hoes, sometimes other hustler, it didn't matter to me. Just to get the money on my side. Fuck that. After a while, I hired a bunch 'a wild niggas down there to help me out. We called ourself the HOP or h-o-p. You know what that means?"

LaCon turned to Vegas. The evil in his eyes seemed to shoot straight through the ski mask. LaCon didn't answer him, but Vegas smiled and continued to speak.

"I know you don't know what that means. That's what you call a rhetorical question." Vegas started chuckling again. "To answer my own question, h-o-p meant House Of Pain. That's all we did was bring pain to niggas. Now, I thought I was a wild motherfucka until I met them. These Kentucky boys showed me some shit. They kidnapped this one asshole one day and for twelve hours this hero would not tell us where the money was. No matter how many cigarettes they put out on his arms and legs. No matter how many punches he took to the stomach, nothin' they did made him crack. So after we realized he wasn't going to tell us shit, one of them Kentucky boys was like *fuck it, since he's not going to tell us shit, let's spinks his ass.* Now I'm thinkin', what the fuck is *spinks*? But before I could ask the question out loud, one of them boys took a crowbar and smashed this asshole in the mouth with it. When I tell you this boy's teeth flew out of his mouth like tic-tacs. I mean his shit went everywhere. And the sad thing is, this Kentucky boy didn't stop wailing on this hero until all of teeth was outta his mouth. Even the motherfuckin' wisdoms. By the time he finished with him, I'm telling you this asshole looked ten times worse then Leon Spinks."

LaCon's eyes began to widen and he was crippled by a heavy fear. Vegas continued to whisper to him.

"So the Kentucky boy ended up burning this asshole alive. He told me later that he spinks'd him so that the cops couldn't identify his dumbass. Now, I just asked you where the money is and you told me. But is there somethin' else, or somewhere else that we should know about?" Vegas' tone grew colder. His eyes intensified with each word. LaCon watched as Vegas reached towards his backside and pulled a hammer from his hip. Vegas put the hammer directly in LaCon's line of sight. LaCon was breathing heavier as Vegas continued to talk. "Now I know this is not a crowbar, but trust me, asshole, this will give you the worse Spinks makeover you could ever have. Now, Imma ask you again. Is there anywhere else we can find the money at?"

Before LaCon could answer him, Shaheed emerged from the closet in a rush. He was choking a black duffle bag and running through the bedroom. His eyes seemed to shine like headlights through the ski mask as Vegas turned to see what the commotion was all about.

"We gotta bounce, man," Shaheed said. "Trust me. Let's roll, Vee. We gotta bail. This nigga's slick."

Vegas turned to LaCon and then back to his cousin Shaheed. He was confused. "What do you mean?" Vegas asked as he stood up. "What happened? You got the money?"

Shaheed was quickly heading for the bedroom entrance. He ran by Vegas and jumped over LaCon. "Yeah, man. I got the money right here. It's in the bag. I think it's like two hundred stacks for real."

Vegas' eyes lit up. A wide grin on his face stretched the ski mask. "Hell yea. That's wassup. So we good then?"

"Nah man. Let's roll," Shaheed said as he was heading for the stairs. Vegas yelled to him.

"Wait, Shah'. Yo, what happened in there?" Vegas asked.

Shaheed turned around. "Man, when I pulled the cover off the air conditioner the money was right there. But when I pulled the duffle bag out I looked in the-"

Vegas was still confused as he cut him off. "So?"

Shaheed started shaking his head. "Man, there was a camera in the air conditioner. It was pointed right at me. So I pulled the side cover off the air conditioner and there was two monitors right there. Man, this nigga got the whole placed wired with cameras. Even in the kitchen. I saw that nigga Troy laying on the kitchen floor and everything. We gotta bounce dog. Let's go."

A red-hot stream of anger charged through Vegas. He was furious. He started to cautiously look around the bedroom for cameras. After a quick scan, Vegas turned to LaCon who was shaking uncontrollably on the floor. A million thoughts ran through Vegas' mind. Shaheed saw his wheels turning and grabbed his arm.

"What the hell is wrong with you, man. Let's go," Shaheed pleaded.

Vegas was still staring at LaCon. "Nah, man...you go 'head. I gotta take care of something real quick." Vegas said.

Shaheed shot his older cousin a confused look. "What? You want me to leave you?"

Vegas turned back to Shaheed. "Yeah, take the money and bounce. I'm good. He got a truck in the driveway I like. Imma get the keys and take that outta here. You go 'head. Pay that bill and make ya shit happen. I'll catch up with you." Vegas turned back to LaCon.

Shaheed looked at his cousin again and shook his head. An overwhelming fear came over him.

"Vee, I'm out. I gotta fuckin go," Shaheed said. "I don't wanna leave you but you on some shit, dog. I'm out."

Vegas never acknowledged Shaheed's words as he slowly walked over to LaCon. Shaheed squinted at his cousin one last time and turned around. The fear of incarceration outweighed his concern for his cousin. Shaheed bolted downstairs. He made it back to the first floor in a matter of seconds. He darted toward the kitchen and headed for the back door. The sight of Troy lying on the kitchen floor made his heart race. He needed to get out of the house and back to the Dodge Charger before things spun wildly out of control. Shaheed hit the back door with lightning speed, but was careful not to draw any unwanted attention. He slowly closed the door and crept down the driveway. Shaheed was passing the mailbox at the bottom of the driveway when he heard a pounding gunshot roar from the second floor of the LaCon residence. A yellow flash made him turn around and stare at the window and his stomach fell to his feet. An unexplainable empty feeling came over him. Without a thought, Shaheed quickly turned around and sprinted into the darkness leaving Vegas alone in the house to take care of LaCon and Troy.

Chapter 13

Friday, November 2, 2007
East Orange, New Jersey

3:54 a.m.

*L*amar felt his eyes becoming very heavy as he sat in his mother's favorite arm chair. He was so tired. It was close to 4:00 a.m. and there was still no sign of Rick. Lamar was just getting comfortable when his phone rang. It was Melissa. He answered the phone, with a slight attitude.

"Why aren't you sleeping?" Lamar barked.

"What? Boy, please!" Melissa snapped. She sounded alert on the other line. "I'm callin' to check on you. I wanna make sure everything is good."

"Yeah, I was trying to take a nap," Lamar said. "I'm cool. So what are you doin'?"

"I can't sleep. I can't believe it's almost four in the morning."

"Yeah I know. And this asshole still didn't show up." Lamar sounded tired.

"So what's up with your mother's boyfriend? Why all the drama, Lamar? You never told me the deal with him."

"Really it's the same ol' shit. He's from the street and my mom is in love with his gay ass. I don't know why. She let him move in here and he really don't do shit. He got a punk ass job down at the Department of Motor Vehicles. But that's it. He's a bumb-ass nigga. I can't imagine why she still chasin' this dude." Melissa remained silent on the other line. She really didn't have an answer for him. Lamar continued to vent about his mother's boyfriend. "I'm definitely gonna go hard at him tonight when he comes here." Lamar's tone grew angry. "I just did eight months over his punk ass and that shit wasn't cool."

On the other end of the phone Melissa was confused. "Wait Lamar, back up." Melissa said. "What do you mean you did that time for him?"

"That's why I got locked up, Melissa," Lamar said. "Pay attention, baby."

"What?" Melissa snapped. "You never told me why you got locked up, remember? You just told me not to come see you. That's all I remember. One minute you stormin' out the house like a mad man and the next minute I'm getting a collect call from you. You never told me what happened."

"Well now you know," Lamar bawled. "Before I went to jail, I came over here because this nigga was raising his hands to my moms. When I got here, he tried to fall back and cop pleas but I wasn't trying to hear that shit. One thing led to another and we just got into it. Only reason I got locked up is because I had that old warrant. If I didn't have that warrant, I don't think the cops would 'a did shit. But it is what it is. Fuck it, it's done."

"Damn, Lamar" she whispered.

"What?"

"I feel like shit," Melissa lowered her tone.

"Huh....why?" Lamar asked.

"Because this whole time I thought High was the reason why you got locked up. All this time I been ready to kick her ass and she didn't even do shit. Wow, I feel like an ass."

There was a brief silence over the phone. Lamar decided to stay quiet. He knew Melissa's issues with Heidi were childish and he wanted her to soak in her embarrassment before he saved her. He waited a few more moments before he broke the silence.

"Yeah, well I don't know why you two are going back and forth like y'all are. Y'all are too grown for that dumb shit. Feel me?" Lamar sharply asked.

"Yeah, but she's still off the chain. I'm not ready to bury the hatchet that quick," Melissa said. "I guess we do need to have a talk though. I don't mind doing that."

"Call her then."

"I don't have her number."

"Okay, I'll text it to you. She still up. She left here about a hour ago."

"Alright, well maybe I'll wait a little and hit her later today on my lunch break or something. But we'll see."

Lamar heard a noise come from upstairs. He sat up in the armchair and instantly became alert. He readjusted himself as he heard the footsteps of his mother Pearl carefully walking down the stairs.

"So what time are you gonna leave your mother's house?" Melissa asked from the other line.

"I have to wait until he gets here," Lamar answered. "I'm probably gonna call his job to see if he goes in around 9 or so. But I gotta talk to him before he sees my mom again. That's the bottom line."

Something in Lamar's tone caused an uneasy feeling to stir in Melissa. She knew Lamar had a bad temper and he was very protective of his mother.

"Okay, baby," she whispered. "But please try to behave yourself. And if something happens, please call me, okay? I don't want a repeat of what happened last time. At least give me a heads up if I have to get bail money or something."

Lamar chuckled to himself. He was amused at Melissa's worried tone. "I can't make any promises, Melissa. Everything is on him. I will fuck him up tonight if he comes in here on that bullshit. So we just have to see." There was a short silence on the phone. Lamar watched as his mother walked into the living room and sat on the sofa adjacent to the armchair. He didn't want Pearl to hear his conversation with Melissa and decided to end the phone call. "Ok, Melissa, I'm 'bout to talk to my mother. She's up now." Lamar said.

"Really? Okay, tell her I said *hello* and please call me later-"

Lamar abruptly cut her off. "Okay, don't worry. Everything is gonna be fine." Lamar said.

Melissa could tell that Lamar's mood was changing and decided not to push the issue. "Alright, Lamar. Call me later if you need me."

"Okay, I will. Bye." Lamar hung up the phone and turned to his mother who was staring blankly toward the front door. She looked exhausted and Lamar felt a sudden sympathy for her. Pearl's issues with Rick were wearing her down. She had been dating him for over five years now and things seemed to be getting progressively worse between the two of them. Despite the drama, the deception and the drinking, Pearl was still willing to take Rick back after any argument. Lamar was frustrated by that, but he loved his mother and he recognized that she needed love, too. He just hated the fact that she was getting the short end of the stick.

"So how did you sleep, Mom?" Lamar asked.

"Couldn't really sleep." Pearl answered quietly. "I thought I kept hearing cars pull up to the driveway and others noises in the house."

"Yeah, I tried to doze off for a few but I kept waking up every ten minutes looking outside," Lamar said.

"Do you want some coffee or somethin'? I can make a pot really quick," Pearl humbly asked.

"Umm, yeah. I can use some coffee. Guess I'm not goin' back to sleep anytime soon." Lamar watched as Pearl slowly got up and walked out of the front room. The combination of stress and fatigue caused her to move even slower. Lamar stood up and followed her to the kitchen. "Mom, how has been Rick acting lately?"

"Like his usual self. Quick-tempered, overbearing, and possessive. But besides that, he's a sweetheart." Pearl joked.

Lamar started laughing. "Nah Mom, I'm serious. Do you think he's cheating on you or somethin'?"

"Child, I don't know. And I really don't care right about now. I'm too old to be chasing some bitch around in these streets over no damn man." Lamar sensed a bit of cynicism in her tone. "Lamar, a man's gonna do what a man's gonna do. Can't no woman force him to stay home and be a good boy. A man's word is his law and sometimes they break they own laws. That's just how it is." Lamar sat quietly and listened to his mother as she put another pot of coffee on the stove. Pearl continued to speak. "I don't know if he's out there shackin' up with some other hoochies. Sometimes I stare at him to see if he would give hisself away and it never happens. Do I think he's cheating? Yes! Do I know who it is? No! But the real question is, do I care?"

"And you don't care." Lamar quickly answered her.

"I don't. As long as he don't bring that shit home to me. I'm done with chasing. I'm tired. The only thing I can't take from his ass is him raising his hands to me. He hasn't done it in a long time. But if he does that shit again I swear Imma call the cops on him. Forget his parole!"

There was a thick silence in the room. Pearl continued to brew the coffee while Lamar sat quietly at the kitchen table. Pearl's last words seemed to echo awkwardly through his mind. Rick's temper and his tendency to lash out at Pearl were really big issues in this house. Rick never touched Pearl when her children were around, but Pearl had told Lamar and Heidi about a number of violent incidents between the two. And tonight Lamar decided that he would do something to make sure that Rick would never touch his mother again without consequences.

"Mom, I got a gift for you." Lamar said. "I left it in the car. I'll be right back."

Pearl turned around from the stove just in time to see Lamar leave through the back door and head to his car. Pearl took a minute to think why her son would get her a gift. Her birthday was months away and there was really no special occasion this evening. *Maybe it's the picture frame that I always wanted.* Pearl thought to herself. *Or maybe a better coffee pot.* She decided to prepare herself for the surprise. She turned the hot coffee off and sat down at the kitchen table, listening closely for Lamar's footsteps at the back door. Pearl smiled in anticipation. Her heart skipped a beat as Lamar came through the door with a small brown paper bag. From the size of the bag, Pearl instantly knew that the surprise could not be a picture frame or a large coffee pot. Lamar had a totally different surprise in store for her. He sat down at the table across from Pearl and gently placed the brown paper bag on the table.

"Mom, I thought about this long and hard and I just have to tell you that I truly believe that this is the best thing for you." His tone was almost apologetic. "Now I know how you are and you probably won't agree with this gift. But I'm worried about you and I think this is somethin' that you can use."

Pearl shot Lamar a suspicious look. She tried to understand where he was coming from but she was unable to. Lamar was practically talking in circles. He slowly put his hand on top of the brown paper bag and slid it toward his mother.

Pearl shot him another peculiar expression. She didn't know what to think.

"Lamar, what is this?" Pearl cautiously asked.

"Just open it, Mom. It's for you." Lamar answered.

Pearl slowly reached for the bag. She picked it up and pulled out the gift. It was a .38 caliber Smith & Wesson revolver. Pearl almost dropped the gun as her hands nervously shook. Pearl had never handled a gun before. She hated guns and was terrified at the mere sight of a pistol. Pearl was noticeably uncomfortable. She aggressively stared at Lamar and put the gun down on the table.

"Boy, why on God's green earth would you bring a gun in my house?!" Pearl asked angrily. "You know I don't like guns."

Lamar anticipated his mother's reaction and decided to explain himself. "Mom, don't look at it like that." Lamar stammered. "I got mad love for you and I just don't want to see you hurt. Just keep the gun in the house somewhere and if Rick gets out of line you can use it to scare him."

"What do you mean scare him?" Pearl asked.

"Mom, c'mon," Lamar snapped. "If he's hittin' on you and you pull out a gun on him he gonna stop that dumb shit immediately. He's no fool. He don't wanna die."

"So you want me to shoot my boyfriend?" Pearl shockingly asked.

The thought of his mother shooting Rick caused a sly smirk to grow on Lamar's face. He tried to mask this delight. "Mom, all I'm sayin' is it's just you and him in this house and nobody else. And if he gets out of line just put him back in his place. I don't think you will have to use it. But if it gets crazy in here again, please do."

Pearl sat quietly on the other end of the table and stared at the gun. Her mind was racing with unspeakable images of the many fights between Rick and herself. And although Pearl could never imagine hurting Rick, she realized that her son Lamar was only trying to protect her with this new gift. After a few moments she reached for the gun and held it in her palm. Pearl was immediately shocked at how light the gun was. She had expected the gun to be a lot heavier. The black rubber grip was very comfortable and she silently marveled at the way the gun fit perfectly in her hand. She carefully put her index finger alongside the trigger and slowly caressed it.

"So is it loaded?" Pearl cautiously asked.

Lamar started to shake his head. "Not yet. I got the bullets right here." Lamar pulled out five .38 caliber bullets. "I wanted to make sure you wanted it first before I loaded it for you."

Pearl continued to stare at the gun. She put a full grip on it and pointed it toward the back door. Lamar noticed her hands were still shaking as she slowly extended her arm and pointed at an imaginary target.

"So I just pull the trigger?" Pearl asked.

"Yes. You just point and then pull the trigger." Lamar said.

Pearl tried to steady her hand as she pointed the pistol at the back window of the house. Her face became serious and she took a deep breath, slowly pulling the trigger. *Click.* She jumped as she imagined a small bullet propelling rapidly through the barrel. She looked at Lamar.

"Try it again, Mom," Lamar quietly said. "This time really concentrate on the target."

Pearl nodded with seriousness. She had experienced a small rush of adrenaline after the first blank shot and wanted to see if the second would produce the same result. She took a deep breath and focused on her target. An angry Rick, raising his fist at her, appeared in her mind. She took another deep breath and pulled the trigger again. *Click.* Pearl let out a gasp. She could clearly hear the shot from the gun this time. She quickly turned to Lamar who was watching in anticipation.

"What if I miss?" Pearl asked.

"You won't miss, Mom. Just aim at his stomach," Lamar said. "Even if you can't handle the kick back from the gun all you have to do is aim for the stomach. Trust me, you will hit that nigga somewhere."

Pearl put down the gun and the solid stainless steel banged on the kitchen table. "Lamar, I can't believe you got me in here talking about shooting my boyfriend."

Lamar started to laugh. "Actually, Mom, the gun is for anybody that's messin' wit' you. But I would prefer you shoot Rick." Pearl shot her son a disappointed look as he continued laugh. She stood up and walked toward the stove again. "So where do you want me to put this at?" Lamar asked.

"In this house you mean?"

"Yeah, you gotta keep it in the house somewhere. How else you gonna get to it?"

"I don't know, where should I put it?" Pearl questioned. Lamar took a second to think. He watched Pearl as she brewed the hot coffee. After a moment, an idea came to mind. Lamar walked over to one of the cabinets and pulled out a huge coffee can that was home to Pearl's thumbtacks, paper clips, and pens. He dumped the contents of the can out onto the countertop. The noise startled Pearl. "What the hell are you doing, baby?" Pearl shouted.

Lamar slyly looked at his mother. "I gotta good spot for you to keep it." He walked over to another cabinet and grabbed a large ZipLock freezer bag. Pearl watched closely as he took the five bullets from his pocket and loaded the .38 special. Lamar carefully closed the cylinder and placed the loaded weapon inside the freezer bag. He squeezed all the air out of the bag and zipped it tight. A playful grin emerged on his face as he looked at his mom. Pearl was not amused. She continued to watch him as he placed the gun in the bottom of the coffee can.

"Mom, how many cans of coffee you have left?" Lamar asked.

"About three of 'em," she answered. "You know I gotta keep some coffee in here."

"Okay, let me get a full can." Pearl walked to the cabinet and pulled out another twenty-six-ounce-can of Folgers. She gave it to Lamar and watched him pour the coffee grounds into the can until they completely covered the gun. Lamar filled the can to the top and showed Pearl.

"The coffee is not going to damage the gun is it?" Pearl asked.

'Not at all," Lamar offered. "The bag will protect it. So you good."

"Ummm hmmm," Pearl grunted.

Lamar slipped the plastic lid onto the can and opened the cabinet. "Mom, I'm gonna put this up here above the sink. Make sure you remember where it is."

"I won't forget it. How could I forget that we have a gun in the house now?"

Pearl sneered at Lamar as he reached above the kitchen sink and placed the coffee can inside of the cabinet. He closed the door and walked by Pearl as he headed for the kitchen table. The room fell silent. Pearl grabbed a cup and poured Lamar some coffee. She poured herself a cup and headed to the table. She sat down next to Lamar as he took a careful sip. A strange feeling of anxiety came over Pearl. The dark feeling caused her to look over to the cabinet where her new pistol sat patiently waiting for drama.

Chapter 14

4:03 a.m.

*J*ust a few miles east on the New Jersey Turnpike, Heidi was still wiping the tears from her tired face when she drove by exit 15. The fight with her mother was fresh on her mind and she needed to get as far away from the house as she could. Pearl and Heidi had fought in the past but tonight their argument had gone well beyond the limits that either of them could have imagined. Heidi would never dare to raise her hands against her mother but tonight the pressure of the evening was pushing her toward uncharted waters. Heidi was still angry from the argument and her slightly shaking hands reminded her of the bitter spat.

An ugly feeling came over Heidi as she imagined the look on her mother's face when she refused to apologize to her. Although she began to feel slightly remorseful about the evening, Heidi refused to brush the chip off of her shoulders. She punched the gas pedal even harder as the SUV sped assertively down the virtually empty expressway.

Heidi turned her attention to the pouch hanging on the back of the passenger seat. After a number of futile attempts to erase the fight from her mind, Heidi finally realized that there was only one thing that could help better her mood. She reached behind the passenger seat and rummaged through the pouch attached to the rear of the seat. After shifting through a pile of papers and CDs, Heidi found what she was looking for.

A devilish smirk grew on her face as she snatched a brown paper bag and pulled it to the front seat. The SUV was speeding by exit 14 when Heidi turned the brown paper bag upside-down and pulled out a bottle of E&J Brandy. Without a thought Heidi turned the bottle to her lips and took two long swallows. The 40%-alcohol-mix seemed to burn through her soul as the liquor rushed down her throat and into her chest. Heidi let out a desperate gasp. The harsh burning sensation was immediately followed by a feeling of euphoria as the effects of the alcohol seemed to ease the tension from her mind. Heidi playfully giggled to herself. The relief was more than she expected. Heidi moved to take another swallow of the Brandy but was interrupted by the buzzing of her cellular phone. She twisted the top back onto the bottle and grabbed her phone. Heidi twisted her face in disgust as she read the display on her cellphone.

INCOMING CALL
Lamar (Cell Phone)

Heidi refused to answer the phone and sent Lamar's call straight to her voicemail service. She knew exactly why her brother was calling, but Heidi was in no mood to apologize to him or her mother and decided not to pursue the issue. She turned her attention back to the E&J Bottle as she pushed the SUV to nearly 70 mph. Heidi was still managing to feel more relaxed now. She twisted the top off the E&J bottle and took another long swallow. She let out another desperate gasp. This time she welcomed the pain. The alcohol was relaxing her.

As the 4runner quickly approached exit 13A on the Turnpike, Heidi got a notion to grab her phone. She decided to call Faith and tell her the news about her fight with Pearl. Heidi disregarded the late hour and phoned her best friend. She listened patiently on the other line waiting for Faith to answer.

Ring. No answer. "C'mon girl, pick up the phone," Heidi whispered to herself. *Ring.* No Answer.

"Damn, bitch! I know you not sleeping over there, not with the night we both are havin'."

Heidi was growing more aggravated with each unanswered ring. When she heard the sound of Faith's voicemail Heidi disconnected the call. She was disappointed. She shook her head and decided to try someone else. She scrolled to the top of her phone book and found Aaron's name. Again, Heidi disregarded the hour and called him. *Ring.* No answer. "Geeez, not this bullshit again," she blurted. *Ring* No answer. "Don't tell me you're sleeping, too, nigga."

After four more unanswered rings, Heidi quickly disconnected the call and slammed the phone in her lap.

"Anything you need, princess, just let me know!" Heidi sarcastically mimicked Aaron's voice. She was visibly disappointed that he hadn't answered the call. She needed someone to talk to about the pressure of the night that was still weighing heavily on her. Heidi grabbed the E&J bottle and twisted off the cap. She took another long swallow of the liquor. This time, the Brandy did more than just burn her chest. Heidi's mood began to change. Her mind started racing with angry thoughts and Heidi felt herself becoming confrontational. She put the bottle of E&J to the side and forcefully reached for her phone once again.

Heidi had a bad habit of calling the one person she shouldn't when she was angry. Tonight was no different. Heidi picked up her phone to dial the number. She didn't need to search her phonebook for this particular phone number. Heidi had committed this number to memory since the first time she saw it almost a year ago. Without hesitation, Heidi dialed the number: 862-487-8537. She sat patiently for someone to answer on the other end. *Ring.* No Answer. "Come on, answer the phone. Please!" Heidi groaned. *Ring.* No Answer.

Heidi began to get frustrated again as the phone continued to ring. A heavy emotion fell upon her as the phone rang for a fourth and fifth time. She started to feel light-headed again, but Heidi decided to ignore the feeling and stayed on the line. After the sixth ring Heidi heard a subtle *click* on the other line. She was expecting to hear the voicemail but to Heidi's surprise, a soft, groggy voice answered on the other line. It was a woman's voice.

"Hello?" The woman answered. "Who is this?"

Heidi hesitated. A sharp feeling of betrayal shot through Heidi's body and she jumped into attack mode. She barked at the woman from the speeding SUV. "You know goddamn well who this is bitch!" Heidi snapped. "You probably got my number saved by now."

Dashawn Taylor

"What?" The woman yelled from the other end of the phone. Her voice was more alive now. "Wait a minute. Who you callin' a *bitch*...bitch?!"

"Listen you nasty whore don't play games with me," Heidi shouted. "I'm sick of you not being straight with me. I know you was fuckin' my fiancé and I just want you to tell me the truth. Stop acting like a coward-"

Before Heidi could finish her thought she heard another subtle *click* from the other line. Heidi quickly looked at her phone and noticed that the call had been disconnected. Without a thought, she dialed the number again and waited for the young woman to answer the phone. After the second ring Heidi was greeted once again by the sound of the woman's voice. This time, the young lady was yelling to the top of her lungs.

"Stop callin' my goddamn phone with this nonsense," the woman yelled. "I don't know who you are. I don't know your man, or your fiancé, or whoever he is to you. This nonsense has gottta stop!"

Heidi totally ignored the woman's pleas and continued with her own accusations. "You don't know my man, huh?" Heidi sarcastically asked. "So why did you send him flowers for his birthday? And why did you send him your phone number? Did you work at his job or somethin'? Or did y'all meet somewhere else? It's out in the open now, bitch. I don't know why you just won't 'fess up to it!"

The young woman continued to defend herself. "Listen, you dumb-ass trick," the woman yelled. "I don't know who you are or how you got my number, but you got serious problems. I mean, you sound like you got some serious mental issues! Why don't you get off of my fuckin' phone and go somewhere before you get yourself hurt, little girl!"

"Get myself hurt? By who?" Heidi yelled.

"By me!" the woman screamed. "You don't know me, bitch."

Heidi was taken aback by the threat. She could clearly hear the anger in the woman's voice, but instead of backing down Heidi went against her better judgment and accepted the woman's challenge.

"Okay, you know what?" Heidi said. "I wasn't gonna go here but I see that you one of those stubborn bitches!"

"What?" the woman yelled.

"Yeah, you tryin' to play me," Heidi yelled. She was getting angrier and growing more impatient with the woman. The E&J was adding to Heidi's hostile mood and her decision to take the argument to another level. "You know I know where you live at, bitch!" Heidi shouted. The woman became quiet on the other line. There was a cold silence on the phone as the two women contemplated on Heidi's shocking news. Heidi cracked a devilish smirk. She waited for the news to sink into the woman's mind and continued to yell at her. "Oh yea, you didn't think I would find out where you lived at? That was my fiancé you was fuckin' with!"

"I'm hanging up now," the woman forcefully said from the other line. "Get some help, bitch."

"Oh no! You the one gonna need some help in a minute," Heidi boasted. "I'm on my way over there, right now!"

"What?" The woman yelled. Her voice began to tremble.

"Oh yea, you're not getting away with this shit *Scott free*. You gonna have to deal with me face-to-face." Heidi yelled. "Newark right? I'll be there in a few bitch so you betta be ready." Heidi's voice was serious and very direct.

The woman didn't say another word. Heidi waited for her to react to her threats but all she heard was another subtle *click* on the other line. The woman hung up again. Heidi grew angrier. She slammed the cell phone in the passenger seat and quickly reached inside her glove compartment. She fumbled through a pile of papers until she found a small yellow business card. She disregarded the company information on the front side and flipped the card over. As she read the young woman's Newark address Heidi slowly nodded her head. She could practically taste the revenge. Heidi turned off the next exit of the New Jersey Turnpike. She pushed her SUV to a break-neck speed as she headed to Newark to finally face the woman she believed had betrayed her.

❖

Chapter 15

Shaheed's legs were heavy as bricks as he jogged through the quiet neighborhood of Upper South Orange. The disturbing images of Vegas killing Sean LaCon and his nephew made his stomach burn. Shaheed was no stranger to violence and street confrontations, but he was far from a murderer. A strange feeling of resentment flowed through his tense body as he rushed to make it back to the car. Shaheed decided to ignore the feeling. As much as he wanted to deal with his cousin's issues, Shaheed elected to deal with the bigger problem directly in front of him. He needed to flee the city before South Orange's finest converged on the scene to investigate the gunshots. Thinking about the police made him run faster. The black duffle bag full of money bounced off of his legs. The pounding impact of the bag seemed to remind Shaheed of the urgency in getting the money safely back to the car and out of South Orange. Despite his fear and the heavy load, Shaheed hit the corner of Harding Street like a track star.

A bizarre feeling came over him as he picked up the pace and darted through the middle of the peaceful street. As he passed the parked cars, Shaheed slowly began to notice that something was terribly wrong. The Dodge Charger was missing from the corner. Shaheed's eyes lit up like a Christmas tree. *Shit.* He abruptly stopped in his tracks and frantically looked around. *Where the hell is Robert? Where is my car?* For the first time tonight, Shaheed panicked. A million and one thoughts ran

- 145 -

through his mind as he thoroughly scanned each automobile on the dark street for the Dodge. It was nowhere to be found. Shaheed pulled off his ski mask in frustration. Through all the commotion, he hardly realized he was still wearing it. Before he could gather his thoughts, Shaheed heard the violent screeching of car tires and turned around to investigate the noise. He was stunned to see a dark car speeding up the street toward him. *I can't believe it's the fuckin' cops!* Shaheed's stomach boiled with fear. The beaming headlights had him frozen in his tracks. There were no flashing lights or blaring sirens but that didn't surprise Shaheed. In order to catch a perpetrator by surprise, the police would never turn on their lights while a robbery was in progress. Shaheed was well aware of their secrets and quickly calculated his odds of escaping. As the speeding car closed in, a fierce stream of adrenaline ran through him. Shaheed decided to make a run for it. He put a tighter grip on the back duffle bag and made a dash toward the sidewalk.

Shaheed heard the roar of the engine behind him as he hustled to get a lead on the car. He was running at top speed on the sidewalk as the car cruised alongside him. Shaheed was petrified. He was so scared that he barely noticed the sound of the car's horn screaming for his attention. Shaheed was focused on escaping the neighborhood. He was cutting through the lawn of an adjacent home when he heard a familiar voice screaming his name from across his shoulder. The voice made him swiftly turn around. Shaheed was surprised to notice that the car cruising next to him was not a police car, and the familiar voice belonged to Robert, who was screaming from the Dodge Charger. In his haste, Shaheed hadn't realized that Robert left the corner of the street to look for his brother and cousin when he heard the gunshots blare from the house.

With little time to waste, Shaheed put his head down and quickly ran over to the car. The expression on Shaheed's face sent an uneasy feeling through Robert. He could tell something had gone terribly wrong.

"Pop the trunk, Robert, we gotta go!" Shaheed yelled to his brother. His voice trembled in fear.

"Yo where's Vegas?" Robert frantically asked.

"He's not comin' with us," Shaheed yelled. "Pop the trunk, nigga. We gotta get the fuck outta here!"

Robert decided not to ask any more questions. He reached towards the door panel and opened the trunk for Shaheed. He sat patiently as Shaheed pulled off his gloves, tossed them in the trunk, and slammed the door shut. He put a tighter grip on the duffle bag as he headed for the back door of the Dodge. He tossed the bag into the back seat and instinctively walked towards the driver-side of the Dodge Charger. As Shaheed approached the driver-side door, Robert opened the window and greeted him.

"I'm good, Shah'!" Robert assured. "I'll drive."

"Nah man, let me drive," Shaheed stammered. "I know these streets better than you, dog. C'mon, them boys gonna be up here any second."

Robert shot Shaheed a confident look. He didn't budge from the driver seat. "Shah, trust me," Robert begged. "For once, trust ya older brother, man. I got you. We gonna make it up outta here. C'mon, let's go!"

Shaheed saw something different in Robert's eyes. An unusual feeling came over him as he stared into his older brother's face. Shaheed desperately looked around the quiet neighborhood. He was clearly against letting this brother drive him to safety. Every nervous twitch in his body was telling him to leap in the car and get behind the wheel. But before he could make another plea to his brother Robert, Shaheed suddenly saw a porch light flash on from across the street. Although he couldn't see very clearly, Shaheed noticed a curtain being pulled back from the second floor window of a large home. Shaheed's heart skipped a beat. Without a thought he scampered around to the passenger side of the Dodge Charger and jumped in the car.

"Shit man, let's bounce!" Shaheed yelled as he fumbled to get inside the car. "I think somebody saw us in that house over there, goddamnit!"

Robert's heart began to race as he listened to his brother. Robert was clearly more nervous than Shaheed at this point. He threw the Dodge Charger in gear and punched the gas. The high-pitched sound of the screeching tires echoed throughout the peaceful neighborhood. Shaheed turned to the house with the porch light illuminated and focused on the second floor. He could see two curtains being pulled back now.

"Yea, somebody saw us, homie," Shaheed whispered, full of regret. He turned to Robert who was focused on the road. "Man, we gotta get out of here. Bust this left up here and take South Orange Ave. all the way out of here. We should be good."

Robert picked up the speed as he hit the corner of Harding Street and South Orange Ave. He blew through the stop sign and made a wild turn onto the main road. The force of the turn threw both men violently to the right. Shaheed immediately regretted having let Robert drive as he was struggling to gain control of the reeling car.

"Rob!" Shaheed yelled.

"I'm good, Shah'. Just trying to get up outta here. Man, I can't go to jail."

"Me neither, nigga. But damn, don't kill us either!" Shaheed carefully watched Robert as the Dodge Charger headed down the empty road. Robert was doing close to 60 mph when Shaheed noticed a lit cigarette burning in the ashtray. Shaheed shook his head in disappointment. He knew Robert had a bad habit of smoking when he was nervous and the sight and smell of the cigarette was another sign that Robert was probably not in the best condition to drive at this point. Shaheed's mind raced as he looked at his brother. "We gotta get another car," he suggested.

Robert shot Shaheed a confused look. "What you mean? Take two separate cars?" Robert asked.

"Nah, we gotta ditch this shit and get another car. If those nosey-ass neighbors saw us peel outta there in this shit, you know they on the phone with the cops right now."

"So you gonna steal one?"

"I don't know. I just know we gonna need a car soon." Shaheed's voice was still trembling in fear. He peered through the window as Robert sped down South Orange Avenue. Robert was totally ignoring every possible traffic law as he tore down the road like a drag racer. The V-6 engine howled as Robert's foot pushed the engine well above the city's speed limit. Shaheed grabbed his cellphone from the glove compartment and looked at the display. He was expecting to see a missed call from his cousin Vegas but there were no messages. Shaheed turned his focus to the black duffle bag in the back seat. He grabbed the bag and pulled it to the front seat. Robert tried to sneak a peek as his brother reached inside the bag and began to count the money. A seductive expression grew on Shaheed's face as he pulled out three thick bundles of crisp $100 bills. Robert couldn't believe his eyes. He had never seen so much cash in his life. The sight sent mixed emotions through him. He was instantly excited and panicky all at once. Surprisingly, Shaheed started to shake his head and shot Robert a disturbing look with the money in hand. "Yo, I think somethin' is seriously really wrong with Vegas." Shaheed said.

"What do you mean? And where's that dude anyway?" Robert nervously asked.

Shaheed turned and looked out the window again. He started to think about what transpired in LaCon's house just a few minutes ago. "First off, I told this nigga not to go in that nigga's house on no bullshit." Shaheed's voice was full of anger. Robert could tell that he was disgusted with Vegas. He felt a slight anticipation as Shaheed continued to tell the story. "So when we first got there, Vegas was damn near salivating at LaCon's truck in the driveway," Shaheed said. "You know how his eyes get all wide when he see a whip he likes and shit. So he staring at this nigga truck like it's a fuckin' turkey sandwich or something." Robert smiled at the joke. He was still very nervous and with the seriousness of the situation he managed to curb his amusement. He continued to listen as Shaheed told the story.

"If it wasn't for this nigga Abdul on my ass, man, I swear I woulda turned around right there. So I'm tryin' to get this nigga Vegas to stay focused on what we gotta do up in there. He lookin' all in the car and shit. So I'm like *yo dog, keep it movin' we gotta get in there and get out*." Shaheed's voice strained with emotion. His agitation increased with every word. Robert could only imagine how this story was going to end. Shaheed felt the car speed up as he continued to tell Robert the story. "So I went into the house first 'cause I had the code to the backdoor."

Shaheed took a deep breath. "I told this nigga Vegas to wait outside until I went in the house and scoped it out. I knew Troy was somewhere on the first floor or in the basement so I started to go inside and check for him." Shaheed's voice began to get lower as he turned to face Robert who was focused on the road. "I wasn't in the basement for no more than two minutes and I came right back upstairs. Rob, why when I came back upstairs this nigga Vegas was in the house standing in the middle of the kitchen. And the funny thing is, Troy was in the kitchen with him."

Shaheed shook his head. "I'm tellin' you man, somethin' is wrong with this dude. Before I could walk over to him, Vegas smashed this nigga Troy in the head with his gun." Robert shot his brother Shaheed a terrified expression. Shaheed nodded. "Yeah, hit this nigga square in the melon with that pistol. Like it wasn't nothin'. That nigga Troy hit the deck in like two seconds."

Robert's heart began to race faster as he listened to the story. His adrenaline was flowing heavily as he envisioned the drama inside of LaCon's house.

"Man, you seen how small Troy is?" Shaheed rhetorically asked. "Vegas cleared that little nigga out. And then I had to stop his dumb ass."

Robert turned to his brother again. He was growing anxious to hear how the story was going to end. He decided to ask for more details.

"So wait, how did y'all get the money if Vegas knocked out Troy?" Robert quickly asked.

Shaheed tried to wave Robert off as he continued to explain that story. "That's what I'm saying." Shaheed said. "Everything could 'a went smooth but this nigga got on some other shit. Now why did he do that to Troy? I don't know, but now we don't know where the money at or nothing. By this time, I'm like *fuck it, let's do it*. So now, I'm following this nigga upstairs knowing he don't know where he going or nothin'. Somethin' was telling me not to fuck with this shit no more and come back to the car. But we in too deep now, know what I'm saying?"

Robert didn't say a word. He just nodded as he glanced over to Shaheed who was still managing to count the money in the middle of his story. The adrenaline was still flowing heavy through Robert and his body reacted by pressing harder on the gas pedal. The car was now doing close to 70mph down South Orange Avenue heading into Newark. Shaheed barely noticed the Charger picking up speed as he continued.

"Robert, when we got upstairs we couldn't see shit, it was crazy dark. And out of the blue this nigga LaCon came out of the room and scared the shit outta me and Vegas!"

"Dammmnnn, so LaCon knew y'all was in the house?" Robert asked.

"Homie, I don't know." Shaheed answered. "It looked like he didn't know we was there. But before I could flinch, man-" Shaheed suddenly stopped talking. A piercing pain shot from his forehead to the back of his neck. Robert looked over to Shaheed who was rubbing his forehead in frustration.

"Shah', you alright?" Robert asked.

"Yeah. I'm cool," Shaheed reluctantly answered. "I just got a crazy headache thinkin' about Vegas' stupid ass. This is so fucked up."

"What?" Robert asked. He was still confused. He tried to keep up with the story but Shaheed was confusing him. "What's fucked up?" Robert asked.

"Vegas' crazy-ass," Shaheed answered. "Man….before LaCon could say a word to us, Vegas shot him!"

"Huh?" Robert grunted.

"Yup. He shot him right in the stomach….BAM!"

Robert put his fist over his mouth. He was in shock and couldn't speak. The news caused his hands to slightly shake as he put a tighter grip on the steering wheel. The gravity of the night began to mount in Robert's mind. He couldn't believe that Vegas shot LaCon in the house. He started to feel light-headed as he quickly glanced at his brother. Shaheed was ruefully nodding his head in the passenger seat. He stopped counting the money and calmly stared at the hundred-dollar-bills in his hands. He felt a strange sense of mixed emotions as he continued to speak to his brother.

"I went in there to get this paper and Vegas went in there to straight kill them niggas for real," Shaheed whispered.

"What!?" Robert yelled. He turned to Shaheed in a panic "He did what?" Robert shook so hard he almost forgot he was driving. "What the fuck, Shah?" Robert yelled. "Vegas killed LaCon and Troy!?"

Shaheed's heart dropped to his stomach as he felt the car propel to 86 mph. He dropped the money stacks as he reached to brace himself against the door. He quickly turned to Robert who was gripping the steering wheel with both hands. He was now driving like a man possessed. The car felt like it was out of control.

"Rob! What the hell are you doing, man? Slow down, yo!" Shaheed yelled.

"Oh my God Shah, I knew I shouldn't 'a came out here with y'all!" Robert frantically barked. His voice cracked with fear. "Goddamit, yo! I'm too close for this bullshit."

Shaheed shot his brother a mystified expression as the car floated down South Orange Avenue. He was getting more nervous as he realized Robert was terrified by the news of the killings.

"Why you flippin' out, homie?" Shaheed yelled. "You gotta slow down man." Shaheed couldn't recognize the expression on Robert's face. He had never seen his brother so scared in his life. Robert was totally ignoring Shaheed's commands to slow down. He tried desperately to get his attention. "Yo, Robert!!!" Shaheed yelled again. "Slow the fuck down man you gonna kill us nigga!" Robert continued to ignore Shaheed. He was shaking his head frantically and gripping the steering wheel with both hands. The sound of the engine roared in contempt as the Dodge quickly approached 93 mph.

"I can't go to jail, man, this is crazy! Not me, I can't do it! Fuck that, I can't!" Robert continued to repeat himself. His voice was very calm and seemed un-phased by his trembling body and speeding car. Images of Vegas killing LaCon and Troy started to flash into his mind and caused him to drive faster. "The cops are probably looking for us right now," Robert frenetically said as he scanned the dark streets. "And I can't go to jail, I just can't!"

The sight of his frightened brother was starting to worry Shaheed. As Robert continued to eerily repeat himself, Shaheed realized that Robert was mentally in another place. A feeling came over Shaheed that made him turn his focus to his seatbelt. He quickly grabbed the end of the seatbelt and pulled it over his body. As he snapped the belt into place, Shaheed made another attempt to reach his brother.

"Robert, we good man!" Shaheed calmly pleaded. "There ain't no cops around. You hear me, dog? Look around. Ain't no cops around."

Robert totally ignored his brother. He was focused on the road and still repeating himself as if he were in a deep trance. He was now doing close to 100 mph down South Orange Ave. The Dodge Charger was quickly approaching the corner of South Orange and Bergen Street when it started to pick up even more speed. Robert was close to 100 feet from the intersection when the light turned yellow. Shaheed looked with alarm at his brother. Robert was not stopping.

"Yo, Robert!" Shaheed yelled. "Don't take this light, yo! This is a busy-ass street." Robert ignored him. "Yo, dog! Don't take this light!" Shaheed yelled again but Robert didn't acknowledge him. Feeling that this was the last chance to get through to him, Shaheed yelled to the top of his lungs. "Rob!!!!! STOP THE FUCKIN' CAR!!!!!"

Robert never said another word. The Dodge Charger sped under the first traffic light as the indicator turned red. Shaheed fearfully placed both hands on the dashboard as Robert continued to punch the gas pedal. A sharp white light flashed into the car just over Robert's left shoulder, illuminating the entire car. Shaheed felt his heart come to a complete halt. He took a deep breath. The world seemed to move in slow motion for Shaheed as he realized where the bright light was coming from. Robert was not the only driver speeding through the intersection of South Orange Ave and Bergen Street.

A speeding SUV was heading straight for them. Both brothers stared out of the driver-side window and into the bright lights of the oncoming traffic. Robert tried to give the car more gas but it was too late. The SUV was too close. Robert instinctively turned the steering wheel to the right and Shaheed let out a terrified scream as he watched the SUV swerve toward the rear of the Charger to avoid a collision. Shaheed and Robert tried to brace themselves for the accident but there was not enough time. The front bumper of the speeding SUV slammed into the rear of the Dodge Charger. The crushing impact forced the rear of the Charger to spin violently to the right. Robert's head slammed into the driver-side window and shattered the glass. He was immediately knocked unconscious. The Dodge Charger continued to spin to the right as the wheels locked. Without warning, the car was airborne. The combination of the high speed and the locking of the tires cause the Dodge Charger to flip through the air like a flimsy pancake. Shaheed couldn't believe what was happening. With the sound of crushing metal and shattering glass, Shaheed continued to scream. His arms were grabbing for anything to stabilize his body, but the force of the flipping car continued to bruise both of the brothers.

After two-and-a-half revolutions, the Dodge Charger finally landed upside down on the adjacent side of South Orange Avenue. Shaheed could hear screams and moans from outside of the shattered windows. He was barely conscious. After a few moments, his vision began to come back into focus. The first thing he saw was a pool of blood dripping from the driver's seat. It was Robert's blood. He was badly hurt. Shaheed frantically looked around the car. He noticed the bag of money had split open. More than half of the crisp one-hundred-dollar-bills were scattered throughout the car. The money was everywhere. Like the Dodge Charger, things were progressively spinning out of control. Shaheed had to act fast. He reached over to his brother.

"Rob...you okay?" Shaheed grunted. His voice was weak. Robert didn't respond. As Shaheed reached for his brother he noticed a large gash on his own right forearm, but he felt no pain. He was undoubtedly too concerned about Robert and the money. "Yo Robert, if you can hear me, hang in there, homie. Everything's gonna be alright," Shaheed whispered as he sprung into action. He could smell the blood in the air mixing with the smell of mangled metal and engine fuel. He screamed in pain as he reached over to free himself from the seatbelt. Shaheed came crashing down to the roof of the car as he successfully unclipped the belt. "Hang in there, bro. Imma get you outta here." Shaheed's twisted body struggled to maneuver in this tight space. "We gonna get up outta here right now."

Shaheed reached for the latch on the passenger-side door. After a few forceful attempts, Shaheed managed to shove the door open. He heard more groans from outside. A small crowd gathered outside the Chicken Shack on the corner to witness the accident. Shaheed ignored the people as he crawled from the Charger and slowly rose to his feet. He stared at the overturned car and was taken aback by the devastation. He couldn't believe he was still conscious after the wreck. Shaheed started to feel dizzy as he took a quick glance around the intersection in search of the cops. There were none in the area.

A feeling of relief came over Shaheed as he turned his focus back to his brother. Shaheed walked over to the driver's side door. The sound of a choking engine startled him. He turned around and noticed that a SUV was partially smashed into a lamppost on the other end of Bergen St. A stark feeling of anger shot to Shaheed's face as he peered at the truck. The female driver of the SUV was visibly dazed and confused. Her jet-black hair was frayed and jaggedly draped over her beautiful face. Her remarkably gentle features were now twisted by the pain of the accident. Shaheed closely watched the young woman as she frantically turned to him. It was Heidi Kachina, also known as *High*.

An ugly feeling hit Shaheed as their eyes met. Shaheed furiously watched as she fumbled with the steering column, trying to restart the engine. Shaheed was confused. *Why is she trying to re-start the truck?* Shaheed thought to himself. *I know this bitch ain't tryin' to bounce!*

Heidi looked around in a panic. Another small crowd gathered on the opposite side of the SUV and winced at the high-pitched sound of the engine struggling to start. Shaheed walked toward the SUV. Pain slowed his pace and he grimaced with every step. Shaheed yelled at Heidi.

"Hey!" Shaheed yelled. "I know you not tryin' to bounce on us. What the fuck is wrong with you?"

Shaheed's angry voice seemed to inject a gallon of energy into Heidi. She took a deep breath as she turned to Shaheed who was heading straight for the truck. Heidi panicked again. She tried to start the engine and this time the engine fired up in a loud roar. Another stream of anger rushed through Shaheed as he realized Heidi was trying to flee the accident scene. He picked up the pace and tried to rush over to the truck. He almost slipped on a large puddle of gasoline that was leaking from the Dodge Charger. Heidi took advantage of the momentary slip and slammed the truck into reverse. The tires screeched with intensity as the rear of the SUV almost hit Shaheed. He managed to dive to the ground just in time to avoid being hit by the rear of the truck. Shaheed yelled in pain as he hit the hard concrete. He couldn't believe Heidi was trying to run him down.

Dashawn Taylor

Shaheed quickly rolled over to get a good view of the truck as Heidi slammed the SUV into gear and punched the gas. This time she was speeding away from Shaheed. The noise startled the crowd of spectators. A feeling of anguish came over Shaheed and he jumped to his feet. He watched the SUV coast up the street and away from the scene. Despite the frenzied escape, the truck was not fast enough to avoid Shaheed's eyes that were focused on the illuminated license plate. A mixed emotion of anger and relief came over him as he read the vanity plates.

"So High?" Shaheed whispered to himself. "What the hell is *So High*?" Shaheed was confused. An image of Heidi's frightened face flashed in his head. Shaheed was confident that their paths would cross again.

A strange noise brayed from behind Shaheed. It was his brother Robert screaming for him from the Dodge Charger. In the mist of all the commotion, Shaheed had failed to realize that his brother had stirred from his slight concussion and was trying to free himself from the mangled car. Shaheed's heart dropped into his stomach as he sprang into action. With little time to waste he rushed toward the Dodge Charger. Shaheed ran quickly to his brother's side. He never noticed the engine fuel spilled out onto the ground. Before he could slow his pace, Shaheed found himself slipping on the gasoline, losing his balance and falling to the hard concrete. The force of the fall momentarily knocked the wind out of him. He could barely move.

Meanwhile, inside of the Dodge Charger, Robert was struggling to free himself. He tried to twist his body enough to crawl out of the mangled car. He was in desperate need of help. He screamed again for his brother but Shaheed never answered. Tears came to Robert's bloody eyes. The pain from the accident and the horrible feeling of helplessness invaded Robert's already limp body. He felt a strong presence upon him as he looked around in a panic to find another way out of the car. Robert's focus was suddenly redirected. Gasoline was pouring out of the rear tank and into the interior of the car. The profound smell of his own blood and the engine fuel filled the air around him. Robert's entire life flashed before his eyes as he noticed the cigarette he'd been smoking earlier was still lit inside the car.

The gasoline from the tank was pouring inside more rapidly now. A thick pool of the engine fuel was heading straight for the cigarette. Robert screamed in horror as he tried to grab it, but couldn't reach it. The cigarette was out of his grasp. Before Robert could blink, the gasoline from the Charger was ignited by the cigarette and the entire car was set ablaze. Within seconds a major explosion lit up the corner of Bergen Street and South Orange Avenue. Robert was killed instantly. The crowd moaned in horror as the intense fire turned everything inside of the Dodge Charger into a memory.

Chapter 16

Friday, November 2, 2007
Plainfield, New Jersey

6:01 a.m.

*H*eidi couldn't stop her hands from shaking as she pulled up to a quiet house in Plainfield, New Jersey. The horrific scene of the accident was weighing heavily on her mind. Heidi drove around aimlessly for nearly two hours after the accident with no destination. After sitting in her car for another forty five minutes, Heidi decided to head to the one safe place she knew she could count on. Heidi slowly emerged from the battered SUV and walked toward the house. The quiet neighborhood seemed to broadcast every step she made to the front door. The sound of her high-heels echoed throughout the complex. Heidi tried to calm her nerves but her body refused to cooperate. She was still visibly shaken and moved quickly to the front door. She was ready to head inside and away from the world when a strange feeling of regret came over her. Heidi motioned to ring the doorbell. Before she could stop herself and rethink her decision, Heidi's fingers were already pressing the bell. The sound of the loud ringing caused her to jump slightly. Within a few minutes, she heard movement coming from inside the quiet home. Her stomach began to turn with anticipation as she waited for the owner to come to the door. After a few seconds, the front door opened and an exhausted man emerged from the house. He was slovenly dressed in a pair of over-worn sweatpants and a milk-white tee shirt. The man was Heidi's Call & Response partner, Aaron.

Heidi shot him a dismal look. Aaron could tell something was terribly wrong and thought better not to question her about the un-announced visit. He opened the front door wider and invited Heidi inside without incident. The thick smell of alcohol and stress followed her inside the house. Aaron offered his disheveled guest a seat on his leather sofa and told her to remain calm. He left the living room and returned with a small glass of iced-tea. The beverage of choice reminded Heidi of the very *cold* night she was experiencing. Aaron handed her the glass and sat down next to her. There was an uncomfortable silence in the room as Heidi slowly sipped the drink. Aaron didn't say a word, waiting until Heidi was ready to talk. Six minutes and two iced-teas later, Heidi was finally ready to open up.

"I'm so sorry to come through here like this," Heidi whispered, "but I am really losin' it, Aaron, and I honestly don't have anyone else to turn to right now."

"It's okay, High. I told you, you never have to apologize to me." Heidi turned to Aaron and he shot her a reassuring smile. He gently grabbed her shaking palm. "Talk to me, Heidi. What happened tonight?"

"I don't know, Aaron. I really don't know." Heidi muttered as she took a deep breath. She turned away from Aaron and dropped her tired head in disappointment. "Tonight I had....absolute control...over nothing." Heidi whispered. The honesty in her confession cut through her words and her voice cracked with pain. Heidi was close to tears as she continued to explain the events of the evening. "I really felt like something ugly was chasin' me tonight, Aaron. I don't know how else to explain it."

Aaron didn't know what to make of Heidi's words. He instinctively wrapped his arms around her and pulled her closer. "Hey...hey....it's okay," Aaron reassured. "Just talk to me. Start from the beginning. What happened?"

Heidi turned to Aaron once again. She could clearly read the concern in his face and body language. But despite his genuine concern for her, Heidi was not ready to open up fully to Aaron. She gently placed her hand on his face and smiled at him.

"Aaron, can we talk about this a little later? I'm exhausted and I just need to sleep this off." Heidi's voice was tired and filled with pain. "I hope you understand."

Aaron nodded his head in agreement. Heidi's defeated expression told only half the story. Aaron wanted so much to hear the other half but he respected Heidi too much to push the issue. He excused himself from the room for a few minutes and returned with a large comforter and a few pillows.

"I don't have much, High, but what I have is yours," Aaron said gently. "At least for tonight."

Heidi shot Aaron a subtle smile.

"Thank you, sweetie," Heidi whispered. "You just don't know how much this means to me. I just want to lie down for a few hours. When I wake up, are you gonna be here?"

"Don't worry, I'll be right here," Aaron said. "I'm gonna call out of work today for you. If you need me, I'll be right upstairs."

Heidi pressed her lips together and nodded toward Aaron. "Thank you," she whispered.

Aaron shot her one final look of support and left the room. Heidi listened as he walked upstairs to his bedroom and closed the door. Heidi slowly sat back on the sofa. She was very happy to finally be in a safe place and at peace. She carefully kicked off her heels and made herself more comfortable. Heidi felt the pressure of her long day mounting on her shoulders and decided to stretch out on the couch. Before she could begin to think about the events of the day, her fatigue caught up to her and Heidi drifted off into a deep sleep.

****

Elizabeth, New Jersey
8:31 a.m.

Just nineteen miles north, in a different part of New Jersey, another young woman was in a deep sleep when the violent sound of breaking glass awakened her. The young woman opened her eyes and sprung to her feet in one continuous motion. She quickly turned on the bedroom lights and looked around in a panic. The young woman was only twenty-two years old but her battle-tested-body made her appear to be closer to thirty years of age. Her stocky yet curvaceous frame was oddly reminiscent of a dainty pit-bull. Her cocoa brown skin was covered in scars and tattoos, traces of a harsh and animated life in the inner city. She wore a short golden-brown afro matching perfectly with her fatigue-print *wife-beater*. The young woman was Shaheed's girlfriend Rhonda.

"Mom?! What the hell was that?" Rhonda yelled from her quiet bedroom. "Mom, was that you?"

After a moment of silence, Rhonda rushed to her bedroom door to investigate the noise. She opened the door and entered the dark hallway. There was no sign of her mother. Before she could rush to her mother's bedroom, another loud crash came from the window inside of her bedroom. Rhonda quickly turned around and darted to the window. She reached it just in time to see a hasty Shaheed hurl another quarter at her window. Despite seeing the flying coin bang into her window, Rhonda was startled by the loud noise.

"Boy, what in the hell are you doin' out there?" Rhonda whispered. She opened the window and yelled to Shaheed. "Nigga, are you crazy? You just broke my window."

Shaheed totally ignored her statement and yelled back to her. "Open the door, Rhonda!" His tone was very aggressive and Rhonda picked up on the vibe immediately. "Come on, Rhonda, hurry up!" he yelled.

"Okay, Shah', here I come." She could tell from Shaheed's tone that something was terribly wrong. She rushed down to the front door and let Shaheed inside the house. As Rhonda closed the door behind him, a strange feeling came over her. "Damn, Shaheed." The empty look in his eyes scared her. She could tell that he had been crying. She backed away and gave him a cautious look. "Shaheed?" Rhonda whispered. "For some strange reason, I feel like I just let somethin' evil inside my house." Shaheed didn't say a word. He continued to stare at her with a distant expression. "Baby?" Rhonda continued. "What happened out there tonight? People been drivin' by the house all slow and pullin' off and Vegas called me like twenty times looking for you. What happened?"

Shaheed turned away from Rhonda and slowly sat down in the living room. His body language made Rhonda very nervous. She humbly watched as Shaheed struggled to find his words, but he could not bring himself to speak. All of the horrors of the evening began to flash into his mind at once. Rhonda hated to see Shaheed fight with his emotions and just wanted to comfort him. She approached him and sat down next to him. As he turned around and looked at her, Rhonda could see that he was on the verge of tears again.

"What time did Vegas call you?" Shaheed asked. The swollen knot in his throat made it hard to talk.

Rhonda shot him a strange look. "Umm.....he called... about a half-hour ago. He sounded crazy though. He kept wakin' me up, callin' my phone back to back to back until I picked up."

"Did he say where he was?"

"No he didn't. But I know he called from his cellphone."

Shaheed balled up his lip as he thought about the last time he'd seen Vegas. He dropped his head in both of his hands and let out a loud gasp of air. Rhonda rubbed Shaheed's back, hoping to soothe him.

"Rhonda, I need you to get him on the phone." Shaheed barked. The tone in his voice sent a chill through Rhonda. "Tell his punk ass to come through here right now. I don't give a fuck if he's outta the country by now. Tell him to get over here right now!"

"You want him to come here?" Rhonda asked.

"Yes. Tell him to come meet me here."

Rhonda was taken aback by Shaheed's tone. She could tell by the anxiety in his voice that he was very serious. Without a thought she jumped to her feet and ran upstairs. After a few attempts, Rhonda finally got Vegas on the phone. She gave him the directions to her house and hung up with him. When she returned downstairs, she noticed that Shaheed was no longer sitting in the living room. He was posted by the front door. Rhonda watched him as he fearfully peeked out of the front window. She could only imagine what Shaheed was running from.

"I'm worried about you, Shah'," Rhonda softly said. "Please talk to me. What happened out there tonight?"

Shaheed's face now showed a look of concern and fear. "I can't tell you everything. But I gotta take care of somethin' today."

"Okay, don't tell me everything," Rhonda said. "But does it have to do with your problem with Abdul?"

"Yes"

"Did you get the money for him?"

Shaheed nodded his head. "I did get the money but then we got into a car accident," Shaheed stammered.

"What? Oh my God! What happened?!" Rhonda yelled. "Are you okay?"

Shaheed put his head down again. "Rhonda, please...don't make me-"

"Okay, I'm sorry. You don't have to talk about it. I'm so sorry." Rhonda walked over to Shaheed and leaned against the front door with him. She gently grabbed his face and made him look at her. "Baby, forget Adbul," she whispered. "Let's just leave. You don't have to pay that nigga."

Shaheed shot his girlfriend an indifferent expression as she continued to talk to him. "Listen, I got $5,000 that I been savin' for a while now," Rhonda said. "Let's just get in the car and leave. I don't even have to pack. Let's just go baby."

Shaheed was shaking his head. "I can't, Rhonda. I gotta take care of this tonight."

Rhonda could sense something unpleasant in Shaheed's last statement. She instinctively reached out to hug Shaheed. "Honey, please don't leave me again," Rhonda whispered as she held him tighter. "Whatever you thinking 'bout doing tonight, please don't. We can take my mother's car and leave right now, baby. I'm pretty sure that nigga Abdul is not gonna chase you halfway across the world for that money. We can just leave and never come back to this place. Just me and you Shah', please."

There was a long silence in the room. Rhonda could feel Shaheed's heart racing as he contemplated leaving with her. With everything that was going on in his life at the present moment, leaving town and avoiding any additional bloodshed was his safest option. But Shaheed was focused on revenge.

"I gotta stay here at least one more day, Rhonda. I gotta tie up this one last loose-end. I'm sorry, baby. After that, we can take your mother's car and leave town."

Rhonda looked up at Shaheed. She decided not to respond. Shaheed's words were no longer comforting to her. She reluctantly nodded her head in agreement and backed away from him. "Okay, baby, I understand." Rhonda said. "What do you want me to do to help you tie up that loose-end?"

Shaheed shot Rhonda a powerful expression. He pursed his lips together and slowly nodded to her. He loved the fact that she was always willing to be a soldier for him from the time they first met. And tonight was no different. "I need you to grab a pen and a piece of paper for me," Shaheed said.

Rhonda headed to the kitchen. After a few minutes she returned with a pencil and a small notepad. "Okay, Sha, what am I writing down?" Rhonda asked.

"I need you to call that guy down at the DMV today and get an address for me," Shaheed instructed. "I saw this license plate tonight and I need to find out where this person lives at."

Rhonda gave Shaheed a worried look. "Okay…what's the license plate?"

"S-O-H-I-G-H," Shaheed continued. "That's the plate number. Just find out who she is and where she live at."

"Oh okay, so it's a female?" Rhonda asked. Her tone grew cold.

"Yeah, it's a female." he barked. Before Rhonda could ask another question, the sound of a loud car horn startled her. Shaheed quickly pulled the curtain back and looked outside the window. He didn't recognize the car but he could see that Vegas was the driver. He turned back to Rhonda who continued to wear a look of worry on her face. "I gotta go," Shaheed said.

"I know." she softly countered. Shaheed motioned to kiss her, but Rhonda pulled away from him. Shaheed was confused. "I don't wanna kiss you goodbye, Shah'." Rhonda said. "When you walk out that door, I don't want this to be the last time I see you." Shaheed stared at her. He was speechless. "I'm serious, Shaheed. You do whatever you gotta do to make it back to me safely, okay?"

Shaheed nodded. The passion in her eyes and in her words seemed to travel throughout his entire body. He looked her directly in the face for a few seconds more, and then headed out the door. Rhonda watched Shaheed as he got inside the car. A gloomy feeling came over her as she watched Vegas and Shaheed speed down her quiet street.

❖

Chapter 17

Saturday, November 3, 2007
Plainfield, New Jersey

4:50 p.m.

"*A*aron!" Heidi yelled. Her voice echoed throughout the second floor bathroom and into the hallway. After a few seconds of silence, Heidi yelled again for her host. "Aaron, sweetie can you come up here for a second?" Heidi yelled again.

The sweet smell of the vanilla-honey bubble bath relaxed Heidi as she lay in the hot water of Aaron's bathtub. All of her problems seemed to temporarily disappear as Heidi felt her mood shifting. It was the middle of the afternoon and Heidi had now been with Aaron for almost thirty six hours. She still had not mentioned the accident. She didn't want to worry Aaron with the details so she remained quiet about the whole ordeal. Heidi yelled again for Aaron who was slowly making his way from the kitchen and up to the bathroom on the second floor.

"Aaron, did you leave?" Heidi yelled.

"No, I'm right here, High." Aaron yelled from outside the bathroom. "You okay?"

"Yeah, I'm good. Can you come in here for a second?"

"You dressed?"

"Boy, just come in here," Heidi joked. "We both grown!" Aaron was taken aback by the request. He took a deep breath and braced himself before walking through the bathroom door. He knew that Heidi was still in the bathtub and he couldn't imagine why she wanted him to come inside with her. "Aaron, don't tell me you scared to come in here?" Heidi joked again.

"No, I'm good, Heidi. Here I come." He gently pushed the door open and entered the bathroom.

A wide smile grew on the faces of both Heidi and Aaron as their eyes met. Aaron's mind raced as he scanned Heidi like a lovely exhibition. He closely observed her golden brown legs as they emerged from the oily water. Her pretty feet rested easily on the edge of the bathtub as she managed to submerge her entire upper-body under the soft bubbles and out of open view. She noticed Aaron was admiring the incredible sight and she smiled at him.

"Damn, boy, I'm glad yo' eyes don't got superpowers," Heidi said sarcastically. "I'd probably be pregnant by now!" They both laughed.

"I'm sorry. You just caught me by surprise. I thought you was gonna be dressed."

"It's okay, really," Heidi said. "I haven't had a man look at me like that in a long time. It feels good to know I still got it. So no offense taken."

Aaron slowly nodded his head and walked across the bathroom. He dropped the porcelain lid on the toilet and took a seat at Heidi's side. He shot her a peculiar look. "So what's on you mind, Heidi?"

"I was lonely," Heidi playfully answered. "I wanted some company."

Aaron shot her another sly smirk. Heidi decided not to speak as she found herself staring at Aaron in a different light. Being around him for the past few days, she found herself growing closer to Aaron. And without realizing it, Aaron was quickly becoming more than a friend to Heidi. As she gazed at his beautiful brown skin tone and his large powerful hands, Heidi decided that it was time to get to know Aaron a little better. She shot him another inviting gesture. He turned away from Heidi and began to look at the wall. Heidi noticed Aaron was struggling to keep his eyes busy and decided to reach for a towel next to the bathtub. She unfolded the towel and placed it over her chest. Heidi readjusted her body and sat up in the bathtub. The sound of the rustling water startled Aaron.

"Come over here, Aaron." Heidi softly said.

Aaron looked over to Heidi who was now sitting straight up in the bathtub and hugging her knees. The towel was perfectly draped over her chest and completely concealing her upper body. Aaron tilted his head to the side and shot Heidi a confused gesture. "I'm not gonna bite you, Aaron," Heidi joked as she shot him a sly smile. "I just need a little bit of help. I can't reach my back and I need you to bathe it for me."

Aaron didn't say a word. A smirk grew on his face as he rose to his feet. Aaron was more than excited to grant Heidi's request. He grabbed the wet loofah and body wash. Without a thought, he sat on the edge of the bathtub directly behind her. As he started to slowly wash Heidi's back, he couldn't help but marvel at her smooth shape and incredible silky skin. Heidi turned her head to the side and placed her face on her knees. She closed her eyes and enjoyed the relaxing sensation of Aaron's strong hands on her back. It was even sweeter than she expected.

"So why did you let me in your house this morning, Aaron?"

"Because I was worried about you." Aaron quickly answered. "I didn't want anything to happen to you and I thought you would be safe here."

"No not like that, Aaron." Her voice sounded strained. "I don't mean like that. I know that. But why me? You don't know me like that yet, I mean I know we are friends....but...you never say *no* to me." Aaron rinsed the soap from Heidi's back as she continued to speak. "Since I've known you, you always do stuff for me that the average man wouldn't. It's like you genuinely care."

"Well, I'll tell you somethin' that I haven't told anyone in such a long time," Aaron said. His voice was low and even as he decided to get very personal with Heidi. She listened closely as he continued to speak. "About seventeen years ago my father worked for the city. He was a landscaper for the Department of Energy. You know....he used to cut down the trees that were blocking the power lines and shit like that. He didn't talk much to his family....but I always knew he was a good man. Good to us and good to his friends. Always lookin' out for people and shit like that. Anyway . . . one day he was called into work on his day off to cut down a tree that was growing through a few power lines in a residential neighborhood. And just like my father he went out and didn't say a word. He never questioned authority and just did what he was told."

Heidi noticed that Aaron's hands were moving slowly now on her back as he began to get deeper into his story. She continued to listen as he spoke about his father. "I wasn't there when this happened," Aaron said, "but the story goes that he was hanging off of the telephone pole and trying to reach out for a branch to cut when his harness malfunctioned. They said he never had a chance to catch himself because the tree branches were so weak. To make a long story short.... my father fell twenty-three feet from that pole and was seriously injured."

"Oh my God!" Heidi gasped.

"Yeah, he fell right there in the middle of the street onto that hard-ass-concrete. He broke his shoulder and wrist, broke six ribs, broke his jaw, and suffered major head injuries. It was crazy how bad that man got hurt that day. So instead of airlifting him to another county...they decided to send my father right there to the city hospital. He lost a lot of blood and he needed a blood transfusion. To make a long story even shorter he looked like he was going to survive those injuries. About four months later...he was still in the hospital and on his way to making a manageable recovery. But do you know that during his fifth month of treatment...they found out that my father got H.I.V. from the blood that was given to him for the blood transfusion."

"What?" Heidi shockingly asked. "They gave your father infected blood?"

"Hell yea." Aaron answered. "For the next two years...we watched my father decline, from a very strong man to a weak little boy, right before our eyes. That shit hurt me to my heart. When he died my father was only about seventy pounds. That's it. Barely skin and bones." Heidi felt herself becoming emotional as she listened to the story of Aaron's father. She picked up her head and put her hands over her face. Aaron continued to tell his story. "The one thing I remember about my father while he was wilting away on that hospital bed...was...my father...was always concerned about us. Always asking his kids about their grades and how things were at home. Like he didn't realize he didn't have long to live." Aaron stopped bathing Heidi and placed his hand on her shoulder. The memory of his father was taking a toll on him.

"When he died...it took a long time for me to get over my father's death. I couldn't believe I couldn't talk to the strongest person I've ever known in my life. He was my superman. For the longest time I couldn't believe that I would have to live the rest of this life without him. I found myself asking the same question over and over. Like a broken record. Just asking the same question to myself-" Aaron fell silent. A hazy feeling came over him. Heidi noticed the change in his mood and turned around to face him. She shot him an empathetic expression as she noticed his eyes were watering.

"What were you asking yourself?" Heidi softly asked.

Aaron gathered himself and continued to reflect on his thoughts. He took a deep breath and turned to Heidi. "Why wasn't I there to catch him?" Aaron softly answered. "Why wasn't I there to catch my father?" Heidi nodded her head as she listened to him. "You remind me of my father, Heidi." His voice was very direct. His mood grew warmer as he spoke about her. "You are a very good person, High. You put a lot of people before yourself and you work extra hard to put a smile on everybody else's face, even if it puts a frown on yours. And that's very rare today. So when I talk to you and when I talk about you the same thread always appears. You are just an all around good person."

"You think so?" Heidi skeptically asked. She was taken aback by Aaron's observation.

"I know so, Princess. So when you ask me *why I let you in*, it's because...I want to be there to catch you, Heidi. I don't care what I have to do and where I have to go....I will never let you fall, Princess, and I mean that."

A very wide smile grew on Heidi's face as she latched onto Aaron's last statement. She was totally impressed by Aaron's honesty. Her heart started to race as their eyes met in a very warm place. She could tell that Aaron's words were sincere. She slowly reached out and grabbed his hands. They were so warm. Heidi was still staring into his eyes when another warm sensation fell over her. Aaron shot her a gentle smile.

"Thank you, Aaron." Heidi whispered. "I will never forget that."

Aaron nodded in agreement. There was a comforting silence in the bathroom. Neither Aaron nor Heidi wanted to say a word. Neither could explain the special moment the two were sharing. For a moment, Heidi noticed that Aaron was leaning into her. She wasn't sure what he was doing and her heart started to race. Before she could react, Aaron leaned into Heidi and slowly kissed her. Heidi melted at the touch of his soft lips against hers. A warm sensation shot through her entire body as the friends kissed as though they had been dating for years. Heidi's sweet tongue sent a chill though Aaron's body. He softly grabbed her by the back of her head as she let out a seductive moan. Aaron felt her body jerk as the electrifying kiss felt like heaven to Heidi. She let out another moan and lifted her hands from the warm water. She reached for Aaron's face and softly rubbed his cheeks as the friends shared a long overdue moment of passion.

Before the friends could take their actions any further, a loud ringing came from the other side of the bathroom. It was Heidi's cellphone. She let out a frustrated gasp. "Goddamit," Heidi barked. "what timing!"

Aaron smiled to himself. He slowly backed away from Heidi and reached for a towel. He dried his hands and passed the phone to a smiling Heidi. They both tried to brush off the momentary embarrassment. "I don't know why people insist on calling at the wrong time." Heidi joked as she reached out to grab the phone. Aaron didn't say a word. He nodded his head again and passed her the phone. Heidi's mood immediately changed as she read the indicator on her phone.

INCOMING CALL
Mom (House Phone)

Heidi let out another frustrated gasp of air as she answered the phone with an attitude. "Mom I'm sorry I didn't call you last night. Everything is fine, I'm feeling much better-" Heidi was cut off by an angry male voice on the other end of the line.

"Listen, Heidi, shut the fuck up!"

Heidi's heart dropped into her stomach when she heard the man's voice screaming at her from the other line. Her hands started slightly shaking as she held the phone closer to her ear.

"Who is this?" Heidi stuttered.

"You'll remember me when you see me, bitch," the voice groaned from the other line. "Don't worry about your mother, she's good. We not gonna hurt her as long as you cooperate. You feel me?" Aaron watched as Heidi eyes began to fill with tears. He didn't know what to think.

"Oh my God, who is this?" Heidi pleaded. Her heart was pounding uncontrollably now. "Where is my mother?"

"I'm only gonna say this once, Heidi, so listen carefully," the voice instructed. "Tonight at eight o'clock you gonna come here to your mother's house to see her. Don't come to the front door. Bring ya ass to the back. We will be waiting for you. Don't bring no guns, no cops, and come alone. If you are ten minutes late or ten minutes early we gonna fuckin' kill her."

"Oh my God no!" Heidi yelled. The tears were flowing uncontrollably down her face now. "Please don't hurt her. Whatever you want me to do, I'll be there…just don't hurt my mother." There was a silence on the phone. "Hello?!" Heidi desperately yelled.

"Don't forget, Heidi. Come alone at 8 o'clock. Don't be late!"

Heidi heard a loud click on the other end of the line. She frantically tried to call her mother's phone again but there was no answer. She tried her mother's cellphone but the phone just kept ringing. Heidi dropped the phone in fear. She was well beyond shocked. Aaron stared at Heidi who was now wearing a blank expression on her face.

"Heidi," Aaron whispered, "what happened?"

"Oh my God." The tears flowed down her face and into the bathtub. She looked up to Aaron who was now standing over her. "Aaron….somebody just…kidnapped my mother."

❖

Chapter 18

Saturday, November 3, 2007
East Orange, New Jersey

6:54 p.m.

*B*ack at Pearl's house, Lamar was screaming at the top of his lungs as a durable plastic bag was swiftly being pulled over his head. His massive body crashed to the basement floor as he wrestled with the two men trying to restrain him. The loud sound of crashing work tools and plywood bounced off the hollow concrete walls in the basement. Lamar couldn't believe what was happening to him. A swift punch to the right side of his jaw dazed him. Lamar's eyes immediately rolled to the back of his head and he faded in and out of consciousness for a few seconds. His attackers were still trying to smother him with a clear-plastic-bag when he finally woke up. Lamar noticed the two men were wearing ski masks and couldn't identify who they were. After a few minutes of struggling with Lamar, one of the attackers started to yell at him in frustration.

"Hold still you fuckin' jackoff!" the first voice commanded.

"I told you we shoulda shot this nigga first, he's a stubborn muthafucka!" the second voice muttered. "I say we shoot this nigga and leave him here in the basement. Nobody would even know."

The two men struggled with Lamar as he continued to try to fight them off. His arms were tied behind his back. With the strength of his upper-body Lamar attempted desperately to fight with the diligent duo. The larger of the two men violently restrained Lamar in a bear-hug and forced him to sit still in the chair. Lamar continued to squirm.

Dashawn Taylor

"Man, just shoot this nigga!" the first attacker screamed as he struggled with Lamar.

"No more shots! No noise this time!" the second attacker grunted.

The first attacker grabbed Lamar by his legs. He pulled a bright white–utility rope from his back pocket and tied Lamar's legs to the wooden chair. Now with Lamar's legs secured, the advantage of the scuffle began to lean to the attackers. The first man quickly pulled out a second rope and tied Lamar's upper body to the chair. Lamar was now totally helpless. He continued to bounce back and forth in the chair but his attempts to escape were unsuccessful. His heart began to race out of control as the second attacker swiftly placed the plastic bag over his head and tied a knot in the back. Lamar shook violently. The feeling of death was closing in on Lamar; he could sense it. His body reacted and searched for air to present to his lungs but there was none left. Lamar's chest contracted in and out but no oxygen was flowing. He was dying. His vision blurred and his neck became as stiff as a diving board as Lamar tried desperately to breathe.

"Look at you now! Not that strong now are you, dog?" one voice eerily taunted. Despite his nearness to death, Lamar continued to fight.

The first attacker moved closer to Lamar and stared into his eyes through the foggy plastic bag. He seemed to be in awe at the sight of Lamar struggling for air. The attacker cracked a devilish smirk through the ski-mask. His lifeless –grey eyes sent a chill through Lamar as he continued to fight for air. After a few moments, Lamar could feel the attacker's hands on both sides of his face. His grin grew wider as he tightly grabbed Lamar's head and placed his thumbs over his mouth. Lamar started to fade away. The lack of oxygen caused Lamar's body to become momentarily paralyzed. He couldn't move anymore. The attacker watched as the fight in Lamar's eyes seemed to weaken by the second. The attacker giggled at the sight. He placed his thumbs closer to Lamar's mouth and pushed against the plastic bag. After a few seconds the attacker managed to poke a large hole in the plastic bag with his thumbs and a refreshing pocket of air rushed into Lamar's lungs as he began to breathe again. Lamar dropped his head forward as he struggled for more oxygen. The sound of laughter could be heard just behind him as the second attacker chuckled at the sight of Lamar gasping for air.

"Oh shit, it feels good don't it motherfucker?" One attacker joked as he grabbed the back of Lamar's head.

"Yeah, it feels good to him." the second attacker added. "Look at him. He's happy to be alive."

Lamar's body was weak. Tears dribbled from his eyes. The fear of dying was overwhelming. The second attacker pushed Lamar's head backwards and stared at him. Lamar could clearly see his grey eyes as his vision became clearer. Without warning, the attacker reached for his ski masked and pulled it off. Although his eyes told a different story, the attacker's baby-face gave him the appearance of a younger man. Still his distant eyes sent morbid chills through Lamar's body. The attacker's name was Vegas.

"Look at me, nigga!" Vegas yelled. His voice startled Lamar as he continued to breathe normally again. "You see how close you came to bitin' that muthafuckin' bullet? Huh?"

Lamar didn't say a word. Vegas nodded to the second attacker who, by this time, had also removed his ski mask. It was Shaheed. Vegas nodded to Shaheed and then back to Lamar. Before Lamar could turn around, a large flash of light came into his brain. Shaheed had punched him on the side of the head. The pain shot to the back of his neck and Lamar groaned in pain.

"Hey, dickhead! Don't be a fuckin hero!" Vegas yelled. "I hate heroes. I'm gonna ask you again. You see how close to dyin' you came, muthafucka?" Lamar slowly looked up to Vegas who was standing in front of him. Lamar slowly nodded his head in agreement. "Right," Vegas whispered as he nodded along with Lamar. "And see how good it feels to be alive?" Lamar nodded again. The pain from the punch caused Lamar to bite his bottom lip and blood dripped down the plastic bag and onto his chest. "Okay hero, here's the rules to this thing," Vegas explained. "You scream for help: we shoot you. You try to escape: we shoot you. You lie to us: we shoot you. And if you do anything that we don't like: we shoot you! Do you understand?"

Lamar's body was overflowing with fear as he stared at Vegas. He slowly nodded his head as he realized the gravity of his predicament. Vegas shot Lamar another devilish smirk.

"Don't worry, dog. We not gonna hurt you. As long as you play it straight with us."

Shaheed remained quiet behind Lamar. He continued to look on as Vegas continued to talk to Lamar. "What's ya name, homie?" Vegas asked.

"Lamar."

"Okay, Lamar, another question. And this one is tricky," Vegas sarcastically said. "Did your girlfriend Heidi tell you to come here?"

"What?" Lamar asked. He shot Vegas a confused look.

"Your girlfriend, nigga! Heidi! Did she tell you to come here?!" Vegas yelled.

"That's not my girlfriend," Lamar barked.

A swift punch came from the back of Lamar's head and connected on his ear. The impact had him screaming in pain. Shaheed was reaching to punch him again before Vegas stopped him.

"Whoa, Shah'!" Vegas yelled. "Cool out, homie. What are you doing, man?"

"This muthafucka is tryin' to be a smart-ass!" Shaheed yelled.

"I'm not!" Lamar screamed as he turned around to Shaheed. "That's not my goddamn girlfriend, she's my sister."

There was a silence in the room. Shaheed quickly stepped in front of Lamar and stared at him. He had fire in his eyes. "You Heidi's brother?" Shaheed angrily whispered. The look in his eyes scared Lamar. "Heidi is ya sister?"

"Yeah, that's my sister," Lamar grunted. He watched as Shaheed reached back to punch him again. He tensed up and braced himself for the hit. Vegas grabbed Shaheed by the arm before he could inflict any more pain on Lamar.

"Not yet, Shaheed," Vegas whispered as he tightly grabbed Shaheed's arm. "Not yet, let's do what we came here to do first." Shaheed shot Vegas an angry glare. He was clearly upset. He took a moment to pause as he turned back to Lamar, who was petrified. Shaheed pulled his arm away from Vegas and reluctantly walked to the other side of the basement. Vegas watched him for a moment and then turned his attention back to Lamar.

"Sister, huh?" Vegas said as he slowly nodded his head. "Okay, so Heidi is your sister. So did she tell you to come here?"

"No, this is my mother's house," Lamar whispered. "I just left to grab something from the store and when I came back, y'all was here." Lamar was in pain. A mix of blood and saliva was building in his mouth. He leaned over to spit it out on the floor. "What the fuck?" Lamar grunted as he shook his head.

"When was the last time you saw her?" Vegas asked.

"She left here late on Friday. I haven't seen her since."

"You know I can tell when someone's lying to me, right?" Vegas added.

"Good for you, man." Lamar sarcastically snapped. "Because I'm not lyin' to you. I saw her Friday night and we had an argument. She was pissed and she left. What do you want me to say?"

Vegas slowly nodded his head as he stared at Lamar. "Okay, hero. I understand."

"Where's my mother at?" Lamar shouted as he looked around the dimly lit basement.

"Don't worry about it, homeboy, she is safe upstairs in her bedroom," Vegas answered. "Like I said, just do what we say and everybody's getting outta here alive." Lamar stared at Vegas. He didn't say a word as Vegas motioned for Shaheed to come closer to him. "So do we understand each other, Lamar?" Vegas asked.

Lamar nodded his head. He was feeling defeated. The thought of him not being able to help his mother made Lamar drop his head.

"Trust me, Lamar, nobody's dyin' today!" Vegas said as Shaheed made his way over to him.

Lamar turned away from Vegas. Something about his last statement made Lamar's blood boil. Before Lamar could react to the statement, Shaheed hit him in the back of the head with his gun. Lamar never saw what hit him. The impact instantly knocked him unconscious. Vegas smiled at the hit.

"Damn, Shah, I know you couldn't wait to do that," Vegas joked.

"Not at all." Shaheed watched Lamar slowly lean forward in the chair.

Vegas walked over to Lamar and put a large strip of duct tape over his mouth. He was not going to take a chance with Lamar waking up and screaming for help. The two attackers headed upstairs. When Shaheed arrived at the top of the stairs, he turned off the lights and left Lamar in darkness and alone. They walked to Pearl's living room where Shaheed took a deep breath and sat down on the sofa. His left hand was shaking uncontrollably. He was clearly nervous about the whole ordeal of holding Pearl and Lamar as hostages. Vegas didn't seem to be worried as he glanced at the family portraits on Peal's walls.

"So you really think this is gonna work?" Shaheed asked as he looked around the house. Vegas could clearly see that his cousin was uneasy.

"I *know* this is gonna work, cousin," Vegas bragged. "Everything is already set up. I told you, my man is very reliable. Me and him made a lot of money together back in the day. And if he says we can get six figures out of this thing, I believe him. Trust me, we don't have to do shit else but wait. Just relax, cousin. After this weekend you'll have crazy money to pay off Abdul and you and Rhonda can be outta here."

"I think we need another person." Shaheed suggested.

"What?" Vegas questioned.

"Yeah." Shaheed quickly answered. "Look, we got this asshole Lamar downstairs. I can watch him. Then we got his mother upstairs. I know you got her. But who the hell is going to watch the doors? I don't think we can hold this place for the whole night."

Vegas took a minute to think. Shaheed was making perfect sense. Vegas sat down on the armchair adjacent from the sofa and there was a loud silence in the living room as the two men tried to come up with the perfect candidate to help them carry out the robbery.

"I tell you right now, Shah, you don't want my peoples to come up here," Vegas said. A devilish grin appeared on his face as he continued to warn Shaheed. "If they come up here, I don't think none of us would make it out of this place alive! Them niggas is fuckin' crazy." Vegas and Shaheed started laughing.

"Nah fam, we don't want ya people up here," Shaheed joked. "You know who I was thinkin' about?"

"Who?"

"Rafeek."

"Abdul's people?" Vegas snapped.

"Yea. Think about it. When I get that money I can just give it to him and keep it moving. I don't have to take a chance with Abdul tryin' to get cute when I go seem him. Feel me?"

"Yup, I feel you." But Vegas' tone was skeptical. "Just know that I don't trust Rafeek, okay? So Imma be watchin' his ass very close."

"Yeah, I know, Shaheed added. "I'm with you. I know he shady as hell but I won't tell 'em much. And I'll tell him to leave his gun at home. We already got enough of them."

"Muthafuckin right!" Vegas said with a sly smile. "But you know he's gonna want some extra money for himself?"

"I know." Shaheed said. "But if your man is right about this six-figure-thing, then Rafeek can have some extra for himself if he wants it." Shaheed nodded his head and walked over to the front door. He peered out the window and surveyed the quiet neighborhood.

"Imma go upstairs and check on moms," Vegas said.

"Okay cousin, imma call Rafeek right now."

Vegas nodded his head and turned around. Shaheed watched him as he headed upstairs to check on Pearl. Shaheed grabbed his cellphone and dialed Rafeek. A strange feeling came over him as Rafeek answered on the other line. Shaheed ignored his intuition and proceeded to ask for Rafeek's help with the hostage situation at Pearl's house.

❖

Chapter 19

Saturday, November 3, 2007
New Jersey Turnpike

7:12 p.m.

*H*eidi tried to calm herself as she headed north on the New Jersey Turnpike on her way to her mother's house. Her hands and legs were shaking so badly that she decided to travel just 45 mph in order to avoid speeding off the road. She had been crying off and on for nearly twenty minutes now when her phone started ringing. She quickly grabbed the phone and noticed that it was Aaron on the other line. Heidi quickly answered the phone.

"Hey, Aaron." Heidi somberly answered.

"Hey you, are you okay?" Aaron asked.

"Yeah, I'm making good time." Her voice sounded drained.

"Are you sure you don't want me to at least drive by your mother's house while you there?" Aaron asked.

"Listen, Aaron, I don't know who these guys are and I don't wanna take a chance like that," Heidi pleaded.

"I'm just worried about you, High. I really don't want anything to happen to you."

"I know, sweetie," Heidi said. "So did you call your peoples from Newark? Did they find out anything?"

"Yeah, that's why I was calling," Aaron said. "One of my dudes from the bricks heard about the accident. He said he thinks one of the niggas died, but he wasn't sure."

Heidi's heart fell into her stomach as she heard the news. "Oh my God, somebody died in the accident?!"

"Yeah, my man told me that there was a big fire and everything," Aaron continued.

"Jesus Christ!" Heidi gasped. "This is crazy. Did he say anything else?"

"Well, no. Not yet. I'm just waiting on him to call me back with some more news. So what do you want me to do?" Heidi's mind was spinning with more damaging thoughts. Hearing the news caused her body to shake even more. There was a long silence on the phone as Heidi was speechless. "You okay, High?" Aaron cautiously asked.

"Yeah, I'm okay. Just a little scared. I'm going to call you back in a few, okay?"

"So you don't want me to do anything?" Aaron quickly asked. "I wanna help you."

"I'm good, Aaron." Heidi snapped. "I'll give you a call back."

Without warning Heidi hung up the phone. She took a quick glance at her watch. Heidi let out a gasp in frustration as she noticed it was close to 7:30 p.m. Heidi needed to make one stop before she got to her mother's house.

****

East Orange, New Jersey
7:18 p.m.

Just a few miles away, Shaheed was standing in the rear of the kitchen at Pearl's house. He was leaning against the back door and carefully watching for any movement in the backyard. The long day was taking a toll on his body. Shaheed was tired and the images of his brother's death continued to haunt him. He was thinking about his brother's face when Vegas walked into the kitchen and startled him.

"Okay, Shah'," Vegas said. "The mom is upstairs in her room. I asked her and she said the same thing, nobody else should be coming to the crib but Heidi. So I think we good." Shaheed slowly nodded his head and walked over to the kitchen table. He took a seat and continued to stare at the back door. "Shah', you sure you up for this, man?" Vegas asked. He shot Shaheed a concerned look. "Look, we can turn around now and keep it movin'." Shaheed turned to his cousin who was standing at the entrance to the kitchen. "I'm serious, cousin." Vegas said. "I told you that I got a couple of stacks saved up for you, man. If you want you can have that and be out. I'm pretty sure that ya girl got some money, too."

"Nah, I'm okay, Vee."

"No you not, cousin." Vegas rebutted.

"Man, I'm good." Shaheed's voice sounded tired and defeated.

"You don't look right, homie. I'm serious. This is serious business tonight. We talkin' six figures or we talkin' sixty years. You feel what I'm sayin?" Shaheed turned to face his cousin. "Oh yea," Vegas continued, "we either gonna get this money, or we gonna get those cuffs tonight if we not on point, you feel me?"

Shaheed rose to his feet and walked towards the back door. "Yea cousin, I feel you."

"So what's really good, Shah'?" Vegas barked.

"Man, I just feel like I crossed the line the other night with Robert. I feel like I coulda done more to help him, man. On the real, I feel like a monster right now."

"What?" Vegas asked. "What you mean you feel like a monster?"

Shaheed turned around and stared at his cousin. His eyes turned beet-red as he imagined his brother dying in the horrific crash. "Vegas, man, I'm not like you. I just can't watch crazy shit happen and look at it like it's nothin'." Shaheed's voice buckled with emotion. "Then the other night, I remember so much pain running through me when I watched that car explode with my brother in it," Shaheed continued. "And you know what's the first thing I thought about when that car caught on fire?"

Vegas shot his cousin a sarcastic expression and shrugged his shoulders. "I don't know, Shah'!" Vegas stammered. "What?"

"The muthafuckin' money," Shaheed whispered. "My brother was burnin' alive in that goddamn car and all I could think about was how the hell I was gonna make it out of Jersey without paying Abdul. And then I thought about my brother second." Vegas remained silent as Shaheed reflected on the crash. "So that's why I feel like a monster. I will never see my brother again because I put money before that nigga."

"Listen, nigga." Vegas interjected. "Get that crap out of your mind, cousin. Shit happens. Your brother died because of the accident, not because of you." Vegas walked over to Shaheed and leaned on the back door directly across from him. "Listen, homie, you didn't kill ya brother. That bitch that smashed into the car did that shit. And she is on her way here. That's it. Nothing more, nothing less. You exactly right about one thing. You did cross the line the other night. You watched your brother die. And you might not ever come back from that shit. Death is real, my dude. But fuck that, we gonna get even for Robert tonight." Shaheed turned to his cousin. His expression began to change as he listened to what Vegas had to say. "But you gotta decide who gonna pay for that shit that happened. Are you gonna pay for that or is Heidi gonna pay for that? That's really it. And if we gonna do it, we gonna do it. All the way! One of them might have to die tonight, and you may have to do it? You feel me?" Shaheed slowly nodded his head. Vegas shot him an angry expression. "Nah man, I'm serious! You feel me?" Vegas barked.

"Yea, nigga, I feel you!" Shaheed yelled.

"That's what I'm talkin' 'bout," Vegas barked. "Shit! Use some of that anger tonight. We gettin' up outta here with that money and that's it."

"And that's it," Shaheed agreed. "No doubt, let's make it happen."

Vegas nodded his head as he walked over to his cousin. He patted Shaheed on the back and turned to leave the kitchen. Vegas was halfway out of the kitchen when he heard a knock on the back door. Shaheed quickly turned around and stared out the window. He couldn't recognize the face but he could tell it was a man. Vegas glanced at his watch and noticed that it was close to 7:30.

"That can't be Heidi this early," Vegas whispered. "Can you see who it is?"

"Nah, I can't see 'em, it's too dark."

"Fuck it. Open the door, I got whoever it is." Vegas said.

Shaheed turned around to his cousin. He noticed that Vegas had his weapon drawn and was pointing the gun directly to the back door. "What are you doing, Vee?" Shaheed whispered.

"I told you, Shah, if we gonna do this we gonna go all the way. Just open the door."

Shaheed shot his cousin a strange look. He shook his head and reached for the doorknob on the back door. Vegas cocked the hammer back on his revolver as he braced himself to greet the visitor. Shaheed took a deep breath and pulled the door opened. A man appeared in the doorway and quickly raised his hands as he noticed Vegas with the gun. He was wearing a black sweat hood and brown work boots. Shaheed took one look at the man and frowned.

"Goddammit, Rafeek!" Shaheed yelled. "I should let my cousin blow your head off for scarin' us like that!"

"Fellas, calm down," Rafeek stuttered. "Don't tell me y'all forgot about invitin' me to the party?"

Vegas lowered his gun and shook his head. He shot Rafeek a disgusted gesture and turned around. "Close the door, Shah," Vegas shouted as he headed to the living room. "And don't forget, nigga. No guns!"

Shaheed pushed Rafeek away from the door and slammed it shut. "Damn, nigga, you was suppose to be here a while ago." Shaheed barked.

"I know, mayne, charge it to the game, slim," Rafeek said. "So how long is this gonna take?"

"Not that long." Shaheed answered. "Alright, 'Feek, turn around man. I gotta frisk you."

"Frisk me for what, slim?" Rafeek snapped. "I'm clean."

Shaheed looked at Rafeek. Both men exchanged an uneasy moment. Shaheed turned to the living room and quickly back to Rafeek who was still wearing an angry expression.

"You 'ain't got shit on you?" Shaheed skeptically asked.

"I told you, slim, I'm clean." A devilish smile came to his face as he nodded to Shaheed. "You told me no guns, right? So I did like you said. My hammer is in the car, slim."

Shaheed gave Rafeek one last glare. Shaheed nodded his head and walked towards the basement door. He motioned for Rafeek to follow him. "Okay, my dude, come on." Shaheed said. "Let me show you what we got going on in here."

Shaheed and Rafeek headed to Pearl's basement. As Rafeek left the kitchen he noticed Vegas was still staring at him from the living room. He quickly turned away from Vegas and followed Shaheed into the basement where Lamar was waiting.

****

New Jersey Turnpike
7:32 p.m.

Ten miles away at a rest stop on the New Jersey Turnpike, Heidi was leaning on the rear of her truck watching the cars come and go. The combination of fear and the cool autumn night caused Heidi's body to shiver. She couldn't stop her body from shaking as she continued to glance at her watch. A cool breeze brushed up against Heidi's chest and she covered up as she noticed a sports car entering the rest area. A warm feeling came over her when she noticed it was her best friend Faith. *Thank God.*

Heidi waited for Faith to pull beside her and walked over to the driver's side. Faith didn't make it two steps out of her car before Heidi rushed to her and gave her a big hug.

"Oh my God, I'm so happy to see you." Heidi moaned.

Faith was taken aback by Heidi's excitement. "Damn, girl. Okay, I guess I'm happy to see you too!" Faith joked.

Heidi continued to hug Faith. She didn't want to let go. "Faith, oh my God girl, you just don't know how glad I am that you came." Heidi's tone grew more fragile. "I don't know what's about to happen but I'm in so much trouble now, girl."

Faith backed away from Heidi. "Is everything okay with you, sweetie?" Faith warily asked.

"No. Everything's not okay," Heidi whispered. "Not at all."

"Damn girl, what happened? Did something go down at your mother's house the other night?"

"Faith, listen. Please don't tell anybody this, okay?" Heidi whispered. The urgency in her voice seemed to intensify every word that left her mouth.

"Okay, girl, what happened?"

"I'm serious, Faith. Please keep this to yourself. I really don't know who these guys are or what they could do."

"I'm your best friend, girl. When I tell you I got you, sweetie, I got you," Faith added. "What happened?"

"Faith, some guys are at my mother's house." Heidi groaned. "They are there right now. I don't know who they are or what they want. But they called me earlier today on my cellphone." Tears bubbled in Heidi's eyes. Faith felt a massive chill rush through her body as she watched her best friend break down. Faith put her hand over her mouth and continued to listen to the news. "They got my mother, Faith, and I don't know what to do." Heidi moaned as the tears began to rush down her face.

"Oh no, Heidi." Faith said. "I can't believe it. Did you call the cops?"

"I can't," Heidi whispered. "I have to go to the house tonight by 8:00. They told me not to tell anybody and come by myself. So you know they are tryin' to hurt us tonight."

"Did you call your brother?" Faith asked.

"I tried calling Lamar ever since they called me, but his phone is off. I think he must be in the house with them right now. I can't find him anywhere."

"Oh no, High, this is terrible," Faith groaned. "I can't believe this. I'm so sorry. What can I do, High?"

"I don't know, girl!" Heidi answered. "I've been thinking about it and I really don't know what to do."

"Do you want me to go with you?" Faith asked.

Heidi turned away in an attempt to regain her composure. She took another look at her watch and noticed that she only had twenty minutes to make it to her mother's house. "I can't, Faith. I can't. They told me to come alone and I just want to do whatever they say, you know?" Faith slowly nodded her head. "But I do have an idea," Heidi said. "Just follow me to my mother's neighborhood. There's a shopping center not too far from her. Just wait there. If I can get to a phone I will call you."

"Okay, but what if you can't get to a phone?"

"Well, give me until tomorrow morning. If you don't hear from me by then, somethin' bad has happened."

Faith shook her head. "No High, don't think like that. If I don't hear from you tonight, I'm comin' in there with the goddamn cavalry."

"No Faith, please. Let me do this my way," Heidi pleaded. "Just give me 'til the morning to come up with something while I'm in there. It's obvious that they want something or they wouldn't have called me. My mother would be dead by now."

Faith nodded her head again. "Okay, Heidi. I gotcha. I'll wait at the store and see what I can come up with. I got your back."

"Thanks, girl. That's all I needed to hear."

Heidi walked over to Faith and hugged her again. Her heart began to race as Faith shot her a reassuring smile. Heidi realized the odds were against her. But having Faith in her corner tonight gave her a better chance of surviving what was ahead. Heidi turned around and jumped in her truck. She fired up the SUV and sped onto the freeway with Faith trailing closely behind. The clock on the dashboard gave Heidi a little over ten minutes to make it to her mother's house. With little time to waste, Heidi pushed the gas pedal to the floor and sped up the dark highway.

❖

Chapter 20

"*H*ey, slim, you makin' this too difficult." Rafeek joked as he smiled at Shaheed and Vegas in the living room. "You said shawty will be here in a minute, right? We don't have a lot of time to negotiate these numbers. Whatever you gonna give Adbul, just throw twenty-five on top of that."

"Twenty-five?" Shaheed yelled. "What the hell you mean twenty-five? You not doin' shit. I just need you to hold down the second floor. And then baby-sit these people. That's it."

Vegas shot Rafeek a blank stare. He was upset that Rafeek was asking for $25,000 to be a part of the heist tonight.

"Listen, mayne, you woke me up out of my sleep beggin' me to do this shit," Rafeek continued. "Mayne, I can get twenty years just for talking about this shit out loud to y'all. It's twenty-five or I walk, slim."

"Well walk then, nigga!" Vegas yelled. He was visibly upset. "We really don't need you!"

Rafeek stood up and turned toward Shaheed who shot him a blank stare. "Nigga, you know you don't wanna walk," Shaheed said. "This is easy money. All you got to do is do what we say and you walk away with the money. It's simple as that. So listen to me, I can give you fifteen easily. And that's it."

There was a silence in the living room as Rafeek thought about the offer. He glanced over to Vegas who shot him a dirty gesture. "Okay slim, make it eighteen and we got a deal,"

Dashawn Taylor

Rafeek said as he shook his head. "At least I can feel like I'm part of the team."

"Done deal!" Vegas barked. "Don't say shit else, Shah'. That's cool, eighteen is cool. We only got a few minutes before Heidi gets here. We gotta set everything up."

Shaheed agreed and walked out of the living room toward the kitchen. Vegas walked toward Rafeek.

"Rafeek," Vegas said. "I need you to go upstairs and sit inside the bedroom in the front of the house. Just look out for any cars or anything suspicious so we can be ready for anything. And keep an eye on mom dukes, too." Rafeek nodded his head as he listened to the instructions given to him by Vegas. "When we yell for you to come downstairs with Heidi's mom, then come downstairs," Vegas instructed. "Other than that stay upstairs, *slim*!" Vegas sarcastically snapped. "You feel me?"

Rafeek shot Vegas a sarcastic smile. He didn't like Vegas' tone but decided not to engage him. Rafeek nodded at the orders and headed upstairs. Vegas shook his head and walked toward the kitchen. Shaheed was leaning against the backdoor when Vegas entered behind him. Shaheed motioned for Vegas to turn off the lights. Vegas obeyed the command and walked over to his cousin.

"So you ready, homie?" Vegas asked.

"I'm ready, cousin." Shaheed answered.

Vegas smiled and continued to look outside of the back door. As the autumn sky grew darker the cousins waited patiently for Heidi to arrive at the house.

****

7:53 p.m.

A few blocks up the street, Heidi was getting out of her SUV and locking the door. She looked around the dark neighborhood and took a deep breath. It was impossible to prepare herself for what she was about to experience, but Heidi tried her best to stay poised. The idea of having Faith as her backup added some relief. She looked around the neighborhood one last time and continued to walk toward her mother's house.

With every step, Heidi felt her legs weakening. Her stomach turned over in circles as she made her way down the dark street. Heidi almost felt a tear come to her eyes when she saw her mother's house. She paused for a second and looked around. A strange feeling came over her as approached the driveway. She thought she saw movement from the second floor window but it was too dark to tell for sure. Heidi shook her head and continued to make her way to the back door. Her heart was pounding through her chest at this point. The fear in her heart traveled swiftly to her legs and she moved carefully, trying to reach the back door.

There were no lights on in the house. This sight made her extra nervous. Heidi said a short prayer to herself and slowly knocked on the door. Before Heidi could catch her breath the back door suddenly swung open. A large man rushed from inside the house and grabbed Heidi's arm. She screamed. Another man quickly grabbed Heidi by the head and covered her mouth. Both men pulled her inside the kitchen and slammed her to the floor. One man quickly closed the back door.

"Shut the fuck up, girl," the other grunted. "Calm down."

Heidi continued to fight as the two men wrestled with her. She tried to scream but the large hand around her mouth was too strong. One man managed to grab both of Heidi's wrists and tie them together. Heidi moaned in terror.

"Stop fighting, bitch! We not tryin' 'a hurt you!" the second man yelled. "You makin' this harder on yarself."

Heidi ignored the man's pleas and continued to fight. She felt one of the men grab her legs and manage to tie them together with a rope. Heidi was completely helpless at this point. One man quickly jumped up and rushed to turn on the lights. The bright flash seemed to temporarily blind her as it illuminated the ragged kitchen. Heidi's vision cleared just in time to see one of the men walking toward her. She was tempted to scream before she realized the other man was on the opposite side of her with a gun pointed in her direction. Heidi was frozen stiff.

"Yeah, please calm yo wild ass down," Vegas grunted. He was clearly out of breath. "I thought we told you to come by yourself?"

"I did," Heidi whispered. "I'm alone."

"Not fightin' like that! I think you got a few souls walkin' with you," Vegas grunted. He took a deep breath and walked over to Heidi, picking her up and awkwardly placing her in one of the kitchen chairs.

"Now Imma un-tie your legs. Don't get cute or my man *will* punish you," Vegas warned. He untied Heidi's legs, then quickly backed away and looked at her. "Okay Heidi, now that we got that bullshit out the way, let me introduce myself to you. I'm Vegas, okay?" Heidi looked up to Vegas as he introduced himself. His grayish eyes scared her. "And him right there? That is my cousin, Shaheed. But I think you guys already met."

Vegas smiled to himself as Shaheed walked closer to Heidi. Her heart dropped to the floor and a cold chill rushed through her entire body as she looked into Shaheed's angry eyes. A deafening memory of the crash flashed into her mind as Heidi recalled Shaheed's face. He could see her wheels turning as he made his way closer to her.

"Yeah bitch, I know you remember me," Shaheed taunted. "You had to know that you was gonna see me again." Heidi didn't say a word. She was petrified. Her body trembled with fear. "Why you so scared now? You mad quiet right now. How come?"

Heidi leaned back in the chair as Shaheed got closer to her. She could see that he was carrying a gun in his hand.

"Please, whatever you thinkin' 'bout doing, please don't," Heidi pleaded. "I'm so sorry about the other night."

"Huh?" Shaheed grunted. "I can't hear you. Are you beggin'?"

"Please, I was drunk. I mean…I was scared…I didn't know what I was doin'." Heidi's voice shook with fear. "I'm sorry for wreckin' your car."

"Wreckin' my car!?" Shaheed yelled with rage. "Bitch you killed my brother the other night! My brother died in that car accident, you fuckin' idiot!"

Heidi's mouth fell open. Shaheed rushed over and put his hand over her mouth. He reached for his pistol and pushed it against the side of her head. Heidi panicked. She tried to break loose from the tight ropes but they had a locking hold on her. Shaheed wrestled with Heidi until he had a tight grip around her neck. He pushed her head back and repositioned the gun to the front of her forehead. Heidi held her breath, sensing the inevitable gunfire. The intensity in Shaheed's eyes sent a shockwave through Heidi's petrified body.

"I'm sorry, Vegas, I gotta end this right now!" Shaheed yelled as he put a tighter grip on Heidi's neck. "I hope you remember this face, bitch, because it's the last you're ever gonna see!"

Heidi watched as Shaheed cocked the hammer back on the Glock 17 Pistol. She closed her eyes and said another quick prayer. Her body tensed up as she braced for the bullet. There was a moment of complete silence in the room. Heidi thought she was dead. She opened her eyes just in time to see Shaheed pulling the trigger on his weapon. *Click.* Heidi's heart stopped as the gun never fired. The men busted out into a boisterous laughter as Heidi struggled to catch her breath. They were playing a cruel joke on her. Heidi put her head down and tried to regain her composure.

"Yeah, bitch, remember how that feels," Shaheed barked. "Like my cousin says, *You see how close you came to dying?*" Heidi still struggled for air. Her heart was racing out of control. Shaheed grabbed her by the head and made her look at him. He pulled out a handful of bullets from his front pocket. "Guess I forgot to load the clip," Shaheed said, "but next time, this muthafucka's gonna be loaded. So do what we say and I'll make sure this is painless." Heidi slowly nodded to Shaheed. He dropped her head and placed one bullet in her pants pocket. "That's for you, bitch," Shaheed grunted. "Just something to remember me by when you out there runnin' that little errand for us." Heidi shot him a confused look. *What errand?* She thought to herself as Shaheed walked over to Vegas.

"Oh yeah, Heidi, or *So High* or whatever you like to call yourself," Vegas began. "It's time to go to work. We got a little errand we need you to run for us tonight. Stand up, bitch, let's go!" Vegas walked over to Heidi and grabbed her under her left shoulder. "C'mon, let's go!" Vegas commanded.

Heidi stood up and followed Vegas to the basement. Her body was still trembling as Vegas pushed the basement door open. He turned on the lights and motioned for Heidi to go downstairs. She turned to Vegas and shot him a worried expression.

"Move, Heidi, I'm not playin' with you!" Vegas shouted.

Heidi's heart pounded as she walked down the stairs. She felt herself getting weaker. Vegas was trailing close behind with his gun pointed to her back. The basement seemed to be extra cold. Heidi felt a wicked chill as she arrived at the bottom of the steps. Her stomach churned with fear as she spotted her brother unconscious in the chair.

"Oh my God, Lamar!" Heidi wanted to run to his aid but she impulsively turned around to locate Vegas.

"Wait right here, don't move," Vegas said as he walked to the rear of the basement. Heidi stood in fear and waited for him to return. She dismissed the notion of trying to escape upstairs because Shaheed decided to stand at the top of the stairs and wait for Vegas to return. Before Heidi could check on her brother Lamar, Vegas returned with a small milk crate. He tossed it behind Heidi.

"Have a seat," He said, turning around and grabbing another chair from the corner of the basement. He placed it directly in front of Heidi. Vegas shot her a sly smile as he sat down. "Okay, Heidi, time to discuss some business."

****

8:12 p.m.

Two floors up in the master bedroom, Rafeek was standing at the doorway carefully watching Heidi's mother. Pearl was sitting on the far end of her bed staring at the floor. Earlier that evening, Shaheed and Rafeek managed to handcuff her arm to the bedpost. Although her legs were free, Pearl was feeling extremely constricted. She said a prayer to herself as she listened to the commotion throughout the house. Pearl was frozen with fear.

"Hey, you okay?" Rafeek asked gently from the doorway.

Pearl was boggled by the question and turned to face him, but she was too scared to answer his question. She turned away again and continued staring at the floor. She was reciting her prayers when a loud yell from the first floor startled her.

"Rafeek, bring her downstairs!" Shaheed yelled

Pearl's heart tightened at the request. She quickly turned to Rafeek who was walking towards her. He didn't say a word. He quickly pulled out a small key and removed the handcuffs. Pearl watched him closely as he left the handcuffs on the bedpost and put the key in his front pocket.

"Let's go," Rafeek grunted, helping her down the stairs.

"What the hell are you doing, Rafeek?" Shaheed snapped.

"What? You told me to bring her downstairs."

"Yea man, but where the 'cuffs at?" Shaheed asked as she shot Rafeek an angry stare. "Why you take 'em off?"

Rafeek turned around and pointed upstairs. "Man, I left the 'cuffs on the bedpost. You are too paranoid for me. I took 'em off so I can bring her down for you. Look at her, slim. She ain't goin' nowhere. She's a scared old lady."

"Nigga, you slippin'. This ain't no goddamn daycare." Rafeek shook his head and waved Shaheed off. Just go back upstairs, nigga," Shaheed angrily whispered. "I'll take her down myself." Pearl watched as the two men exchanged fierce stares. Rafeek shook his head and turned around. Shaheed shot him a disgusted gesture and pulled Pearl by her arm. "Alright, little lady, get downstairs." Pearl walked down the stairs with Shaheed following close behind, watching her as she made her way down into the basement. Vegas turned around just in time to see Pearl cover her mouth at the sight of her son.

"Sit down over there." Vegas motioned for Pearl to sit next to Lamar.

"Mom, everything's going to be okay," Heidi blurted.

"Yeah, Mom, everything is going to be okay," Vegas sarcastically snapped.

The sight of her terrified mother brought tears to Heidi's eyes. Pearl turned to her daughter and slowly covered her mouth. "Heidi, what's going on baby?" Pearl cried out. "What's this about?"

"Lady, please sit yo' ass over there and shut up," Vegas barked. Both women frightfully turned to Vegas as he continued. "Yes! Sit down and shut up. I said nobody's gonna die tonight and I mean it. Just cooperate with us and everything's gonna be fine."

Pearl quickly obeyed him and rushed to sit next to Lamar. Shaheed slowly walked downstairs and took a seat on the bottom step. He carefully watched Pearl as Vegas turned his attention back to Heidi.

"Now like I was sayin'," Vegas continued. "This is gonna go as smooth as butter if you want it to. You understand?"

Heidi nodded. She tried her best to ignore her fear but she couldn't stop her body from trembling. The seriousness of the night was weighing heavy on her right now.

"Now, my cousin back there wanted to blow your goddamn head off when he first talked to me about you," Vegas whispered. "You killed his brother and we can't bring him back."

Heidi reluctantly turned to Shaheed. She felt another cold chill in her body as he shot her an evil stare. His lifeless eyes seemed to send shockwaves through her.

"But I told him to fallback. I told him that we could use this as an opportunity for all of us to make some money." Heidi shot Shaheed a strange look. "Oh yea," Vegas said with a sly smirk. "You can make some money too in this. Feel me?"

Heidi didn't know what to say. She was confused. She turned to her mother Pearl who shot her a concerned look. Heidi used every muscle in her tired body to resist the urge to break down in front of her mother. She turned back to Vegas and slowly shrugged her shoulders. "I'll do whatever you want me to do. Just don't hurt my family. What do you need from me?"

Vegas nodded his head and smiled at Heidi. "Good girl. Okay let's do business. Have you ever heard of a company called Datakorp.com?" Heidi quickly looked up to Vegas. Her eyes were wide with emotion. Pearl turned from Lamar and quickly looked at Vegas. "Of course you heard of Datakorp.com, your ex used to work for them, right?" Vegas said. Heidi's mouth fell open as Vegas made the stunning connection. "Don't be shocked, Heidi, you'd be surprised what two grand and two days can buy you around here."

Heidi dropped her head in frustration. Thoughts of her fiancé Jayson crept back to her as she tried to figure out who had given Vegas this information "What do you want from me?" she asked.

"I want you to go in there and rob the place." Vegas answered.

"What?" Heidi snapped. "That's impossible."

"It's not impossible!" Vegas yelled. His powerful voice startled her. "You not usin' your head, Heidi."

"I can't rob Datakorp.com." Heidi sarcastically snapped. "It's a brokerage firm. They don't even have money in the building."

"No doubt. I know that. But guess what tonight is." Vegas asked.

"I don't know."

"It's daylight sayings tonight. And the time goes back one hour at 2:00a.m." Vegas said as a slick smile grew on his face.

"What are you gettin' at?" Heidi was growing more frustrated with every word. "I don't know what the hell you sayin' to me. You still didn't tell me what I'm doin'." Pearl turned to Heidi. She could tell her daughter was growing impatient with Vegas. She offered her a calming expression but Heidi never looked her way. Vegas stood up in front of Heidi and walked away from her.

"Alright you impatient bitch, listen real closely," Vegas snapped. "This is what the hell you doin'. Tonight at one o'clock, I want you to be at Datakorp.com. There's a security guard that's gonna be downstairs when you first get to the building. He's gonna let you in. Take a key from him to get insde the Datakorp Processing Office. Don't ask him any other questions. And don't try to get cute up there, he's gonna be watchin' you the whole time."

"Okay." Heidi said. "What am I doing in the processing office?"

"There's gonna be two computers in the office that handle the maintenance fees for the company. Use the one on the left side of the office. When you turn on the computer you don't have to worry about no passwords or nothin' like that. The system is already on." Vegas slowly walked back over to Heidi and sat down in front of her again. "Now make sure you get

Dashawn Taylor

there by one o'clock okay? If not, it's going to be real bad for your family. You understand what I'm sayin'?"

Heidi balled up her lip and slowly nodded. She understood clearly what Vegas was insinuating. "So what am I doing at this computer?" Heidi whispered.

"Okay, at 1:15 you gonna log into the system. There's a folder that says schedule Maintenance Fees." Open that one. Basically, all you gonna do is reschedule the maintenance fees for the accounts. That's it. Change the date to tonight's date and put the time for 1:30 a.m. That's it. It's gonna ask you to confirm the change and confirm the account number. Now here comes the tricky part." Vegas turned around and motioned to Shaheed. "Hand me that paper again, Shah'."

Shaheed stood to his feet and walked over to Vegas. He handed him a small business card with writing on the back. Vegas took the card from Shaheed and turned back to Heidi who was trying to focus on the writing. Vegas pulled the card away before she could read any of the details.

"Now Heidi, the computer is gonna ask you to confirm the account that you want the maintenance fees to be forwarded to. I know you gonna write this number down before you leave but I want you to send the money to account number 862-487-85"

"3-7," Heidi quickly whispered. Vegas quickly looked up to Heidi in amazement.

"How did you know that was the number?" Vegas said as he sharply stared at Heidi. "Where do you know that number from?"

Heidi heart skipped a beat as she stared in Vegas' eyes. His intensity seemed to freeze her whole body. The entire memory of the 10-digit number ran through her mind at lightning speed. She had to think fast to throw Vegas off.

"I...saw it...on the card you got right there." The fear in her eyes confused Vegas. He looked down at the business card again and looked back to Heidi. "You had the card right there in front of me." Heidi added. "You expect me not to look at it?"

Vegas shot Heidi another confused gesture and turned back to Shaheed. "Yeah, we gotta quick one here, Shaheed." Vegas said. "Gotta watch this one." Heidi cracked a nervous smile. Her heart was racing out of control but she managed to maintain her composure as Vegas continued to instruct her. "Okay, so that's the account number. Don't forget, just put the account number in there and change the date and time. Stay there until the money transfers into the account. It should take less than five minutes. After that, change the date and account numbers back to the original information. And that's it. You're done. Come back here and everythin' will be fine."

Heidi made eye contact with Vegas as she processed all of the instructions. "Sounds like a good enough plan." Heidi said. "But how do you expect to get the money out of the Datakorp account? They'll just freeze the account once they find the error. Then what you gonna do?" Vegas slowly shook his head and smiled at Heidi. His confidence confused Heidi for a moment.

"Damn, Heidi you still not usin' your head, girl," Vegas taunted. "Tonight is daylight savings time. So when you change the account number and the time of the transaction, it will be 1:30 a.m. Now think about this for a moment. The money will go into the account at 1:30 a.m. right? But at 2:00 a.m. the time will reverse back to 1:00 a.m. again on the computer clock. Your transaction will be totally erased from the records but the money will be in the account already. So by the time anyone notices that the money was re-routed to another account we will be long gone with the money. Understand now?" Heidi was at a loss for words. The genius of the plan impressed her. Vegas shot her another smirk and continued to speak. "Yeah this shit is serious, Heidi. So don't fuck this up or somebody's getting fucked up. You feel me?" Vegas snapped. His voice became very direct. "Datakop.com got almost 300,000 customers. They charge each customer $5 a month. So you do the math. That's six figures and better. And don't worry, we will take care of ya family. We put everything on that."

The basement fell silent. Heidi replayed the plan in her mind to ensure that she remembered every detail. A rush of adrenaline ran through her as she thought about pulling off the job for Vegas and Shaheed. She still had so many questions to answer. *How did Vegas get all of the information on Datakorp and where did he get the account number?* Heidi quickly turned and looked to Vegas.

"So what happens to me?" Heidi whispered.

"What do you mean?" Vegas asked.

"If I go in there tonight, the camera system is gonna catch my face and I will definitely go to jail behind this shit."

"Don't worry about that." Vegas continued. "The guard will handle the alarm and camera systems. All you have to do is go up there and do your job. That's it. Nothing more nothing less. When you done, just come back here and we out. That's it. Think about it for a second. Imma give you some time to think it over." Vegas said. "Don't get cute down here. There's more guns upstairs than you think. Don't make us use them tonight."

Vegas rose to his feet and walked toward Shaheed. Heidi followed him with her eyes and caught Shaheed's soul-piercing stare. He was still upset about his brother and he wanted Heidi to know it. She quickly turned away from him. Vegas tapped Shaheed on the shoulder and they both proceeded to walk upstairs. Heidi listened closely as they closed the basement door and left her alone with her family to discuss the heist.

Chapter 21

Saturday, November 3, 2007
East Orange, New Jersey

9:26 p.m.

A strong gust of wind shook Faith's car and startled her as she waited impatiently for Heidi to return from her mother's house. Faith was parked just a few blocks from Pearl's house but she felt like she was a world away. The possibility of someone hurting Heidi and her mother took Faith's senses to high alert. Her nerves caused her body to tremble slightly. She continued to rock back and forth in the driver's seat, trying to calm herself as the hours passed. Faith looked at her cellphone again. A small grin appeared on her face as she noticed that she'd already entered a *9* and a *1* on her cellphone. This was an old trick she learned after years of working the graveyard shift. With her thumb slightly hovering over the number 1 on her keypad, Faith carefully scanned the dark neighborhood for any signs of trouble. Any slight movement from the street or in the neighborhood would trigger Faith's thumb to quickly press that last *1* and call the police. Faith was still scanning the area when her cellphone began to ring. The loud ringtone startled her momentarily and she rushed to see who was calling. She frowned at her screen as she read the information.

INCOMING CALL
(Restricted Caller)

Faith looked around in frustration. She couldn't imagine who would be calling her this late from a blocked number. After the third ring, Faith answered the call with an attitude.

"Hello," Faith answered. She was greeted by a soft female voice on the other line.

"Yes, is this Faith?" the voice softly asked.

"Yes it is, and who is this?" Faith snapped.

"Just call me Dee." The young woman on the phone sounded like she was disguising her voice as she continued to speak. "You called over here looking for a gift for tonight's party right?"

Faith took a few moments to think.

"Okay, Dee…I'm sorry…yes...yes…I do need a gift for a party tonight." Faith said as she recalled an earlier conversation.

"Is the party still going on?" Dee asked.

"Yes it is." Faith countered. "So what is this gift going to cost me?"

"My boss is asking for five thousand." Dee said.

"What?" Faith yelled. "What do you mean five thousand? That's robbery!"

"Faith, you only got a few hours to get here to pick up the gift. The price is non negotiable due to your history with my boss. If you want the gift, it will be here for you until we close. Thanks." Before Faith could negotiate the price she heard a subtle *click* on the other line. The young woman disconnected the call.

"Hello!" Faith blurted. "Hello? Dammit!" She put the phone back in her lap and let out a frustrated hiss of air. She quickly looked at her watch and noticed that it was quickly approaching ten o'clock. *Where is Heidi?* Faith thought to herself. She looked up the dark street and waited for her best friend to emerge from the darkness.

****

9:44 p.m.

Back in Pearl's basement, Heidi was trying to emerge from a different sort of darkness. She was grappling with the mystery of that infamous phone number she'd committed to memory so long ago. She had just ten minutes before Vegas and Shaheed would make their way back into the basement. Heidi was pacing back and forth hoping something would help her to figure out the puzzle. Her mother Pearl continued to tend to Lamar. His head injury was getting worse and he was still unconscious. Pearl wrapped a white t-shirt around his head, but it was quickly turning red with all the blood he was losing. Heidi walked over to her mother and knelt down next to her.

"I knew I should have put a window or something down here in the basement," said Pearl apologetically. "We coulda just ran outta here and went for help."

"I know, Mom," Heidi softly said. "How's he doing? Think he's gonna pull through?"

"Yea, he's just losing a lot of blood. I can't imagine what they hit him with. He hasn't woke up yet." Pearl explained.

"Mom," Heidi whispered. "There's something deeper going on her tonight."

The sound of Heidi's tone made her mother cautiously turn to her. "What do you mean?"

"That account number that Vegas gave to me, I saw that number last year."

"What?" Pearl stammered.

"Shhhhhh, Mom you gotta lower your voice," Heidi cautioned. "I saw that same ten-digit-number last year at Jayson's job. Somebody sent him flowers and I thought it was a phone number."

"Heidi baby, I don't follow you," Pearl whispered. "What are you talking about?"

"Mom, last year right before Jayson died, I went to his job to see him." Heidi explained. "Before I left the job, somebody sent him flowers and told him to contact them with that same ten-digit-number. I took the flowers and the card thinkin' it was some chick trying to get with him. I called the number all year but I didn't get nowhere with the number. There was a girl at the phone number but she didn't know shit about what I was talkin' about. But I know that number by heart. But I didn't know until tonight that it's not a phone number. It's the same number that the account number is under at Datakorp."

"Are you sure, Heidi?" Pearl asked. Her body began to feel uneasy as Heidi explained her story. "So you think those men upstairs killed Jayson?"

"I don't know, Mom."

Pearl dropped her head and tried to regain her composure. "So what are we gonna do?" Pearl whispered.

Heidi walked back over to Lamar. She sat down next to Lamar and Pearl and cautiously looked upstairs. "Well, Imma go do the Datakorp switch for them." Heidi said. "But judging by what somebody did to Jayson, they are not going to let us out of here alive. So I gotta come back here with some help."

"They said no cops," Pearl whispered.

"I know but I'll think of something." The sound of the basement door startled the two women. Heidi quickly turned to Pearl who shot her a terrified look. The sound of footsteps could be heard just a few feet away. Heidi moved closer to Pearl. "Mom, just keep Lamar alive and try to stay calm. We will make it out of this. I promise." More tears came to Pearl's eyes as she watched Heidi stand up and wait for the men to come downstairs. Vegas was the first to approach her.

"So what's the verdict, Heidi?" Vegas sharply asked.

"I'm in. Just make sure my family is taken care of."

"Sure thing," Vegas agreed. "Okay, go 'head upstairs so you can get ready." Heidi walked by Vegas and headed up the stairs. Vegas turned around and noticed that Pearl was crying. "Cheer up, little lady," Vegas taunted. "I told you that nobody was gonna die tonight and I mean it. Everything's gonna be fine."

Pearl didn't say a word to Vegas. She watched him as the two men left the basement with her daughter. Pearl dropped her head into her shaking hands and prayed that her daughter would make it back to her safely.

❖

Chapter 22

"*D*on't forget, Heidi, if you mess this up we *will* kill your family," Vegas barked from across the kitchen table. Heidi endured nearly two hours of constant instructions from Shaheed and Vegas about the robbery at Datakorp.com. She was amazed at how much information the duo knew about the company. From the security system to how many local offices were in the building, Vegas seemed to run off random facts about the company as if he'd worked at Datakorp.com in upper management for a few years. Heidi tried to calm herself as she picked up the last of the instructions from them. Shaheed snapped his fingers to get Heidi's attention. She turned to him and listened closely as he continued to explain the security codes in the Service Department of Datakorp.

"Okay that's it, you should be good," Shaheed said as he stared at Heidi. "Don't go in there and do somethin' stupid or we will kill ya dumb-ass tonight, Heidi. We not playin' with you."

Heidi nodded her head. She knew that Shaheed was not making idle threats. He was clearly upset about his brother's death and he was just looking for a reason to take his revenge. It was just a matter of time before Shaheed's true intentions were going to be revealed. Heidi's mind was racing as she thought about ways to save her mother and her brother. She knew the injury to her brother's head was going to get worse and she didn't know how long her mother's nerves were going to stay intact. As Shaheed continued to stare in Heidi's direction, she took a quick glance at the clock on the wall. *12:09*, Heidi thought to herself. She nodded her head one last time to Shaheed and quickly turned to Vegas.

"Okay y'all, I get it," Heidi whispered. "Can I go now?" The room fell silent as Shaheed and Vegas cautiously looked at one another. "C'mon fellas," Heidi said in frustration. "You want me to be back in less than two hours? It's gonna take me about twenty minutes to get down to Newark-"

"Yea, you can go," Vegas cut her off. "Like I said, don't get cute out there. They say mothers are supposed to die before their daughters. Feel me? But don't force my hand tonight, Heidi."

Heidi balled her lips up and nodded to Vegas. The stark image of Vegas killing her mother made her face twitch slightly. Her body began to heat up with anger but she quickly realized that right now was not the time to save her family. The odds were totally against her. Heidi knew she would have to come up with a solid plan to get her family to safety, but first she turned her attention to Datakorp.com and changing the information for Vegas and Shaheed. Heidi slowly stood up and headed to the back door. Without saying a word Vegas and Shaheed watched as Heidi left the house. Shaheed walked toward the door and closed it behind her. He peered through the window and watched as Heidi headed to her car.

"You shoulda let me kill dat bitch, Vegas." Shaheed said as he continued to look out the back window.

"You gonna get ya chance, homie. Don't worry," Vegas sneered. He walked toward the living room and motioned for Shaheed to follow him. "C'mon, Shah'. Let's get everything ready." Shaheed turned around and shot Vegas a blank expression. He walked toward Vegas without saying a word. "Don't worry, cousin." Vegas said as he shot Shaheed a devilish grin. "You gonna get ya chance."

****

12:21 a.m.

With a little over a half-hour to make it down to Datakorp, Heidi hustled back to her truck. The adrenaline in her body heightened all of her senses. She could feel the heavy pound of her heart as it thumped in unison with her jogging pace. Images of her mother and brother flashed in her mind and made her run faster. She didn't want to waste another minute. She knew exactly how dangerous Vegas and Shaheed could be and she didn't want to leave her family alone with them. Heidi rushed to her truck and jumped in the driver's seat. The engine barely had a chance to heat up before Heidi was forcing the truck into gear and darting up the street. The screeching tires could be heard throughout the quiet neighborhood. Heidi didn't care who heard her at this point. The truck was moving at break-neck speeds as it tore into the quiet streets.

Heidi reached under her seat and pulled out her cellphone. She quickly noticed she had eleven missed calls. All from her best friend Faith. Heidi opened her phonebook and scrolled down to Aaron's name. She needed all the help she could find tonight and Aaron was the first person she thought of. Without hesitation she clicked on Aaron's name and dialed the number. *Ring.* No answer.

"C'mon baby, pick up the phone," Heidi whispered as she rocked back and forth. *Ring.* No answer. "Aaron, Aaron, Aaron. Where are you? I need you now, baby boy. Where you go that quick?" Heidi pushed the phone closer to her ear as the phone continued to ring. Heidi waited until his voicemail activated and decided to leave a message. "Aaron, it's me. When you get this, please call me right away. I'm in a lot of trouble and I know you know what I'm talkin' about. I need you to do something for me. So please, when you get this call me. Bye."

Heidi hung up the phone and slammed it in her lap. She needed a major favor from Aaron tonight and she was praying that he returned her call before she came back to her mother's house. Heidi turned her attention back to the road. She thought about Faith's missed calls as she continued to speed down the street. She knew that Faith was more than eager to help her tonight and Heidi was hoping that Faith was still in the parking lot where she agreed to wait for her. Heidi ignored all of the traffic lights and continued to speed to her destination.

As Heidi pulled up to the shopping center, a warm feeling came over her. She quickly spotted Faith's car and let out a gasp of relief. She was happy to see that Faith was still there. Heidi quickly pulled up beside her and jumped out the truck. Faith got out of her car and walked over to Heidi. Before Heidi could say a word to her, Faith quickly reached out and embraced her. She was so happy to see Heidi still in one piece.

"Hey girl, I'm so glad that you made it out of there." Faith squeezed Heidi with all her might.

"I know." Heidi countered. "And I'm so glad you didn't leave me, girl. I really need you right now."

Faith felt herself getting emotional as she pulled back from Heidi and stared at her. "I'm here, High. What do you want me to do? Just give me the word."

Heidi pursed her lips together and shook her head. "Faith, the niggas found a way to get into the Datakorp system." Heidi said.

"Datakorp? Didn't Jayson work at Datakorp?" Faith asked as she leaned against the car. "What does that have to do with you and your mother?"

"Girl, these idiots is on some baby-back-bullshit for real. They snatched my moms because of some other shit and now they want me to go down to Datakorp to do somethin' for them."

Faith shot Heidi a blank stare. "Heidi, you know I'm lost right?" Faith whispered with a confused expression. "I don't know what the hell you sayin' to me. What do they want?"

"Money." Heidi snapped. "These niggas want money. That's it."

Both women fell silent as Faith reflected on this information. She noticed that Heidi was growing agitated with the entire ordeal. She closely watched her best friend as Heidi took another quick look at her watch. She continued to shake her head and looked over to Faith again.

"Girl, to make a long story short they found a way to transfer all the monthly maintenance fees from the brokerage accounts to one account that they control."

"The maintenance fees? You mean from the whole company?"

"The whole company. They want me to go down there and change the account information so that they can get the money out of it."

"Holy shit," Faith gasped. "How much money?"

"At least $2,000,000" Heidi whispered.

"Jesus Christ."

"Tell me about it."

"Well that's just dumb. When the company finds out that you changed the account information, they gonna get caught. I'm pretty sure the people at that company are not that stupid."

Heidi put her head down and giggled to herself. A strange feeling came over her as she began to feel like she had experienced this before. She looked back at Faith. "Faith, listen to this fly shit," Heidi said. "Tonight is daylight savings, right. So imma change the account information at 1:30. The money will be transferred like fifteen minutes later. But when the time goes back at two o'clock, the entire transaction will be erased. Just like that."

"You have got to be kiddin' me, Heidi. Are you serious?"

"Very serious." Heidi whispered. "By the time they figure out where the money is, them niggas will be long gone."

Faith shot her best friend a sharp look. It didn't take long for Faith to realize that the plan was well thought-out and well calculated. She had expected to hear something crazy from Heidi but this was well beyond what Faith could have ever imagined.

"So they holdin' ya mother until you come back tonight, right?" Faith asked.

"Yup," Heidi answered as she slowly nodded her head. "I'm bout to rush down to the main office at Datakorp right now, but I need you to do something for me."

"Just name it. What you want me to do?"

"I need you to get me a gun. I don't have time to get one myself. I was trying to get one from Aaron but he is not picking' up his phone."

"I'm way ahead of you, girl. I'm on top of it."

Dashawn Taylor

"That's why you my nigga, Faith. Thank you so much. I swear if they so much as breathe on my mother the wrong way tonight imma kill they ass for real."

"No you not," Faith ordered as she shot Heidi a serious stare. Heidi cocked her head to the side and shot Faith a confused expression. "You can't kill them niggas, High," Faith barked as she emphatically shook her head. "'Cause imma kill they ass first."

Heidi smiled at her best friend and gave her a hug. "I'm outta here, girl. Meet me back here in two hours. I should have a plan by then."

Both women exchanged nervous smiles and headed back to their vehicles. The sound of screeching tires could be heard as Heidi peeled out of the parking lot first. She had less then twenty minutes to make it down to Datakorp.com and hold up her end of the deal with Vegas and Shaheed.

Chapter 23

The 700th block of Broad Street in Newark was oddly empty on this particular evening. Usually a main drag for partygoers, policeman, and late night stragglers, Heidi was surprised to see none of these sorts out and about as she pulled up to the main entrance of the Datakorp building. An eerie feeling came over her as she looked at the entrance to 744 Broad Street. A funny feeling always came over her when she drove by this place. It always made her think of Jayson, and tonight was no different. Heidi felt a heavy presence around her as she quickly took a glance at her watch and noticed she only had three minutes to get inside the building and check-in with the security guard.

Heidi looked around the quiet street one last time. She jumped out of the car and rushed into the building where the security guard was impatiently waiting for her. Heidi was only three steps into the building before a tall and lanky man came rushing over to her. Heidi paused for a moment and looked him over as he hastily approached her. His uniform didn't fit right and he almost seemed to be out of place in the plush lobby. Heidi looked around the man's hip and noticed that he was wearing a standard issue utility belt accompanied by a loaded pistol. Heidi momentarily froze as the guard reached out for her.

"Let's go, lil' mama," he barked, grabbing Heidi by the arm. "You only got five minutes to make it upstairs before I gotta turn the lobby cameras back on. You are late, goddamit."

Heidi quickly pulled away from the security guard. She shot him a hard stare and shook her head. "Don't touch me, nigga," Heidi snapped. "And I'm not late. Just tell me where I need to go and I'll go."

"Look here, you feisty bitch." The security guard snapped. "If I didn't want this money so bad I woulda kicked ya stupid ass back out on the street and let them hooligans kill ya peoples." The guard shot Heidi a hard stare. His tone was dead serious. The security guard gave Heidi a disgusted once-over and pointed to the elevators. "Get on elevator number five and go to the twenty-second floor. When you get off the elevator go to the right and go into the second door on the left side. That will be the office you need." Heidi continued to stare at the guard as he instructed her. "Be back down here in an hour!" the guard continued. "That's all you got. An hour. After that, you on ya own. You dig?"

Heidi chuckled to herself and shook her head again. "Yea, I dig!" Heidi sarcastically snapped. She pushed the guard out of her path and headed to the elevators. Heidi's mood was unexpectedly calm. She knew exactly what she had to do and how she needed to do it. She had replayed the scenario a dozen times in her mind and now it was time to execute the plan. Heidi pushed the elevator button and waited for it to arrive. Within seconds the elevator doors were opening. Heidi paused for a second and took a deep breath. There was no turning back now. Heidi slowly walked into the elevator and pressed the button. She said a quick prayer as she felt the elevator shoot her up to the twenty-second floor.

****

Patterson, New Jersey
1:14 a.m.

Meanwhile, in Patterson, New Jersey Faith shook her head as she pulled into the parking lot of Dirty Betty's Go-Go Bar. She could hear the loud music blaring from the nightclub, signaling a busy night. She grabbed a thick envelope from her handbag and jumped out of her car. Faith didn't want to see Dirty Betty again but she knew this was the only way she could help out Heidi. Faith ignored her pride and rushed to the front door of the club. One of the bouncers immediately recognized Faith and stopped her at the door.

"Hey, Faith, I can't do it tonight," the bouncer said. His tone was very apologetic yet firm. "You know Betty banned you from the club."

Faith put her hands up and shook her head. "Nigga stop playing. She knew I was coming tonight." Faith barked. "I'm just here to pick up somethin' from her.

The bouncer raised his forearm to Faith and impeded her progress. "I can't do it!" he shouted.

Faith ignored the bouncer and tried to push her way by him, but he was too strong and Faith couldn't make it through the entrance. Another bouncer saw the commotion at the door and rushed over to the scene. It was Rueben, the head bouncer at the club. Faith felt a stream of relief hit her when she saw him. Rueben was always kind to her and even when she had the problem with Dirty Betty, Rueben was the first to come to her aid and even helped Faith to the car with her things.

"Rueben, can you please tell this dickhead that I have to see Betty?" Faith commanded. "Imma be here for five minutes and I'm leavin'. That's it. I swear."

Rueben nodded his head and grabbed the other bouncer by the arm. "She's good dude. Let her in."

Faith twisted her face up to the other bouncer as he dropped his guard. She quickly rushed inside looking for Betty. Rueben was trailing not too far behind. Faith instinctively looked over to the stage. She didn't recognize any of the new girls that were seductively swaying on the stage and luring the hard-earned-dollars from their admirers' pockets. Faith turned away from them and set her attention to the back office wishing Betty would be there. As Faith approached the office, she quickly realized that her intuition was correct. From a few feet away, Betty could be seen taking a long pull of a half-burned cigarette and talking on the phone. Faith cautiously walked in front of her view and gently knocked on the door. Betty looked at Faith and shot her a dead stare. Both women remained silent. Betty extinguished her cigarette and motioned for Faith to come inside. Faith slowly walked into the office and sat at the desk.

Dashawn Taylor

"Imma call you right back," Betty snarled as she continued to stare in Faith's direction. She quickly hung up the phone and reached under her desk. "Let's make this quick."

"Sounds good to me" Faith said as she watched Dirty Betty pull out a brown shoebox from under her desk. Betty slid the shoebox over to Faith and shot her a hard stare.

"You brought the money, right?" Betty asked.

"I brought the money." Faith answered as she nodded her head. "I can't believe you charging me $5,000 for this shit."

"Take it or leave it, Faith." Betty snapped. "But I know you need it and I got it. So if you want it, give me the money."

"You know what, Betty, I refuse to sit here and argue with you." She took out the envelope of money and tossed it to Betty. While Betty opened the envelope and counted the money, Faith looked into the shoebox and caught a glimpse of two intimidating 9mm "Baby" Desert Eagle Pistols. She was tempted to reach in the box and grabbed one of the guns but she resisted the urge. She looked up to Betty who was still counting the money.

"The guns are not traceable and I gave you four extra clips," Betty said as she focused on her money. "With that many bullets you can shoot-up the whole neighborhood and reload a few times."

Faith nodded her head. Betty was still counting the money. Faith grabbed the shoebox and rose to her feet to leave. "Don't worry, Betty, it's all there." Faith said.

"I know." Betty whispered as she continued to count the money. Faith watched her as she seemed to be mesmerized by the look and feel of the crisp one hundred dollar bills. Faith took a moment to herself and walked toward the door. She slowly turned back to Betty.

"You know, Betty," Faith said, "I never cheated with Maya's man. That was all a big mis-understandin'."

"I know," Betty whispered. Faith shot her a confused look as Betty's eyes slowly rose from her desk. "I fired that bitch last night. Too much drama," Betty said as she shot Faith a devilish smile and turned her attention back to the envelope. She never lost count of the money as she stacked the cash in small piles on her desk. Faith smiled to herself and looked at Betty. She put a tighter grip on the shoebox, turned around, and headed for the door. But before she could make it out of the office, Betty yelled her name and she turned around.

"Faith," Betty said. "I don't know what you got goin' on tonight out there. But-"

Betty stopped herself and leaned back in her chair. Faith shot her an alarming expression. She didn't know what to expect from the most dangerous woman that she had ever known. Betty nodded her head and shot her a warm smile. Faith was taken back by her expression. "Good luck." Betty said.

Faith shot Betty a wide smile. "Thank you." Faith turned around and headed for the front door. Rueben followed close behind her and walked her to the car. Faith smiled at Rueben as she fired up her engine. She took one last look at the front of the club and peeled out of the parking lot. She quickly reached for her cellphone and called Heidi. As the phone started to ring, Faith was praying that everything was going as planned.

Chapter 24

Sunday, November 4, 2007
East Orange, New Jersey

1:26 a.m.

$\mathscr{B}$ack at Pearl's house, the sound of moving furniture and breaking glass could be heard just above Pearl's head. With each *thump* and *crash*, Pearl's heart burned with anxiety. Time was running out on Pearl's family and she could sense it. Shaheed and Vegas were expecting Heidi to return within a few hours and Pearl could only imagine what was going to happen once the job was completed. From the moment she looked into Vegas' dead eyes she could tell that the men were very dangerous. With every passing minute, the chances of Pearl's family escaping the house were getting slimmer and slimmer. With no windows in her basement and no other exits, Pearl had no choice but to come up with a plan of how to escape through the first floor of the house. But the thought of confronting Vegas and Shaheed made her more nervous.

Pearl's heart became heavy with emotion as she turned to her son Lamar who was still unconscious from his head injury. She walked over to her helpless son and sat next to him. She grabbed his hands and put a tight grip on them.

"Please baby, hang in there" Pearl whispered. Tears began to bubble in her eyes as she gazed at her son's peaceful face. "I don't know how Imma do it, but Imma get us out of here. You just hang in there, Lamar. You hear me? Just hang in there, baby."

Pearl turned away from Lamar and looked around the basement. She was praying that a reasonable idea would come to her soon as she stood up and quickly gazed around the basement in search of any type of blunt object. Pearl moved to the rear of the basement and searched through a few boxes that were scattered about the floor. She let out a loud gasp as she noticed that there were nothing but papers and old clothes in the boxes. She tossed the clothes to the side by the handful, hoping to find a knife or a screwdriver inside. There were none. Pearl was about to give up her search when she found a small cigar box under a few pair of jeans. She quickly snatched the top off of the shoebox and shuffled through the contents.

"Dammit!" Pearl screamed as she shuffled around the box and noticed that it was filled with just incense and a few cigarette lighters. Pearl shook her head again as she grabbed one of the lighters. "What the hell am I suppose to do with this?" Pearl sarcastically muttered. She raised the lighter to her ear and shook it. With the sound of the half-empty lighter, Pearl tossed the shoebox in disgust. Before she could toss the lighter a loud bang came from the top of the stairs. It was the basement door opening. Pearl's heart skipped a beat as she saw Vegas running down the stairs. Pearl quickly put the lighter in her pocket and rushed over to her son. Vegas made it downstairs quicker than she thought he would. He shot her a suspicious look as Pearl continued to walk towards Lamar. Her eyes widened as she stared at Vegas.

"I heard some noise down here," Vegas barked. "What the hell are you doin' down here?"

Pearl shook her head in fear. "Nothin'. I'm not doin' nothin'. I don't know what you heard," Pearl stuttered.

Vegas shot her another suspicious stare and looked around the basement. At first glance everything seemed to be in order but Vegas took a few more moments and looked around. He turned back to Pearl and shot her another suspicious look. Pearl didn't budge. Vegas ignored his instinct and decided to leave. Pearl watched him as he walked upstairs and headed for the door. Pearl recognized this new opportunity and decided to take advantage. She hustled towards the stairs and took her chance.

"Umm, excuse me." Pearl softly said. "Please, give me one second."

Vegas turned around and looked down at Pearl. His large frame seemed to take up the entire doorway. He shot her a semi-interested gesture. "What?"

Pearl nearly retreated from Vegas' tone but she knew that this was her last chance to make a move. She quickly regained her courage and looked up to Vegas. "Well for one, I have a serious medical condition and I need to eat somethin' very soon and-"

Before she could say another word, Vegas cut her off. "Okay, we'll bring somethin' down to you" he said as he motioned to close the door.

"Wait!" Pearl yelled. "I haven't been to the bathroom all night. And I don't think I can hold it, seriously." Vegas looked down at Pearl. She shot him a sympathetic look. The basement fell silent as Vegas blankly stared at her. He didn't say a word as his body language began to change. "You guys are in charge here. I know that. I just need to go to the potty and that's it. What the hell can I do to y'all?" Vegas' expression never changed. His grey eyes froze Pearl for a moment. She didn't know what to think as she stared back at Vegas. Pearl shot him another look of concern. "Well?" Pearl whispered.

Vegas slowly nodded his head and motioned for Pearl to come up the stairs. He walked away from the opened door as Pearl made her way up the flight of stairs. As she entered the hallway her jaw dropped at the chaotic scene. She couldn't recognize her house. Her kitchen was in total disarray with all of the chairs flipped over and her kitchen table blocking the back entrance to the house. The trashcans were emptied out onto the floor and papers were scattered everywhere. Pearl quickly turned around to catch a glimpse of her living room. She was shocked to see her sofa turned upside-down and blocking the entrance to the front door. It appeared that the men were getting ready for a major stand off and didn't want anyone to rush into the house.

"What the hell are y'all doing to my house?" Pearl whispered under her breath. Before she could look around any longer, she noticed Rafeek was quickly approaching her from the living room.

"Take her ass upstairs to the bathroom and that's it." Vegas ordered. He shot Rafeek a hard stare and Rafeek returned the gesture.

"Like I said, slim, you don't have to yell at me," Rafeek barked. "I can hear you loud and clear."

Rafeek waved Vegas off and grabbed Pearl by the arm. He shoved her toward the stairs. Pearl bucked against his aggression.

"Hey!" Pearl yelled.

"Just go upstairs," Rafeek countered. He was obviously upset.

Pearl decided to avoid any further confrontation with Rafeek and headed straight to the second floor bathroom. As she moved up the stairs she cautiously looked around. Rafeek was following close behind. Pearl quickly noticed that all the furniture in the second floor hallway was turned over. It was hard for her to maneuver. She couldn't imagine why the men would practically destroy her house. As she approached the entrance to the bathroom, she turned around to Rafeek.

"Umm, I have to do this part alone." Pearl said. "Please don't follow me all the way into the bathroom."

A small grin emerged on Rafeek's face as he chuckled to himself. "Oh yea, that's fine with me. You can go in the bathroom by yourself. I know you not goin' nowhere."

Pearl shot Rafeek a peculiar look. As she opened the door and walked into the bathroom she quickly noticed why Rafeek was wearing his slick grin. The men had taken both wooden cabinets from the bottom of the bathroom sink and nailed them against the windows. Pearl had no chance of breaking through the wood in an attempt to escape. A dark feeling came over her as she closed the door behind her. She slowly sat down on the edge of the bathtub and contemplated another way to escape from the house.

****

Newark, New Jersey
1:42 a.m.

Meanwhile, back at Datakorp, Heidi waited patiently in the office as the final transactions were being completed. The silence made her very uneasy as she watched the computer transfer thousands of dollars per second. The screen flickered as hundreds of names, addresses, and account numbers flashed on the screen and maintenance fees poured into the new account. Heidi was amazed at the sight. As the transactions began to wind down, Heidi took one last look at the final tally. What she read on the screen made her heart drop to the floor:

Total= $2,345,342.00
Transfer Completed

Heidi slowly shook her head and gazed at the screen. She leaned back in her chair and thought for a moment. A funny feeling came over her as she continued to ponder this enormous amount of money. Heidi quickly sat up in her chair and grabbed the mouse on the desk. She clicked off the top screen and opened another window. Heidi looked at the time on the computer clock as her mind started to race. Her fingers started typing on the keyboard at a record speed as images of her mother and brother flashed into her mind.

Before Heidi could complete another transaction, her cellphone started buzzing in her pants pocket. Heidi quickly reached for the phone. She was shocked to see that it was Faith calling. Heidi quickly answered the phone and continued to type on the keyboard.

"Hey girl, tell me something good," Heidi whispered.

"We good, High," Faith said from the other line. "Betty gave me two of them things and we even got some extra magazines with them. So how's it going on that end?"

"We are good, girl. Trust me, we are so good." Heidi said. She continued to type on the keyboard as a sly smile grew on her face. "So how you want to do this, girl? How far are you from my mother's house?"

"I can be there in less than a half hour." Faith assured.

"Okay, this is what I want you to do. I want you to park around the corner from my mom's house and wait for me. Imma be there within the hour."

"Within the hour?" Faith asked.

"Yeah, don't worry. I'll be there. Just wait for me."

"Okay. I'm on my way."

"Bye."

Heidi hung up the phone and looked at the clock. It was quickly approaching two o'clock and Heidi had completed her last transaction just in time. She quickly shut down the computer and headed for the door. She pulled her baseball cap lower on her head and rushed to the elevator. Heidi didn't have a minute to waste as the elevator quickly opened for her and took her down to the lobby of the building. The same security guard greeted her and she shot him a disgusted look and headed for the front door.

"Wait!" the security guard yelled. Heidi turned around and looked at him. "Aren't you forgetting something?" he asked.

"Huh?" Heidi grunted. She was confused.

"Aren't you forgetting this?" the guard asked as he walked over to her and handed her a black briefcase. In her haste to reach the door, she never noticed he was carrying a black leather briefcase with gold trimming. "Before you leave, you gotta take this with you," the guard said. "Make sure Vegas and Shaheed get this. And tell them that my boss already called me and verified the transaction so we are square."

Another rush of adrenaline shot through her body as the guard handed her the briefcase. It was heavy. "Okay," Heidi whispered. She was beyond confused. "I will do that." Heidi turned around and headed for the door. With little time to waste, she jumped into her truck and fired up the engine. The sound echoed throughout the barren street. Heidi slowly placed the briefcase in the passenger side seat and looked at it. After a few moments of contemplation, Heidi curiously reached for the two golden latches and opened the case. Her eyes lit up with astonishment as she gazed at over $1.5 million in one –hundred – dollar bills. Heidi was frozen at the sight of the money. "Jesus Christ" she whispered as her heart skipped a beat.

Heidi frantically closed the briefcase and looked around. She slammed the truck into gear and sped off. As her SUV ripped down the empty street, Heidi grabbed her cellphone. Now that the briefcase was added to the equation, Heidi realized that her family was in a lot more trouble than she and Faith could handle alone. She was going to need more help. Heidi scrolled down to Aaron's name and dialed the number. To Heidi's dismay, Aaron's phone continued to go straight to voicemail.

Heidi couldn't believe it. *Where are you?* Heidi wondered to herself. She called his number a few more times, but she continued to get the same results. After her fifth attempt to reach him, Heidi decided to leave a message for Aaron.

"Aaron, this is me." Heidi frantically said. Her voice sounded defeated and worried. "Please call me back. I'm on my way to my mother's house and I need you to meet me there. Call me back so I can give you the address. Okay? Bye." Heidi hung up the phone and turned her attention back to the road. As she punched the gas pedal and picked up the pace Heidi tried to brace herself for what was waiting for her once she returned to her mother's house.

Chapter 25

Sunday, November 4, 2007
East Orange, New Jersey

1:02 a.m.
(Daylight Savings Time)

*B*oom, *Boom, Boom*! The sound of Rafeek's hard fist banging against the bathroom door startled Pearl who was sitting on the edge of the bathtub in the second floor bathroom.

"Okay lady, let's go in there" Rafeek yelled. "You been in there for too damn long now. What the hell you doin'?" Pearl didn't say a word. She fretfully turned towards the door and stared at it. *Boom, Boom, Boom*! Rafeek banged on the door again. "Can you hear me?" Rafeek yelled again. "I said let's go!"

"Yes!" Pearl yelled from the other side of the door. She quickly stood to her feet and looked around. An ominous feeling came over her as she contemplated a way to make it outside of the house to get help for her family. She was near tears as she frantically looked around the bathroom hoping some sort of idea or premonition would come to her. An idea jumped into her mind as she reached behind the toilet and grabbed the plunger. She unscrewed the wooden stick and looked at it. She threw a couple of imaginary swings but quickly realized that this would not work; it was too thin and frail to be used as a weapon. Pearl shook her head and tossed the stick to the back of the toilet.

Boom, Boom, Boom! Rafeek banged on the door again. "What are you doing in there?!" Rafeek yelled. "Let's go! I'm not gonna knock again. Imma kick this bitch down in a minute!"

Pearl knew that Rafeek's patience was wearing thin. She was in the bathroom for over ten minutes now and she was running out of options. Pearl tried again to pull the cabinets off of the windows but the nails wouldn't budge. She turned her attention to the medicine cabinet above the sink. She scoffed at the sight of her q-tips, nail-files, and hairspray. Another dark feeling came over her as she realized there was nothing in the bathroom she could use to escape. She looked under the sink but there was nothing there either. Rafeek banged on the door again but Pearl continued to ignore his threats. She turned around one last time to the medicine cabinet and slowly looked at everything that was in there. Pearl's expression changed as an idea came to her in a flash. Without a minute to waste, Pearl sprung into action.

"Hey!" Rafeek yelled. He was beyond angry at this point. "What the fuck, lady, lets go!" There was no answer from the other side of the door. Rafeek placed his ear against the bathroom door but he couldn't hear a thing. He banged on the door again. *Boom, Boom, Boom!* There was still no answer. Rafeek grabbed the doorknob and tried to open it but the door was locked. "Okay lady, I see you wanna play games." Rafeek yelled. "You better hope you can make it out of that window before I get in there."

Rafeek stepped back from the door and sized it up. He lifted his right leg and cocked it back. Without a thought, he gave the bathroom door a heavy kick just above the doorknob. His heavy foot caused the wood around the deadbolt-lock to crack. Rafeek expected to hear a scream from the other end of the door, but he heard nothing. He cocked his right leg again and decided to give the door a heavier kick this time. Rafeek took a deep breath and kicked the door again. This time the lock partially gave way and the bright light from the bathroom shined through the crack in the door. Rafeek nodded his head and frowned. "You see, bitch, you made me angry now!" Rafeek yelled. "I hope yo' ass is halfway down the street. ''Cause if it 'ain't, Imma drag it back downstairs."

Rafeek sized up the door again. He took a few more steps back and lowered his shoulder. With all of his strength, Rafeek charged the bathroom door like a linebacker charging a quarterback. He hit the door with an enormous force. The impact cracked all of the wood around the deadbolt lock and Rafeek stumbled into the middle of the bathroom. The loud crash could be heard throughout the house. Rafeek was slightly knocked off balance by the swinging door. He regained his composure and quickly turned towards the bathroom window. A confused look grew on Rafeek's face when he noticed that the wood from the cabinets was still nailed to the window. Rafeek's heart dropped as he heard a slight noise from his left side. He quickly turned around just in time to see Pearl standing in the bathtub. She was pointing something at him. His mouth fell opened in shock. Rafeek pulled his face back to get a better look at Pearl. A quick feeling of relief came over him when he noticed that it was a can of hairspray and not a gun pointed at him. A sly smirk grew on his face. "What the hell you gonna do with that?" Rafeek nervously mumbled. Before he could say another word, Pearl revealed the cigarette lighter that she had found in the basement. She quickly raised the lighter in front of the spray can. "Oh shit!" Rafeek yelled.

He froze as Pearl simultaneously sparked the lighter and sprayed a thick stream of hairspray toward him. The combination created a huge fireball that exploded all over Rafeek. He screamed in pain. The intense fire began to burn the skin off of the left side of his face. Pearl continued to spray the home-made-blow-torch toward Rafeek as he tried his best to back away from her. The bathroom was too small for him to escape. He screamed at the top of his lungs as the fire burned his hands, face, and hair. Pearl refused to show any mercy. She continued to spray the intense fire into Rafeek's face as she watched him yell in pain. He tried to get the fire off of him but the flame was too powerful. Rafeek fell against the sink and managed to grab hold of the bathroom door. With his arms flailing and his head on fire, Rafeek fled from the bathroom like a bat-out-of-hell.

Pearl stopped the attack and listened to Rafeek stagger through the ransacked hallway. Her heart started pounding through her chest as she quickly realized that an opportunity to escape was now available. She knew it was just a matter of time before Vegas and Shaheed heard the commotion from the bathroom. She cautiously walked out of the bathroom and watched Rafeek stumble towards the stairs. She could smell his flesh burning.

"Shaheed, oh my God, please help me!" Rafeek yelled. "Somebody please help!"

Dashawn Taylor

It was hard for Rafeek to maneuver in the despoiled hallway, crippled by the relentless flames ravaging his entire body. Shaheed was the first to hear Rafeek screaming from the second floor. He was in the kitchen when he heard Rafeek yelling for help. He quickly ran towards the bottom of the staircase where his eyes lit up in amazement at the site of Rafeek's entire upper body engulfed in flames.

"What the fuck?!" Shaheed yelled. "Vegas, get over here man! Somethin's goin' on upstairs."

Vegas turned to Shaheed from the living room and ran over to him. His mouth fell open at the sight of Rafeek stumbling towards the stairs with his chest and head on fire. Before Shaheed could make a move up the stairs he quickly noticed that Rafeek's fortune was about to turn for the worse. Pearl was trailing closely behind Rafeek as he stumbled towards the top of the stairs. She waited for him to reach for the banister and cocked her right leg back. Before he could get a firm grip on the banister, Pearl kicked him square in the back with all of her strength. The force sent him flying down the stairs in a heap. Rafeek yelled in pain as he tumbled down the entire flight. Shaheed grimaced at the sound of Rafeek's bones cracking with every tumble. Pearl turned around and rushed to her bedroom. She slammed the door behind her and locked it. She could still hear Rafeek yelling in pain from the fall. She frantically looked around the bedroom and turned her attention to the front window. Pearl took a deep break and shook her head. Freedom was just beyond the second floor window and she could sense it. Without a second to lose, Pearl smashed the window and made her way to the roof.

Vegas heard the sound of the window smashing on the second floor. He turned to his cousin but quickly noticed that Shaheed was too busy dousing the flames that continued to punish Rafeek. Vegas leapt into action and darted up the stairs. His heart was racing as he approached the bedroom door. He wasn't surprised to find the door locked from the inside. Fearing that he was already too late, Vegas lowered his shoulder and smashed the door open. His heavy body almost knocked the entire door off of the hinges. Vegas' jaw dropped as he entered the room. Pearl was nowhere to be found. A cool breeze rushed through the broken window and confirmed Vegas' fears. Pearl had escaped. Anger flooded Vegas' body as he realized things were spinning out of control. Rafeek was hurt badly on the first floor and the men had managed to lose a hostage. Vegas aggressively turned around and headed towards the staircase. He was visibly irritated as he rushed down the stairs and stood over Shaheed and Rafeek.

"We got a problem," Vegas barked. Shaheed remained quiet as he looked up to his cousin. "I'm going to call *him* and tell him to get his ass down here." Vegas said.

Shaheed shot his cousin a confused look. "What!?" Shaheed yelled. "Are you sure you want him to come down here?"

"This is not our muthafuckin' problem anymore." Vegas barked. He was clearly upset. "If that nigga wants his cut of this money he's gonna have to come down here and get it. Fuck that."

Shaheed could see the intensity in his cousin's eyes. The expression on Vegas' face told the whole story. Shaheed slowly dropped his head and closed his eyes. Vegas walked into the living room grabbed his cellphone. He aggressively dialed ten digits on his phone and waited impatiently for someone to pick up on the other line.

****

1:27 a.m.
(Daylight Savings Time)

Heidi and Faith made it back to Pearl's neighborhood in record time. Heidi's adrenaline was causing her body to shake uncontrollably when she pulled up to the corner of her mother's block. Heidi tried to disregard her emotions but the gravity of the evening was too intense to ignore. Faith's car pulled up tightly behind Heidi's truck as they both turned off their headlights. Heidi jumped out of the 4runner and walked over to Faith's car. Faith watched closely as Heidi walked towards her with a black briefcase in her hand. Faith shot Heidi a confused look as she got out of her car to meet her.

"Girl, what's that?" Faith asked.

"The guard gave me this for Shaheed and Vegas." Heidi answered.

"Money?"

"Yup." Heidi answered. "A lot of it."

"Jesus Christ. What are you gonna do? What's the plan?"

"I don't have one," Heidi answered as she gazed down the dark street toward her mother's house. "I'm gonna use the money as a bargaining chip for my family. I have no idea what these niggas is capable of though. You got somethin' for me?"

"I sure do," Faith eagerly replied.

Heidi watched as she reached into her back seat and grabbed two loaded handguns. Her eyes lit up as Faith handed her one of the jet-black pistols. The feeling of the cold steel in her hand made her heart race even faster.

"Goddamn girl, this thing is heavier than I thought," Heidi whispered.

"Yea," Faith agreed. "Betty wanted to make sure we could bang these niggas out if we had to."

"I see," Heidi said as she took another deep breath. She took one final look down the dark street and turned back to Faith. "You ready?"

Faith nodded her head. There was a chilling silence in the air as both women exchanged nervous stares. Heidi decided not to say a word as she turned around and headed towards Pearl's house. Faith followed closely behind.

As the women cautiously approached the house Faith made a shocking discovery. She heard a feeble moan that made her stop in her tracks. She grabbed Heidi by the arm and forced her to slow down.

"Did you hear that?" Faith whispered.

Heidi turned around in a panic. "No. What was it?" Heidi stammered.

"I don't know," Faith answered. "I thought I heard somethin' comin' from the bushes on the side of the house." Faith raised her gun and walked towards the sound. The darkness of the area made it hard for her to see. The moan became louder as Faith got closer to the trees. Oh my God Heidi, come here!" Faith howled. "It's your mother."

Heidi rushed over to Faith, immediately dropping the briefcase and covering her mouth at the sight of her mother suffering in the bushes. Tears began to pour down Heidi's face as she ran over to Pearl. "Mom, what happened?!" Heidi cried. "What are you doin' out here? Did they hurt you?"

Pearl was nursing her right ankle as she lay on her back. She shot her daughter a reassuring look and smiled at her. "I'm okay, Heidi," Pearl whispered. "I had to climb down from the second floor roof and I slipped. I think I messed up my ankle."

"Jesus Christ, Mom, what the hell were you thinking?" Heidi snapped.

"I'm okay, child, really." Pearl continued. "I was just trying to get my wind back."

Heidi frantically looked around as she helped her mother to her feet. "Are you okay to walk, Mom?" Heidi asked.

"Yea, I can walk. And it's only two of them now. I took care of the third one. We can take care of the other two now."

"We? What are you talkin' about, Mom?" Heidi snapped. She reached in her pocket and grabbed the keys to her truck. "Mom, take these keys and go to the hospital. My truck is parked down the block. Just go to the emergency room and check yourself in, please."

"I can do this, Heidi, I'm okay," Pearl protested.

Heidi emphatically shook her head, "No, mom!" Heidi said. "Please. Do as I say. Just take the keys and go to the hospital. We can take care of this. Is Lamar okay?"

Pearl turned away from her daughter. "I don't know. God, I hope so." I just took the first opportunity that I saw and I got out of there."

"It's okay, Ms. Pearl. Don't feel bad," Faith said as she walked over to Pearl and Heidi. "We gonna go in there and finish this thing."

Pearl turned to Faith. The look of determination in both of the young women's faces made her proud. Pearl turned to Heidi and nodded her head. She grabbed for the keys to the truck and squeezed Heidi's hand.

"Lamar is still in the basement," Pearl whispered. "Don't let them hurt my baby."

"I won't," Heidi promised. Pearl pursed her lips together and shot her daughter a confident look. She took the keys from Heidi and headed to the truck. Heidi watched as she hobbled down the street toward the 4runner. Once her mother was clear out of sight, Heidi turned to Faith. "Two of them, huh?" Heidi whispered. She turned to the house again and looked at the pistol. She took the safety off of the trigger and turned to Faith again. "Let's go finish this shit," Heidi grunted. Faith nodded her head. Heidi grabbed the leather briefcase and headed to the back door of the house with Faith following close behind.

****

1:36 a.m.
(Daylight Savings Time)

Inside of Pearl's house, Rafeek was still yelling in pain as Shaheed and Vegas tried to move his wounded body to the kitchen. Shaheed managed to smother all of the flames, but the pain from the attack continued to torture Rafeek.

"You gotta shut the fuck up, dog!" Vegas screamed as he pulled Rafeek into the kitchen by his legs. "Nigga, you gotta stop yellin'. You gonna get us caught out here for real."

Rafeek ignored Vegas. He continued to moan in pain from the second-degree-burns all over his body. Vegas slammed Rafeek's legs to the floor and walked towards the back of the kitchen. Angry and confused, Vegas didn't know what to do. Taking Rafeek to the hospital was out of the question and neither he nor Shaheed knew how to handle these kinds of injuries. Vegas turned to Shaheed and stared at him.

"What?" Shaheed snapped.

"I told you we didn't need his ass," Vegas argued.

"Man, what the hell we gonna do about it now?!" Shaheed yelled. "He's here now."

Vegas shook his head and turned to Rafeek who was now balled-up in pain. After a few minutes the yelling from Rafeek suddenly stopped. The pain from the burns sent his body into a shock and Rafeek passed out. He was now unconscious on the kitchen floor. Vegas gritted his teeth and walked over to Shaheed who quickly stood to his feet.

"Look man, this is what the hell we gonna do," Vegas grunted. "We gonna take his faggot-ass downstairs. We can't have him wakin' up again and screamin' like that. ''Cause if he stays up here, you better believe somebody's gonna hear him."

"Okay, let's do it then. That's cool with me," Shaheed mumbled.

Vegas looked as his watch and shook his head. Without saying a word, Vegas shot his cousin a disgusted look and walked towards Rafeek and grabbed his legs. Shaheed was making his way over to Rafeek's arms when a loud crash came from the back door. Vegas dropped Rafeek's legs and pulled out his gun in a panic. He peered at the back door with his weapon pointed straight at the window. Shaheed's heart skipped a beat as he wondered who could be outside.

"You think that nigga made it down here that quick?" Shaheed asked.

"Not a chance," Vegas whispered. "That's somebody else." Shaheed pulled out his gun and cautiously walked towards the back door. He pushed a few chairs away from the door and took a quick peek through the window. "Who is it, Shah'?" Vegas asked as he slowly approached the middle of the kitchen with his weapon drawn.

"I think its Heidi. But I see somebody else with her." His voice began to tremble with fear. "Yeah, she brought somebody with her, Vegas, some other chick."

Vegas gritted his teeth again and put a tighter grip on his pistol. "Fuck it, let 'em in. The more the merrier," Vegas sarcastically grunted.

Shaheed pushed the kitchen chairs away from the door. Vegas took a few steps back as he watched his cousin reach for the doorknob. Shaheed warily unlocked the door and backed away with his gun raised. "The door is open!" Shaheed yelled as he put a tighter grip on his weapon.

Before Shaheed could take another step backwards, Heidi and Faith rushed into the kitchen with their guns raised. The bravery of the two women startled Shaheed as he continued to back up. He didn't know what to expect from them. The look in Heidi's eyes was foreign and full of determination. She was breathing heavily with excitement and fear as she purposefully pointed her gun directly at Vegas. He didn't budge as their eyes met.

"What the fuck is this, Heidi?" Vegas barked as he glanced over to Faith. "What's up with the surprises?"

Dashawn Taylor

"That's funny, I was gonna ask you the same thing." Heidi yelled. "Which one of you motherfuckers touched my mother?"

Shaheed shot Heidi a twisted gesture. "Bitch, ain't nobody touch ya-"

Before Shaheed could finish his rant, Vegas cut him short. "Shaheed, fall back, homie!" Vegas yelled. He gave Shaheed a hard stare and turned back to Heidi who continued to point her gun in his direction. "Heidi, this shit right here ain't got nothin' to do with ya mother," Vegas said. "Now why don't you put that gun away and pass that money to me so we can be outta here."

"Where's my brother?" Heidi barked. She tried to hold her hand steady but her body continued to shake in fear.

"He's downstairs," Vegas answered as he continued to point his gun directly at her. "We didn't touch him. We left him the same way you left him. Now stop pointin' that gun at me and give me the goddamn briefcase."

Vegas was growing more upset and everyone in the kitchen could feel the tension building. Faith moved closer to Heidi as she kept her gun on Shaheed. She was growing more nervous by the second and Vegas could sense it.

"I'm not giving you shit, Vegas." Heidi said. "Y'all gonna leave my mother's house right now. And I'll give you the money when y'all get outside."

"One of my partners is hurt over there, Heidi," Vegas continued. "You want us to pick him up and just walk him outta here?"

"I don't give a shit what you do!" Heidi yelled. "Just get the fuck out of here and I'll give you the money when y'all get outside, that's it."

"So that's the deal?" Vegas whispered. His intense grey eyes were fixed on Heidi.

"Yea, motherfucker. That's the deal" Heidi barked.

Vegas slowly nodded his head. The expression on his face never changed. He looked at Heidi one last time and glanced at Faith. He could sense that both women were determined. But more importantly, he could also smell the fear on the women as they began to tremble in unison. Vegas slowly turned back to Heidi and shot her a dead stare.

"I wanna show you somethin', Heidi." Vegas whispered. "I'm 'bout to turn around and walk over to Rafeek. Now don't shoot me. I just want to show you somethin'." Heidi gave Vegas a confused look as he slowly turned around and walked over to Rafeek. She could see that Rafeek was clearly hurt. Half of the skin was burned off of his face and his clothes were torn. Rafeek was now unconscious and laying on the kitchen floor. Vegas slowly approached him and knelt down beside him. "You see this, Heidi?" Vegas sharply asked. Heidi didn't say a word. Something in Vegas' eyes scared her. She watched him closely as he lifted Rafeek's head. "You watchin' Heidi?" Vegas whispered. Heidi didn't budge. She continued to watch Vegas as he lifted Rafeek's half-burned face and showed it to her. "Now Heidi, watch closely," Vegas barked. "Imma show you what the motherfuckin' deal is."

Before Heidi could blink, Vegas quickly put the cold hard pistol to Rafeek's face and pulled the trigger.

BOOM! The sound of the gunshot nearly shook the entire kitchen as Rafeek's head exploded like a balloon from the gunshot. Blood and skull fragments splattered to the back wall and all over the kitchen floor. Heidi screamed in terror and frantically backed against the wall near the back door. She couldn't believe what she was witnessing. The look in Vegas' eyes froze her as he slowly turned to her without blinking an eye. Faith nearly fainted at the site of the massive blood stains on the kitchen floor. Without warning, she began to vomit uncontrollably. Vegas quickly rose to his feet and point his gun back at Heidi. "Don't move, bitch!" Vegas yelled.

Shaheed sprung into action and rushed over to Faith. She was still vomiting in the corner a few feet from Heidi. Before Faith could regain her composure, Shaheed smashed her on the side of the head with his gun. She was instantly knocked unconscious. Heidi made a move to help her friend but the sound of Vegas' voice stopped her in her tracks.

"Don't move, Heidi!" Vegas yelled. "Take another step, and I'll blow your fuckin' face off."

Heidi froze with the command. Her body trembled with fear as she slowly turned back to Vegas. Her gun was partially raised but she was clearly shaken by the whole ordeal. Shaheed kicked the gun away from Faith's limp body and turned his attention to Heidi. Vegas nodded his head as he slowly wiped the splattered blood from his face.

"Now here's the deal, Heidi," Vegas grunted. "First off, drop that half-ass pistol before somethin' bad happens to you." Heidi didn't move. She continued to stare at Vegas. "Don't be stupid, Heidi. Just drop the gun and the money and we can all go our separate ways. Don't try to be a hero. I will make a mess outta you in this kitchen, Heidi. Trust me."

Heidi's lip quivered as the fear started to get the best of her. The sight of Rafeek's slaughtered body made her knees weak. She slowly turned away from Vegas and glanced over to Shaheed. She could tell that Shaheed was nervous but he still managed to point his gun directly at her. Heidi turned her back to Vegas. His gun was pointed directly at her. Although Vegas was across the room, the gun felt like it was two inches from her face. Heidi gritted her teeth in anger. It took all the strength in her body to open her mouth, but Heidi managed to whisper something to Vegas.

"I can't give you this money," she whispered.

Vegas shot her a confused stare. "What?" Vegas stuttered.

"If I give up this money, you gonna kill us right here. I can't give you this money."

"I'm not gonna hurt you, Heidi," Vegas barked. His deep voice vibrated throughout the kitchen. "Just put the briefcase down. Don't do nothin' stupid."

"No," Heidi whispered as she shook her head. Tears began to flow down here face. She was so scared. "I can't die like this. Not like this."

Vegas put a tighter grip on his gun as he stared at Heidi. The look in her eyes sent a chill through his body. For the first time tonight, Vegas' heart began to race with anticipation. He didn't know what to expect from Heidi. "Put the goddamn gun down, Heidi. I'm not gonna tell you again."

"No!" Heidi shouted.

She raised her gun higher and pointed it directly at Vegas. She shot him a cold stare as the tears continued to flow down her face. Vegas' eyes widened with anger as Heidi continued to defy him. He watched her closely as she put a tighter grip on her weapon. Heidi took a deep breath and slowly exhaled. She cut her eyes over to Shaheed again and sized him up. The look in her eyes scared Shaheed and made him turn away from her.

As if possessed by a higher power, Heidi began to regain her composure and her body stopped shaking. She cut her eyes back to Vegas and stared at him. Vegas gave her another intense stare as he realized she was sizing him up. The look in her eyes continued to make him feel uneasy. Heidi recited a short prayer to herself as the kitchen fell into dead silence. *Ye, though I walk through the valley of the shadow of death, I will fear no evil. For You are with me; Your rod and Your staff, they comfort me.* Heidi was ready. Giving up the briefcase and her gun was not an option. She would have to find a way to pull off the impossible.

"Heidi," Shaheed whispered, his voice trembling with fear, "just give us the money and we-"

Before Shaheed could finish his statement Heidi made an unexpected decision. A loud gunshot rang out from her pistol. Vegas was caught off guard by the gunshot. He tried to duck out of the way but was hit in the shoulder by the bullet. The impact knocked him to the kitchen floor. Vegas screamed in pain. Heidi continued to blindly shoot at Vegas as she made her way to the back door. Shaheed frantically pointed his gun at her and pulled the trigger. Heidi flinched in terror and closed her eyes. Her heart stopped as she tried to brace herself for the bullet. *Click* Shaheed never got a shot off. Heidi quickly opened her eyes. She watched Shaheed as he awkwardly glanced at his pistol. He never realized that he had jammed the safety on the gun when he hit Faith with it. Heidi took advantage of the mishap and fired a shot directly at Shaheed. The bullet caught him square in the stomach and threw him to the kitchen floor.

"Oh my God!" Shaheed yelled as the hot bullet entered his mid section.

Heidi let off two more shots toward Vegas and darted out the back door. A rush of adrenaline went through her body as she stumbled down the stairs. She managed to brace herself on the back porch to regain her balance. Heidi knew she needed to make it away from the house and to safety in order to save her family. She quickly regained her balance and rushed toward the back gate.

Dashawn Taylor

Heidi was nearing the front of the house when the dark silhouette of a man appeared in front of her. She screamed in terror at the sight of the tall man. She frantically raised her gun to him and slowly backed away. The darkness made it hard for Heidi to seem him.

"Who's there?" Heidi frightfully asked. The man was silent. Heidi's mouth fell open at the eerie shadow. She put a tighter grip on her gun and continued to back away. The man didn't budge as Heidi squinted to take a closer look. She couldn't identify him. "Who are you?" Heidi cried out. "What do you want?"

"I'm sorry, Heidi," the man whispered.

A confused look emerged on Heidi's face as she tried to identify the man. It was still too dark for Heidi to see him. She lowered her head and took a closer look at him. As their eyes finally met, the man quickly revealed his gun and let off five shots in Heidi's direction. *Boom, Boom, Boom Boom, Boom*! The gunfire echoed throughout the quiet neighborhood. Heidi yelled in pain as three of the five bullets cut into her body. The impact threw Heidi to the hard concrete and she grunted in pain as she landed flat on her back.

"Please don't kill me," Heidi groaned as the hot bullets burned her insides.

The man suspiciously looked around as he walked over to Heidi. He kicked the gun out of Heidi's hand and looked down at her. Heidi shot the man a horrific expression. Blood began to leak from the corners of her mouth as her internal injuries quickly turned serious. The man knelt down directly over Heidi and finally revealed his identity. An intense chill rushed through Heidi's body as she looked into the man's cold eyes. She started to shake uncontrollably with fear. She couldn't believe that he was the one.

"Aaron?" Heidi whispered. A dark feeling came over her as she tried to appeal to him. "What are you doin'?"

"I'm sorry, Heidi," Aaron whispered. He pursed his lips together and shook his head. "I can't let you leave with my money." Aaron grabbed the briefcase from Heidi's grip and opened it. His eyes widened as he seductively gazed at the crisp one –hundred –dollar bills neatly stacked in the leather case. A devilish smirk emerged on his face as he seemed captivated by the sight of the money. Aaron slammed the briefcase shut and rose to his feet. He stood directly over Heidi and gave her a cold stare. Heidi was frozen with fear. She opened her mouth and made an attempt to plea with Aaron one last time, but he never gave her a chance to speak. Aaron coldly pointed the gun at her chest and let off two more shots. The bullets hit Heidi's frail body like a ton of bricks. Aaron expected her to scream in pain but the bullets tore through her skin and entered her lungs. Heidi couldn't breath. Her body began to convulse as she tried desperately to live. The fatal gunshots were too much for her to handle.

"Goodnight, Princess." Aaron whispered.

He coldly stared at Heidi as she began to fade away. Her body stopped shaking and Heidi let out one final gasp of air. Aaron gazed at Heidi's lifeless eyes and pursed his lips together. He slowly backed away from her as he realized Heidi was finally dead. Without a second to lose, Aaron sprinted away from the crime scene and disappeared into the darkness.

Epilogue

Sunday, November 4, 2007
East Orange, New Jersey

5:38 a.m.
(Daylight Savings Time)

*D*etective Harold Williams turned off the high-pitched sirens on his Crown Victoria as his unmarked police cruiser pulled up to Pearl's house. Half asleep and mostly irritated, Detective Williams slowly put the car in park and let out a frustrated gasp of air. Twelve years on the East Orange Police force and one long night of partying were to blame for the tired expression that seemed a part of Detective Williams' normal face. His tired eyes peered through the passenger side window as he took a quick survey of the massive crime scene and shook his head.

"I hate working Sunday mornings," Detective Williams mumbled to himself.

He took another sip of his lukewarm coffee and sat back in his car seat. He knew he was in for a long day. Sunday morning homicide cases were the worst. Media resources, leads, and police manpower were always decreased on the weekends. He took one final sip of the coffee and jumped out of the police cruiser.

Detective Williams was immediately greeted by Officer Denise Richards who was the first person called to the scene. She quickly approached Detective Williams and reached out to shake his hand. He politely returned the gesture.

"Good morning, Detective," Officer Richards offered as she shot him a pleasant smile. "Sorry to wake you so early. But these things seem to happen at the most inconvenient times."

Dashawn Taylor

"Tell me about it," Detective Williams sarcastically blurted. "So what do we know right now?"

"Well, it looks like a home invasion that then turned into a kidnapping," Officer Richards explained as the pair proceeded to walk into the front entrance of Pearl's house. "We got two dead in the kitchen, one dead in the basement and another dead outside."

Detective Williams felt a knot form in his stomach as he walked into the kitchen. Blood was everywhere. The entire house was turned upside down and the smell of death was in the air.

"Do we have an I.D. on these two?" Detective Williams sharply asked as he pointed to Rafeek and Faith who both lay dead in the middle of Pearl's kitchen.

"We did find a wallet in his pocket," Officer Richards confirmed as she pointed at Rafeek. "His name is Rafeek Simmons. The female's name is Faith Jowler. We did find some car keys on her and a few officers are looking for her vehicle now."

"And the one downstairs?" Detective Williams asked. His mood was growing darker as he continued to gaze at the bloody carnage in the kitchen.

"Yes, the male downstairs has been identified as Lamar Kachina. Well, as of right now it seems to be his house. There are photos of him on the walls and in a few rooms upstairs," Officer Richards continued. "He was tied up in the basement when we found him."

"Dead?" Detective Williams asked.

"Confirmed. Gunshot wound to the head. Point blank range."

"This isn't pretty," Detective Williams mumbled.

"Not at all," Officer Richards agreed. "There's a broken window in the second floor bedroom. It looks like the burglars came in through that window. And whatever they came for seems to have been very important."

"Yes," Detective Williams said. "Important enough to kill for."

"Let me show you the basement, Detective," Officer Richards said. "I think you will find this interesting."

Detective Williams turned around and headed to the basement. Before he could leave the kitchen he heard a loud crash coming from the back door. He quickly turned around to investigate the noise. A young paramedic rushed through the back door with a look of concern on his face. Detective Williams quickly walked over to assist him.

"What is it?" Detective Williams asked as he reached out for the young man.

"Who's in charge here?" the young man blurted. He was out of breath.

"I am for the moment," Detective Williams answered.

"Good. You gotta see this."

Detective Williams watched as the young man turned around and ran out the back door. Officer Richards was trailing close behind as they followed the paramedic outside the back door and around to the side of the house. Detective Williams' mouth fell open at the site of a beautiful young woman lying on the concrete. It was Heidi. His eyes widened at the massive blood that covered her body. Three other paramedics were tending to her.

"What's going on here?" Detective Williams frantically asked.

The young paramedic knelt down next to Heidi and gently grabbed her hand. "She took five shots to the chest, sir. But she is still breathing," the young man whispered.

"Jesus Christ, five shots?" Detective Williams groaned as he looked at Heidi's peaceful face. "Is she gonna make it?"

"I believe so," the young paramedic whispered as he gently rubbed Heidi's warm hands. He turned around to Detective Williams and shot him a reassuring smile. "She's a strong woman…I believe she's going make it."

-order more copies-

Full Name _____

(street address) _____

(City) _____ (State) _____ (Zip Code)

(Phone Number) *optional* _____

(Email Address) _____

(Check All That Applies to you!)
- [ ] Avid Reader
- [ ] Vendor
- [ ] Book Club
- [ ] Student
- [ ] Distributor
- [ ] Teacher
- [ ] Inmate
- [ ] Author

PRICING INFO

- [ ] 1-10 Books ($15.00/Book)
- [ ] 11-100 Books ($10.00/Book)
- [ ] 101-500 Books ($7.00/Book)

I Would Like To Order _____ Book(s)
(Amount)

: : : : FREE SHIPPING ON ALL BOOK ORDERS : : : :

Special Instructions (Schools, Correctional Facilities And/Or Vendors)

_____

_____

_____

Please Send Your Check Or Money Order To:

Dashawn Taylor
c/o KISSED BY THE DEVIL
PO Box 8644
Newark, NJ 07108

PLEASE ALLOW 5-7 BUSINESS DAYS FOR SHIPPING WITHIN THE USA

A Novel by:

DASHAWN TAYLOR